THE RIVER'S EDGE

Lenore McKelvey Puhek

THE RIVER'S EDGE

Libby Townsend Meagher
and
Thomas Francis Meagher

Their Love Story

Lenore McKelvey Puhek

iUniverse, Inc.
New York Lincoln Shanghai

The River's Edge

Libby Townsend Meagher and Thomas Francis Meagher Their Love Story

Copyright © 2006 by Lenore McKelvey Puhek

iUniverse books may be ordered through booksellers or by contacting:

iUniverse
2021 Pine Lake Road, Suite 100
Lincoln, NE 68512
www.iuniverse.com
1-800-Authors (1-800-288-4677)

ISBN-13: 978-0-595-37847-0 (pbk)
ISBN-13: 978-0-595-67575-3 (cloth)
ISBN-13: 978-0-595-82221-8 (ebk)
ISBN-10: 0-595-37847-1 (pbk)
ISBN-10: 0-595-67575-1 (cloth)
ISBN-10: 0-595-82221-5 (ebk)

Printed in the United States of America

First Edition: December 2005
First Edition Softcover: December 2005
First Edition Hardcover: December 2005

Cover art designed by: © Ellen McKelvey Murphy for both soft cover book and hard cover book
Photography: © Missouri River, near Fort Benton, Montana: Lenore McKelvey Puhek
Back page art: Merelyn K. Brubaker, Watercolor © Missouri River, Fort Benton, Montana 2005

This book is dedicated to the memory of
Thomas and Libby

—True Soul mates—
Then and Now

Thomas Francis Meagher 1865   Elizabeth Townsend Meagher
(Used with permission Montana Historical Society, Helena, MT)

C O N T E N T S

▼

PART II: THE CIVIL WAR YEARS 1861–1865

PART III: MONTANA TERRITORY1865–1867

List of Illustrations

Cover design: by © Ellen McKelvey Murphy (Graphics) 2005
Cover: Photo of Missouri River © Lenore McKelvey Puhek, 2005
Title: © By Lenore McKelvey Puhek, 2005
Back Cover: Watercolor © by Merelyn K. Brubaker, 2005

PART I

▼

NEW YORK CITY
1852–1866

To love at all is to be vulnerable. Love anything, and your heart will certainly be wrung and possibly be broken. If you want to make sure of keeping it intact, you must give your heart to no one... Wrap it carefully with hobbies and little luxuries; avoid all entanglements; lock it up safe in casket... of your own selfishness... (There) it will not be broken; it will become unbreakable, impenetrable, irredeemable.

—*The Four Loves*

C. S. Lewis

CHAPTER 1

▼

MEAGHER OF THE SWORD

The Irish meeting hall on lower Fourteenth Street filled quickly as Irishmen, caps in hand, took seats to hear their famous orator from Waterford, Ireland, Thomas Francis Meagher. Come hear *"Meagher of the Sword"* screamed out from the handbills plastered all over the lower east side. Posters were tacked up in the slums of New York, where the Irish filled the tenement houses just like the rats filled the sewers and streets. A few women also waited in anticipation, wanting to see and hear for themselves this man that their husbands talked about as they sat on the stoops and fire escapes for their evening pipes.

Most of the men recognized and acknowledged each other with a wave or a head nod. For years, thousands of their countrymen had left Ireland's shores. Men worked on freighters to pay their way over the ocean, while their families stayed behind to save the money to book passage on unsafe and overcrowded boats. All paid outrageous fees for the opportunity of living in "Amerikay." What they got for their money after walking down the gangplanks shocked even the toughest of their lot.

Contrary to a popular myth, the streets were not overflowing with gold nuggets for the plucking after a rainstorm. The Irish were not welcome immigrants. Housing and jobs were scarce. None of them came close to realizing the true conditions of their relatives who had come before them; relatives that encouraged and cajoled and begged for other family members to follow across the pond. Yet for many, being in New York City still held a promise of a better life, and even though most were half-starving in the slums, they were at least banded together in hope and freedom.

The famine years of the 1840's forced the men, women and children to action. Their dignity gone, stripped of all hope, only the promise of continued hunger hung like a pall in every corner of Ireland. It was now more than ten years later and the conditions in their beloved homeland were no better.

"Leave us behind!" shouted old men and women in sheer desperation. "There isn't enough food. Every day the miles of trenches are being filled with the dead from the night before." Their pleas rang in the ears of the young men and women. "Go before your children belong to England. Flee to Amerikay." Sadly, listening to their elders' advice, hundreds of thousands of the younger generation did leave their beloved Ireland.

Their families "waked" them for the last time. Grieving mothers and fathers, clinging to the old ways, now declared their beloved sons and daughters dead. They knew the ocean was so deep and wide and the opposite shore so far away they would never see them again. My God! Their grandchildren, their future, would be lost forever. While the sacrifice was overwhelming, there still burned a tiny flame, a spark of light. Their kin would be safe and happy in a new world.

They would need a strong Irish leader—one that would not disappoint them. Many had put faith in Thomas Francis Meagher from Waterford, Ireland. During the famine, *Meagher of the Sword* had made promises of a better future for all of them, and had failed. Now he, too, was in the New World. For the Irish to succeed there they would need solidarity. Maybe this time, Meagher would be the leader he was born to become. In New York City the halls filled wherever the orator took the stage. He hated to see the plight of his fellow countrymen.

Two ruddy-faced construction workers waved their large, rough and calloused hands to many others in recognition as they filed into the hall.

Seán Daly from Waterford, and Patrick Sullivan from Limerick, stood close together.

"Dia dhuit." They greeted each other, both preferring the Irish. Their native tongue sounded comfortable to their ears. It was the English that sounded harsh and impossible to learn. Amazingly, their wives and children were quickly picking up the English language. It was easier for them since they were working as maids and cooks and their children were mixing with New Yorkers in the public schools. The English language, resisted like death itself in Ireland, had now become an essential tool for survival in America.

"Do you think Meagher can help us?" asked Sullivan.

"Help us? Help us? What? He's a miracle worker?" asked Daly. "The man is a silver-tongued Irishman, out to make a living the only way he knows how," said Daly. "He uses his talents, he does. You and I both paid our fifty cent piece to get in today, right?"

"Yeah, yeah, that I did. Took it right out of my baby's mouth, I did. But I do listen, and he gives me a glimmer of hope," said Sullivan. "I've been in New York all this winter past and can't get anything but an occasional day job layin' the bricks." Sullivan looked out over the crowd.

"It was my Aíne that got the dream to come. Her older sister, Déirdre and her husband Mike, kept writing for us to come. *Leave from Cobb. Live with us until you get on your feet,* they wrote. "Now Aíne is going to have a baby, and I can't even buy her a warm shawl to wrap up in."

Sullivan had raised his right arm while he talked to Daly, and suddenly he realized his temper had flared. He let his hand drop listlessly to his side.

"Ten of us squashed into a two-room tenement flat, so rundown we don't even have runnin' water to drink or cook with." His blue eyes dimmed with sadness at their plight. "We thought we were leavin' all that behind in Limerick."

Just then a mighty roar went up inside the hall and jarred the men back to the reason they were here sweating in the July heat.

"Here he comes! Hooray! Hooray!" the crowd shouted. Meagher, his curly black hair neat and tidy, was dressed in the proper black coat and boiled white shirt. Confidently he strode, seemingly larger than life, through the isles of men and a few women, toward the stage and the podium. He appeared much taller than his five-feet-nine-inches, and for a moment, he quietly checked out the room, while he waited for the crowd to quit shuffling their chairs and their feet.

"Na Géanna Fiáine." Meagher stretched his arms over his head, his hands balled into fists. *"Na Géanna Fiáine,"* he shouted, his orator's voice clearly heard in the four corners of the hall. The crowd exploded at the call of "The Wild Geese."

Today Meagher would give his speech twice, first in Irish—then repeat it in eloquent English. He never knew exactly what brothers filled the chairs in front of him. He remained ever hopeful that someone in the audience would be from the political arena, or that a beating heart from an industrial giant would soften to the cry of the oppressed.

The odor from the unwashed men was stifling as the afternoon wore on, but Meagher apparently was not bothered by it. He remained deeply engrossed in fighting with words for his cause of helping his own, the Irish.

The orator's reputation hung on the fact that he was *Meagher of the Sword*. He used the symbol of the "sword" to emphasize the position of the Irish against the government; he cut to the chase with words, whether back in Ireland, or now for his daily cause here in America.

Standing in the back of the hall, near the exit, was an auburn-haired young woman, well-dressed and looking out of place. She seemed mesmerized by the great orator. The woman was Elizabeth Townsend, a New York City socialite, and the daughter of Peter Townsend, an industrial giant in the steel business. She had attended many of these hall meetings with great intentions of wanting to help somehow in the slums, even though her father forbade any such talk from her.

Elizabeth preferred to stand near the exits. She could catch a bit of fresh air and yet still hear every word Meagher had to say. The hours passed swiftly as Meagher finally brought the speech to a close.

"We need the attention of the industrial giants of this great city, and by God, I'll get us the help we need."

The clapping and whistling subsided and the jostling began. Men hurried out into the late afternoon sun, their spirit renewed once again with hopes for a good summer. They believed what they heard in the meeting hall. Meagher had promised to go to the giants in the industrial field and seek jobs and better living conditions. At least he was offering suggestions, new hope.

The lady, conspicuous in her fashionable clothes, exited the building and started walking toward Fifth Avenue and home. Her mind filled with the orator's brazen words. She knew full well he could incite the men to riots in the streets and what would come of that?

A sleek, black Brougham pulled up alongside Elizabeth at the street curb and stopped.

"Elizabeth? Elizabeth. What on earth? What are you doing in this part of town?" asked a familiar male voice. "Why are you alone? Where is Katie?" The door swung open as Elizabeth stopped walking to peer into the carriage. The elderly, rather portly gentleman motioned for her to join him for the long ride home.

"Hello Father." Elizabeth looked surprised to see him, but she gratefully climbed into the buggy and sat opposite him. "Thank you…I was wilting in this horrible heat…and what are *you* doing in this part of town, yourself?" Her voice held a lilt as she asked the question.

Peter Townsend spoke again, this time in a stern, concerned fatherly voice. "You know I forbid your activities down here, Elizabeth. This is the roughest part of New York. It's not fitting for you to be down here mingling with riffraff." His voice grew softer. "Why do you persist in disobeying me?"

Elizabeth laughed. "Mingling with riffraff? Why, Father, I'd hardly call my attending a lecture by the mighty orator, Thomas Francis Meagher from Ireland, mingling with riffraff."

She reached for her father's arm.

"Have you ever attended one of these town hall meetings? I've been coming…Oh! I know you don't want me to." Elizabeth paused and looked out the window at the passing scenes.

"Father, these people need your help. They need you and all the other employers to open doors for them." She paused, studying her father's jaw. She saw it was set in that stubborn line that meant enough said. This conversation was not going well, not at all.

"Elizabeth, you have heard me talk about this problem many times. These Irishmen are half-crazy…foreigners with strange customs and ways. They are Catholics for goodness sakes. You are out of your element down here. What do you think you are going to accomplish by coming here?" he asked. "Look at yourself. You dressed in a summer frock while most of the other women I saw coming out of that hall were dressed in rags. Do you ever look around you? Have you no self-respect?"

Elizabeth sat back into the deep cushions of the carriage seat. Just barely over twenty-two years of age and highly educated in the best schools, she had been sent on a yearlong trip to Europe. Culture and money being her birthright, her parents had hoped she might find a Count or a very wealthy European for a life mate while on the extended tour. Unfortunately, for them, that did not materialize. Elizabeth had no intention of leaving American soil. She could not, would not, shut her eyes to what was happening in her own city of New York.

One stop on the voyage had been in Belfast, Ireland, and Elizabeth enjoyed her stay on the Emerald Isle for several days while bookings back to America were completed. It was long enough for her to succumb to the Irish charm and fall in love with Ireland. The shipyards of Belfast bustled with activity. The eastern side of the island was flourishing since the worker's hands and body were enslaved to England. But never would an Irishman's soul belong to the Queen.

Peter Townsend glanced over at his beautiful daughter and looked into her blue sparkling eyes. How healthy and glowing she looked this day. She worried him. For several months he had hired a bodyguard to follow his daughter and report to him. It was not a coincidence that he just happened to be driving this street on this day. He knew where Elizabeth was spending her afternoon, and he didn't like it.

He was a man of quick decision and action, a leader and builder in the community. He yielded a stern hand in his business dealings and with the myriad employees in his mines and factories. Yet with his daughter, he could not seem to control her or talk sense into her head. He feared that Elizabeth's future somehow was going to be intertwined with the Irish slums of New York.

Thomas Francis Meagher, a man used to large crowds and the dull masses of suffering humanity that filled the lecture halls, saw a flash of green dress barely visible in the heavy layer of stale smoke that hung in the hall. He turned to his aide.

"See that woman?" He pointed toward the exit. "There, in the back. Who is she?"

The aide shook his head. "I don't know her name, but she attends your lectures regularly. Thomas, I'd say you have a secret admirer." The two men laughed.

Thomas left the stage and followed the young woman outside and watched as she disappeared into the fancy carriage of a rich man. A carriage pulled by matching bay horses, decorated in shiny brass harness. The coachman, intent on controlling his team, sat high up in the carriage. He wore the typical uniform of white shirt and black tails, with a top hat made from beaver pelts. The black man's white gloves orchestrated in circles and fine lines as the driver held the reins in his left hand and cracked the whip over the horses' heads with his other hand.

Meagher felt an unexplained but overwhelming sense of loss as he watched the carriage whisk the young woman away from him and out of his sight.

CHAPTER 2

▼

TWO MEN MEET

The Wednesday night meal consisted of roast beef, potatoes, carrots, onions and fresh hot bread, followed by English trifle. Bridget had poured him his favorite evening beverage, an Irish coffee with a dollop of fresh, thick cream. Dining alone, Mr. Peter Townsend, his appetite satiated, looked about the quiet room in his Fifth Avenue mansion. Elizabeth had gone to visit her married sister, Alice, and to spend the evening in the Barlow home.

I wish you'd get home, my dear wife. Elizabeth is going off into unknown waters, and she needs some female, womanly guidance, he thought. Peter pushed himself away from the table and crossed the hallway to enter his well-decorated study. He saw Bridget, his cook of ten years, working in the kitchen putting away pots and pans.

"Bridget, a fine meal as usual. Thank you."

Bridget was eager to clear the table and finish her nightly chores. Her arthritis had flared up this morning, and the heat of the day had worn her out. Being the cook in the Townsend household was not usually a difficult job, but lately Bridget found herself wondering how much longer she would be able to perform all of her tasks.

When Mr. Townsend had brought the Irish teenager, Katie, into the household staff two years ago, Bridget was slightly relieved and also slightly agitated. The young girl, Katie McBride, spoke hardly any English, and was so timid just a scowling face from Bridget would send her hiding in the pantry. But things had worked out, and under Bridget's tutelage, Katie McBride was a valued employee and member of the Townsend staff. She and Miss Elizabeth had an easy relationship. That was most important since the Townsend's other daughter, Alice, had since married into the Barlow circle of high society, and moved into her own mansion.

Peter always retired after the evening meal to his study to relax with a good Cuban cigar and a brandy. As was his routine, he sank into his oversized brown Corsican leather chair that carried a permanent imprint from his rotund body.

He enjoyed this quiet time, sitting in the manly library where he could look at the book titles, and inspect the many European bronze sculptures that he had managed to collect over the years. Collecting sculptures was one of the few luxuries he allowed himself, being a man who controlled his personal life with a strict discipline, the same as he did his businesses, his employees, and even to some degree, his wife and family.

The front door knocker clanked three times. He watched his faithful butler, Milton, walk with a slow but steady purpose to the front door. Milton kept himself busy in the kitchen usually, helping Bridget with chores, running errands, and overall, being a very useful and perfect employee. Milton had been in the Townsend household for at least fifteen years, arriving for work as a young man from England not long after the Townsend's had moved into this present Fifth Avenue mansion.

He and Mr. Townsend were amiable toward each other, but there was not a hint of a friendship. Milton was the perfect image of an English butler. He carried himself ramrod straight and had a long, rather pointed nose. He wore pincers for eyewear, and that gave him the expression of one looking down his nose when he wanted to give a haughty appearance.

He enjoyed the thought that the Townsend children, Miss Elizabeth and Miss Alice, had been afraid of him when they were very small chil-

2

2

dren. He never gave them cookies and milk like Bridget, saying they did not need favors before dinnertime.

"Are you expecting company tonight, sir?" he asked as he walked past the open glass doors of the study.

"Yes, Milton. Bring him right in." He did expect a visitor this night, and was pleased to see the man punctual.

Well, he's prompt, he thought, as he pulled open his pocket watch to check the time. He loved looking at this ornate gold watch. It had been a gift from his father almost 25 years ago. *All those years ago—when he was about the same age as the visitor knocking at his front door.* With a clasp of his fingers, he snapped the lid shut and automatically tucked the watch back into his vest pocket. He stood to greet his visitor.

Milton opened the exterior front door just as the stranger was about to knock again. The fist in his face startled Milton.

"Yes? Can I help you?" asked the butler. He stood stiff and proper in his black and white butler's uniform. He recognized the stranger, but gave no sign of it. In fact, he took a snobbish approach to the man.

"Good evening, sir. I have an appointment with Mr. Townsend. I am Thomas Francis Meagher."

"One moment, sir." Milton deliberately left the handsome man standing on the step.

"Sir, there is a Mr. Thomas Francis Meagher to see you?" said Milton.

"Well show him right in, Milton, don't leave him standing outside."

Milton shuffled back to the door and this time smiled at the stranger.

"Won't you come in sir? Mister Townsend is in his study. Follow me."

Meagher meekly followed the elderly man down a polished hallway, where not a speck of dust showed itself in the lamplight glow.

"Thank you, Milton. Please close the doors."

"Yes, sir," said Milton, as he backed out of the room, shutting the glass sliding panels as he did so.

"Welcome to my home, Mr. Meagher. Your message sent to my office by the young lad arrived around five o'clock today. What urgency brings you to my study this night?" Townsend walked behind his ornate mahogany desk, and pointed to another leather chair. Meagher sat.

"This is truly a gentleman's room, sir. You must be totally comfortable surrounded by such an intellectual décor." He pointed to the wall shelves loaded with the Classics. "Books…I, myself, love reading and spent many hours in libraries as a young scholar," said Meagher.

Townsend had not expected that information and was taken aback.

"Are you *the* Meagher of the Sword?"

"Indeed, that is I." Meagher fidgeted with his cuff. "And sir, excuse my boldness, but my name is pronounced MaHer, the Irish way, not Meegher, the English way."

Townsend very slowly pitched his fingertips together and peered over them at the man opposite his desk.

"Again, I ask, what brings you here to my home this night, MaHer?" Townsend practiced saying the name correctly, and this brought a smile to Meagher's face. The two men, formalities now out of the way, started talking in earnest.

"Mr. Townsend, without a doubt you are a friend to the Irish. You hire them in your factories and even give employment to Irish women here in your beautiful mansion." Meagher continued. "But we need your help in a most dire matter. We need to clean up the living conditions in the Irish slum sections of New York City."

Townsend's eyes blinked rapidly, and he dropped his hands to his desktop, feeling for the edge of his blotter. He said nothing for a moment, mainly because the man had tossed him a curve with his introduction of the subject matter. The men took turns, listening, offering suggestions, trying to find solutions to the horrible squalor the Irish immigrants were forced to accept. The hours ticked away. When the hall grandfather clock chimed nine times, Meagher called a halt to the meeting.

"Sir. I did not mean to take up your whole evening. Please forgive me this intrusion. However, I do feel we have made some progress, at least, as to what needs we Irish have for jobs and housing for our families." With that, the two men shook hands.

"We'll meet again very soon, young man. I give you my word something will be done to bring about change. I like your style and your energy, Meagher."

Little did Meagher and Townsend know just how very soon they would meet again. For just as Thomas opened the front door to step out into the hot July air, a vision clouded his pathway. Before him stood the woman from the hall meeting earlier in the day, still wearing the same green dress.

"Good evening!" he blurted out.

"Hello?" she managed to say.

Townsend, amused by the situation of the chance meeting, stood back and watched his daughter.

By now, Elizabeth had regained her composure. She recognized the man standing on her father's front steps.

"Hello. How nice to see you, sir." She didn't know what else to say or do.

Meagher suddenly realized he was blocking her entrance into her own home.

"Excuse me, Miss. I believe I saw you this afternoon? At the meeting?"

Elizabeth looked at her father. He was not smiling now.

"Yes, Mr. Meagher, you did see me. I enjoy listening to you speak. You have a just cause to fight for your people's plight." Again she glanced in the direction of her father.

"Father…? Were you two discussing…?" But Townsend cut her off.

"Now, Elizabeth, you know I don't discuss business deals away from the office." He looked at Thomas.

"Meagher, this is Elizabeth, my daughter. Thank you for coming to me with your suggestions, and good night."

With that bit of a carrot dangling before him, Meagher left the Townsend home. He paused once, only to hear the click of the door lock being slid into place.

Elizabeth Townsend, you and I will meet again soon…very soon, I promise you and myself, he thought. Glancing up into the still hot night sky, he hoped a good Irish fairy would carry his words to the young woman he sensed watched him depart.

Had he turned to look, he would not have been disappointed, for a delicate lace curtain was slightly ajar in the upstairs hall window that faced the street.

Meagher couldn't believe his Irish luck this day. He had held the attention of hundreds of men in a full hall, had a few coins in his pocket this hour, had made a serious connection with an industrial giant, fulfilling his promise made in his speech that very day. And, best of all, he'd just met his *Anam Cara*, the love of his life.

CHAPTER 3

▼

THE INVITATION TO DINE

Only one day had passed when the invitation arrived, via the young freckle-faced, red-haired courier, all of nine years old.

When Milton answered the knocking at the front door, he was forced to look down at the lad standing straight and important-looking on the steps.

"I have a letter for Miss Elizabeth Townsend," he said. "And, I am to wait for her answer."

Milton ushered the boy into the foyer. He sought out Elizabeth who happened to be in the parlor at the time.

Miss Elizabeth, there is a young messenger to see you," he said, and stepped aside so she could view the lad in the foyer.

There stood the boy, hopping from one leg to the other, hat in hand, staring all about him. Elizabeth smiled at the scene.

"I am Miss Townsend," she said, as she walked toward him. "Do you have a letter for me?"

"Yes ma'am." He handed her the white, plain envelope. "And I am to wait for your reply." He hesitated. "Please ma'am, I can wait."

Elizabeth accepted the envelope from the young boy. The bold, hand-written unfamiliar script puzzled her. She instinctively knew that it was from Mr. Meagher. She carefully opened the sealed flap and stared at the writing on the single white sheet of paper, also written in the same bold script.

"Well, now. This is so sudden," she said aloud, and then realized the boy was standing there, waiting for her reply.

Mr. Thomas Francis Meagher

Requests

The

Pleasure

Of

Your company

At

Dinner this

Saturday Evening

At

7:00 P.M.

RSVP.

"What is your name, son?"

"Patrick Walsh, ma'am."

"Well, Patrick, wait here and I will write my reply." Elizabeth disappeared down the hallway, making a detour into the kitchen. The cook was chopping vegetables for their evening meal.

"Bridget, I am glad you are here. There is a rather skinny-looking young boy in the hallway. Would you please take him a handful of your cookies that I smelled baking this morning, and a glass of cool milk?"

She turned on her heels and hurried into her father's study. She sat, mainly to collect herself and her thoughts.

An invitation from the great orator…still clutched in her hand…how was she to answer this bold invitation?

Oh! Why not? I'll be brazen one time. It will be fun to be seen in public with the man, and I would like an evening out. Thus rationalized Elizabeth as she penned her acceptance on the reverse side of the sheet of paper.

> *Dear Mr. Meagher*
> *Thank you for the invitation to dine with you this Saturday.*
> *Seven o'clock would be a fine time to call.*
> *Sincerely,*
> *Miss Elizabeth Townsend*

She hurried out to the boy, who looked sheepishly up at her, obviously enjoying the cookies and milk.

"Patrick, do you work for Mr. Meagher?"

"Yes ma'am, that is for sure. Mr. Meagher is a friend of me da."

Elizabeth handed him the letter.

"See to it you do not lose this important letter, young man. You must deliver it to Mr. Meagher this afternoon."

Patrick handed Elizabeth the empty glass, and he stuffed his pockets with the rest of the cookies on the plate before surrendering it to her.

"Yes, Ma'am, you can count on me." And he ran out of the hallway and out the open front door, and down the path as Elizabeth watched until he disappeared from her sight.

CHAPTER 4

▼

ELIZABETH DRESSES FOR DINNER

It seemed to Elizabeth that the week would never end and then, suddenly, as if time had played a trick on her, it was Saturday. The upstairs maid, a young Irish girl from Sligo, stood near the open wardrobe doors, watching rather helplessly as Elizabeth tossed dresses onto her four-poster canopy bed.

"What shall I wear? It's so hot! Oh, Katie, I need your help."

Katie McBride opened her mouth, and then closed it again. What could she say? She walked to the bed and picked up a pale blue dress, gossamer-type material, full-length to the floor with flowing lines and flowing sleeves and an open neckline. A dress Elizabeth had purchased in Paris, but not worn since she returned home.

"Pardon me, Miss Elizabeth, but this would do nicely. You have satin slippers to match, and with a string of soft white pearls...well, Mr. Meagher won't be able to take his eyes off you."

Elizabeth turned and stared at Katie.

"You know who my dining partner is for tonight?"

Katie didn't know quite what to say, but she knew she had to be honest.

"Yes Ma'am. Everyone knows in the Irish community that you are taking your dinner tonight with Mr. Meagher." She covered her mouth with her hand, but went on. "You will probably be the top story in the society pages in tomorrow's *New York Times*." Katie giggled at this bit of news, but Elizabeth did not.

"There will be no such story. I am just having a nice evening out with a gentleman, Katie. Mind your mouth." Then, looking at the dismay on the poor girl's face, Elizabeth softened and with just a touch of mischief said, "I'm still going anyway." She smiled at the thought of being seen on the arm of Thomas Francis Meagher, Meagher of the Sword.

"Let's hope you are wrong, but maybe it will be all right, if you are right. Oh! I don't even know what I am saying anymore today." She picked up the blue dress and handed it to Katie to freshen and press.

"Katie, sometime will you tell me why you left Ireland? I know I have never really asked you about your childhood or how you got here. I only know that Father has you as an indentured servant because he paid your passage." She looked at the girl. "Please, I don't mean to pry, but it seems my life is taking a twist, and I want to know what I need to about the people in my own house."

With her hand covering her mouth to stifle a cry, Katie turned and fled the room. Elizabeth stared after the girl. *Now what have I gone and done?* She thought. Her nerves were on edge and it was already three o'clock. *He* would be here for her in less than four hours.

Father was not happy with her news that she was dining publicly, but she had worked her way around him. He would be pleasant when Mr. Meagher came to call. They had exchanged words earlier in the week about Elizabeth stepping out without a chaperone. But, as Elizabeth pointed out to her father, she had traveled extensively, and after all, was of age.

For jewelry, she opened her special case and peered at the brilliant stones given to her for various birthdays and Christmas gifts. She decided that Katie was right. A single strand of pearls at her throat would have a cooling effect. She drew out the pearls and laid them on her dressing table.

Next, she went in to the bathroom and started the water, making sure the temperature remained tepid. The city still steamed under the intense summer heat, and there was little relief in the evenings. Elizabeth looked at the boudoir clock. As she slid into the cool water, scented with glycerin and rose petals, a feeling of inadequacy came over her.

What was *she* thinking? What in the world would they talk about? He being so worldly, a widower for heaven's sakes, and so well known, respected, even loved by the people. What was *he* thinking, for heaven's sakes? She being from an English background and non-Catholic to boot. But the healing waters soon soothed her nerves and she felt restored. A short nap would take care of her anxieties.

A short nap? I haven't time for a nap. I still have my hair to arrange, and... she heard a soft tapping at her door.

"Excuse me, Ma'am. I am returning your dress ready for you to wear. Can I help you arrange your hair?" asked Katie. Elizabeth was grateful for the girl's calming influence.

"I think I'd like it up on top of my head, off my shoulders, with a few straggly curlicues tonight. Let's give this Mr. Meagher something to look at, Katie." And for the first time all day, Elizabeth laughed out loud at that thought.

As the grandfather clock chimed 6:30 p.m., Elizabeth found herself in the parlor. She clasped and unclasped her hands and called for Katie.

"Katie, please, I need you. Hurry!" said Elizabeth. "Would you be so kind as to fetch me some hand lotion? I don't want to go back upstairs in this gown."

Katie raced up the stairs for the lotion. She made a quick sweep of the bedroom and spotted two very important pieces lying on the bed: a beautiful lace fan with pearl beading and tassel loops for Elizabeth's hand to slip into. And a white beaded bag, just large enough for a handkerchief, a small bottle of rose water, and maybe a small compact with a mirror. Katie carefully picked up these delicate items and carried them downstairs to the waiting Elizabeth.

"Miss Elizabeth, I think you meant to bring the purse and fan downstairs with you?" asked Katie in such a sweet voice. She knew how nervous her mistress was at the thought of keeping this invitation to dine.

The hall clock chimed seven, just as the doorknocker clapped three times. Milton, waiting patiently to open the door, did so with an elegant flare, and Thomas strolled into the wood-paneled hallway.

"Good evening, sir," spoke Milton.

"Good evening to you, too," said Thomas.

Mr. Townsend, waiting in the parlor with Elizabeth, called out a greeting to the gentleman caller.

"Milton, show Mr. "MaHer" into the parlor, will you please?"

"Good evening to you, sir," said Meagher, and the two men shook hands.

But it was Elizabeth standing near the unlit fireplace, like a vision of loveliness, that caught him off guard.

Elizabeth saw Thomas catch his breath as he came into her presence in the parlor. She felt an unfamiliar but pleasant stirring in her.

I will remember this moment forever, thought Elizabeth as she took a step towards Thomas.

"And didn't she look splendid?" said Katie to Bridget as they retreated to the kitchen. They heard the front door shut and both gave a heavy sigh.

"The man would have to be a perfect *ejit* not to see her beauty glowing from within her soul tonight." Bridget nodded in agreement.

"I'm predictin' a wedding in the Townsend house," and Katie sighed again.

"Be off with you, now." But Bridget knew there was not a woman in New York City who did not envy her mistress this night.

"Truly a wonderful sight, the two of them," chimed in Bridget.

They both heard Mr. Townsend approaching the kitchen door and turned their conversation to the duties at hand. Bridget looked at Katie and sent her the message, "Ye be keepin' those crazy thoughts to yerself, now child. No talkin' about this night outside this house."

"Ah! Mr. Townsend, sir. 'Tis a fine Shepherd's pie I have for ye for your dinner tonight. Surely ye will be happy to have the Missus home from the country by next week's end, now won't ye?"

If only you knew just how happy I will be, thought Peter Townsend as his thoughts strayed back again to his daughter and how utterly captivating she looked on the arm of *Meagher of the Sword.*

CHAPTER 5

▼

ELIZABETH VS. HER FATHER

Lulled by the warm sun shining through the window of the maid's quarters, Katie stretched her body like a cat coming awake. It took her a minute to rouse from the wonderful dream in which she found herself taking part. She didn't want it to end. In her dream, the handsome Seán Daly, from Waterford, was in the bar part of the pub. He and her brother Patrick were having a Guinness. She could see him looking her way and wondered what Patrick was telling him. Seán was flirting with her as she sat in the snug, where she visited with the other ladies. He approached her and asked if she would like something from the bar.

"*Ar mhaith leat deoch?*" he had asked, and Katie said, "I would like a glass of water, please." Seán had laughed in a good way, but she was happy that she remembered to speak in English. Even in her dreams she was learning English.

Now he was walking her home and what a fine walk it was indeed. Was he going to kiss her?

Katie sat bolt upright in her single bed in the tiny space tucked under the eaves on the third floor of the Townsend mansion. Now fully awake, she remembered it was Sunday. Her day off to spend a few hours with her brothers, who lived together only a few short blocks away in a rat-infested tenement apartment building down on the lower eastside. But there was something else on her mind this morning that needed her full attention. She had to see Miss Libby.

Katie shook her hair freely in order to clear her head. It was Sunday, her day to be with her siblings and attend Mass.

Well, they will just have to miss me this morning, she thought. *I've got to make a breakfast tray and take it to Miss Elizabeth before she gets dressed.* Katie hurried through her morning toilette, dressed in a cool wrap and ran down the back stairs to the kitchen. There she found Bridget already at the stove, the coffee ready, a pan of hotcakes, scrambled eggs in a covered pan to keep them warm, and the bacon sizzling in an oversized iron skillet.

"Good morning, Bridget." Katie's English skills over the past two years had become nearly perfect, and she was proud of herself for learning the language so fast. Only on occasion, when she was excited or worried, did she slip into Irish. She also taught her siblings English phrases to help them find better jobs.

"Good morning to ye, Katie. What has ye in the kitchen so early?" Bridget looked at the clock on the wall. "Better yet, why are ye here at all? This is Sunday, did ye forget?"

Katie gave her a big wide grin. "Oh! No. I didn't forget. I'm here to fetch a breakfast tray for Miss Elizabeth." Katie leaned her elbows on the huge kitchen counter. "Aren't you just a little bit curious about Miss Elizabeth and last night?"

Now it was Bridget's turn to smile. "Now listen here, missy, don't ye go bothering Miss Elizabeth with questions." But the tone of her voice was cheery, and in a low voice she said, "Yes, I'd luv to know, too."

Elizabeth had stayed out later than expected last night on her first outing with Mr. Thomas Francis Meagher. Katie intended to find out all she could about the famous orator and their evening together, knowing full well it was none of her business.

But it is my business, she reasoned. *Miss Elizabeth has to be properly tended to, and it is my job to see she is prepared for every occasion.* With that thought keeping her guilt at bay, Katie fixed the breakfast tray. She used special doilies and linen napkins; two fancy cups and saucers, silverware, a glass of orange juice, a slice of hot bacon and three tablespoons of scrambled eggs. She did not take pancakes, even though they were ready. Miss Elizabeth preferred toast and strawberry jam, which Katie added to the tray. She filled a small coffee pot decorated with hand painted roses, and smiled at her job well done.

Carefully balancing the breakfast tray, Katie made her way back up the stairs to the second floor and stopped in front of the closed door of her mistress.

She listened for sounds of stirring and was pleased when she heard Elizabeth up and about. She knocked on the door, opened it with her free hand, and entered the elaborately decorated bedroom.

"Miss Elizabeth, It's Katie," she called out. "I brought you breakfast." She set the tray on a small round table in front of the large window. She reached up and pulled the cords, opening the heavy velvet dark green drapes.

Elizabeth came to the table and sat, grateful to Katie for the breakfast tray and the younger girl's thoughtfulness.

"Katie, this is Sunday. You should be gone by now," said Elizabeth. Seeing the extra cup and saucer on the tray, along with a larger-sized coffee pot and Katie's face, told Elizabeth why Katie was still at the Townsend mansion this Sunday morning.

"Katie, I thank you for this quiet time. Do you want to visit with me?"

Katie scurried around the chair and sat.

"Let me pour the coffee, Ma'am," said Katie in the sweetest voice she could muster.

"I thought you'd like to start this day in your cool room. The kitchen is already hot, what with Bridget down there cooking on the stove. She is putting a huge roast in the oven today for the noon meal." Katie stopped jabbering and looked right at Elizabeth.

"Miss Elizabeth, please tell me about last night." When Elizabeth didn't interrupt, Katie continued. "Where did you go? What did you eat? What is HE like? Oh! You were so beautiful last night, I just have to know. I am dyin' with the wantin." Katie took a breath. And Elizabeth sipped the hot coffee.

Elsewhere in the mansion, Peter Townsend also was up and dressed and ready for breakfast. He walked down the wood-paneled hallway, and paused at Elizabeth's door. He saw Katie and his daughter in a cozy conversation, and he continued on his way to the kitchen.

I'll bet they are going over her dinner invitation from last night, he thought. *Well, I have some ideas about how to squash this relationship in the bud. Right after I eat my breakfast.* He padded on down the carpeted front steps, greeted Bridget with a hearty good morning and ate his breakfast in the dining room, alone.

Elizabeth wanted to share her evening with Katie as much as Katie wanted to hear about it. The two young women were more like sisters than mistress and servant. Katie had grown so much under Elizabeth's tutelage and a genuine friendship had resulted. They shopped together and worked about the house together. On occasion, Elizabeth would take Katie out to a fancy hotel for an elegant luncheon. She called them "rewards." It was a toss-up as to who was the more rewarded, as they both enjoyed these outings very much.

Elizabeth took Katie's hands in her own. She had a glow about her and a special look in her sea-blue eyes that Katie had never seen before. It was a softness that had been missing. A softness that results when a woman drops her defenses and looks at the man she will love the rest of her life.

"It was wonderful, Katie. Mr. Meagher helped me into the waiting buggy. Then he followed me inside, being very careful not to sit on my billowing skirts." Elizabeth giggled at the memory. "I used my fan to cool my skin all the way uptown."

Elizabeth blushed a bit as she remembered the feeling. "I wasn't even sure the source of the heat, but it was apparent all night long. I am sure my cheeks were flaming."

"Go on, don't stop," said Katie. The cups of coffee were now growing cold on the tray. Elizabeth tilted her head a bit, looked at Katie and continued.

"We went to Delmonicos and it was so invitingly cool there. The maitre' de welcomed us, calling Mr. Meagher by name, and there were friends of Father's dining also. Everyone stopped and stared when we entered the dining room, and…" Elizabeth caught her breath. "I loved every minute of it, Katie. He is a perfect gentleman, so full of stories about life in Ireland, and…" as if that sentence reminded Elizabeth of something, she turned directly to Katie.

"Katie, I really do want to know about your life in Ireland. I know I brought it up yesterday, and it was upsetting to you but when the time is right, will you tell me?"

Katie nodded in agreement, but she didn't want to talk, she wanted to listen.

"I'll tell you what I remember, Miss Elizabeth but please, go on with your story about last night. What did you order to eat?"

"The table service, the waiter in his handsome black tuxedo coat, his white gloves, it is all etched in my heart," said Elizabeth. "Mr. Meagher ordered for us, and guess what? He ordered a French Bordeaux wine. A wine steward came with a key around his neck, and he opened the bottle. He had Mr. Meagher taste it first. If it had not been good, he would have brought us another bottle. It was just all so exciting. Oh! You should have seen the long stemmed crystal glasses filled with that rich red wine."

Unaware of the comparison, Elizabeth reached for the little squat glass on her breakfast tray and drank some orange juice. She fidgeted on her chair a bit.

"When the waiter came with our order, I was so impressed. We ate pheasant under glass. It was served on a huge plate covered with greens, and had a glass dome over the top of it. Such elegance. Even during my trip to Europe I did not receive such attention by the staff." Taking a breath, she continued.

"Mr. Meagher smiled and greeted all the people who came by our table just to say hello to him. I think some came to take a closer look at me, too." Katie saw a secret smile curve ever so slightly at the corners of Elizabeth's mouth. She was happy for Elizabeth, for it seemed that Thomas Francis Meagher was already moving into that special space that only one person can occupy in a young woman's heart.

"After we ate the pheasant and a vegetable plate, and coffee was served, three violinists walked over to our table. They played Mendelssohn. Elizabeth began to smile broadly at an untold memory from the previous evening.

"What? What is so funny? Please tell me," begged Katie.

"Well, Mr. Meagher stood up and whispered a request in the lead violinist's ear. The musician grinned, and he whispered something to the other two men. They broke into a spirited Irish jig, and the entire room picked up the energy from the music. Mr. Meagher leaned over and explained to me that any classically trained violinist can play Mendelssohn, but only a fiddler can play a jig. Those three violinists were turned into fiddlers, and they looked nearly as happy as I felt. I didn't want the evening to end but, of course, it had to eventually. How much coffee can a lady drink without some after effects? And, my corset was so tight I thought it would burst the seams and embarrass me to death."

Katie giggled at that and covered her mouth. After a minute, she continued.

"What did the wine taste like? Was it sour or sweet? How many glasses did you have? Did you toast each other with the stemmed glasses?" The girl just couldn't stop the flow, or wait for answers. Katie didn't want the evening to end for Miss Elizabeth. She was mesmerized and fancied herself on the date with them.

"Did he ask you for another evening?" Katie dropped her head and looked to the floor. *How can I be so bold?* she thought. But Elizabeth just smiled.

"As a matter of fact, he did. He will come calling one week from today to take me to an outdoor concert to be held as a fund raiser for the Irish slum dwellers."

"And?" Katie waited. "Did you say you would accompany him?"

"Now, what do you think I said, Katie?" She paused and looked at the girl.

"You will have to help me chose a special frock for the afternoon lawn party, Katie. I said 'yes' to the invitation."

Katie jumped from the chair.

"Let's plan to go shopping for a new white lawn dress Miss Elizabeth, and we'll find a blue satin sash the color of your eyes, and you can wear that frilly, silly hat you brought back from Europe, and..."

"Whoa! Slow down, Katie. We have all week to think about it," said Elizabeth, but secretly she was already dreaming and planning for the occasion herself. "Hat? The one with all the feathers and roses? Yes! That is the one I shall wear."

Meanwhile, her father waited patiently in his study for Elizabeth to come downstairs. While waiting, he had penned a letter to his wife. He advised her to stay in the Catskills until the end of August or even longer, since the hot weather continued to hold the city in its tight and forbidding grip. He would personally post this letter, right after his little talk with Elizabeth.

"Ah!" He heard her in the parlor. "Elizabeth." He called her to come to him in his study.

"How was your evening with Mr. Meagher?" He deliberately called him "Mee-gher."

Elizabeth smiled. "Good morning to you, too, father." She sat in one of his leather wing-backed chairs. "It was a very nice evening, father. Mr. Ma-her was a perfect gentleman. Father, he is well-educated and very well-mannered."

"Elizabeth, I have something very important to ask of you." He picked up a piece of paper, pretending it was from her mother vacationing in the Catskills. "Your mother needs to stay out of this intense heat and has asked you to come and join her for the month of August or perhaps longer into the fall." He looked directly into Elizabeth's eyes. He saw a crushing disappointment hiding there. "I want you to go and stay with your mother for as long as need be. I have made arrangements for you to leave tomorrow, Monday. Take Katie with you."

"But Father…I…" Elizabeth could not speak, as a tear had caught in her throat. "Can it wait one week? I have plans."

Just as I suspected, thought Peter. *I am doing the right thing by separating these two.*

"It is already arranged, Elizabeth. You have today to ready your things, and I noticed Katie did not go to her family today, so she will be here to help you. In the Catskills, you will have a whole month or more to meet interesting young people, and be out of this intense heat. I would go myself, but I just cannot take the time away from the foundry."

Elizabeth turned on her heel and left the room. She fled back upstairs and pulled the bell for Katie.

The young girl appeared immediately at her bedroom door.

"What is it Miss? Why…what has happened? You look as if you had seen a ghost? Are you ill?"

Elizabeth was in such a state of agitation that she hardly heard the words Katie spoke. Her brain was spinning furiously. She opened her wardrobe door, and then slammed it with a bang. It suddenly dawned on her what her father was up to. Her mother was supposed to be coming home this week.

The whole trip was a ruse to get Elizabeth out of town and away from the likes of Thomas Francis Meagher. Her father was trying to distract her. She knew her father was intractable once he had set a plan in motion, but she could be equally stubborn.

"Why, how dare he interfere in my life like this?" She thought of her concert lawn party invitation from Mr. Meagher.

"Katie, I need you to run an errand for me and do it quickly." She reached for pen and paper, and hastily wrote a note to Mr. Meagher.

> *Dear Mr. Meagher,*
> *I regret that I have to cancel our plans*
> *for next Sunday afternoon. It seems my mother,*
> *who is vacationing in the Catskills, is in need*
> *of my assistance. I will be gone for at least the*

month of August and perhaps into September.
I was looking forward to attending the lawn party.
Perhaps another time.
I remain,
Faithfully yours,
Miss Elizabeth Townsend

"This letter must reach Mr. Meagher today. He lives at the Metropolitan Hotel, and if he is not there, try his law office on Alice Street. Do not leave the letter with anyone but Mr. Meagher." Elizabeth sealed over the flap. "Then hurry back here. We have packing to do. You and I are going to take a vacation in the Catskills."

Katie could not believe her ears. "A vacation? The Catskills? I'm to accompany you? I've never been on a...."

The anticipation and excitement at the thought of a vacation in the mountains quickly dimmed when Katie saw tears welling up in Elizabeth's eyes. "You can trust me to deliver your letter, Miss Elizabeth. I'll hurry back."

CHAPTER 6

▼

KATIE'S STORY

Because she was an indentured servant to Mr. Peter Townsend, Katie had a better life than her siblings. She still couldn't believe her good luck. For two years now, this tiny room, comfortable and to her liking, had been her home.

Her parents, Joseph and Kathleen McBride, unable to provide for all of their children because of the never-ending Irish famine, were forced to send away their younger children to live with relatives in the Wicklow Hills. As if that wasn't enough to break their hearts, English taxes weighed heavily upon their backs. The English landlord confiscated what crops they were able to raise. Thus, at the end of the farming season, the McBride's found their cupboards bare despite a rather good crop.

Uprisings were secretly being planned. McBride's neighbors were leaning toward a rebellion and wanted Joseph to join in. It was not a good time to live in Ireland. He was content, however, knowing his four sons, who had escaped Ireland's famine and fled safely to Amerikay, would not become martyrs for the cause, joining with the Young Rebellions lead by Thomas Francis Meagher. Look what that had cost Meagher? The last Joseph had heard Meagher was exiled from Ireland forever.

The older sons had worked their way to America, saving every penny they could spare in order to send for the next brother to follow suit.

This system had worked for a while, until their mum died from malnutrition; their youngest sister, Katie, remained with their da. He had needed her help on the farm. But that all changed when, at age fourteen, Katie was thrust into the role of an orphan. She awoke one morning to a silent, cold house. She found her da stiff on his cot, dead from the consumption. For weeks his coughing had turned to a bloody mass, and she had suspected his days were numbered upon this earth.

A few weeks earlier, Katie had searched the cupboards and dresser drawers looking for the treasure box that held all the important papers and letters. She had written to her brother Patrick in New York City about the death of their mother and of her terrible premonition that she would soon be facing life alone and unprotected in Sligo. Now a new letter would also find its way to Patrick.

> Dear brother Patrick, (1851)
>   Please Patrick, can you help me escape this terrible life
>   I am forced to lead? Da is dying every day, Patrick.
>   By the time you read this, I'll be alone. I'm scared."
>   Devotedly, and goodbye,
>   Your sister,
>   Katie.

While Katie tried to fend for herself, the English landlord paid her an unannounced visit. Sitting astride his prancing black stallion decorated with hand-forged silver tacked to the leather saddle and bridle, the evil man deliberately tried to intimidate the young girl.

"Hello the house," he yelled, cupping his hands to his mouth. He summoned the frightened girl out of the cottage away from the safety of its walls. There, in the yard, the English landlord issued an ultimatum, reading from the unrolled "Notice of Eviction" document.

"Your father failed to pay the necessary taxes before he died," he shouted using flawless Irish. "You must be off this property by the end of this month. Your father failed to pay the taxes or produce a crop. You are standing on land that belongs to England. You can not take anything but personal belongings, you cannot take any animals, equipment or furniture." He matter-of-factly held out the official-looking document and Katie took it with trembling hands.

In America, her brother, Patrick, alarmed at the letter he'd received, fretted about what to do. He could not leave Katie in Ireland. She had no place to go, except to the neighboring farm where that old man would bed her. Her conditions were worse than his, even if he was living in the slums. He had a good job with Townsend Iron Works.

Wait! Maybe old man Townsend will help me with enough money to get her here, he thought. He'd been a faithful worker for four years, and maybe his boss could help bring Katie to New York City. He'd try by asking for more hours, so he would be able to pay back the loan.

Armed with a new determination and courage for his cause, Patrick borrowed a fairly new wool pea coat, wore his best trousers and shined his boots as best he could. When the lunch shift alarm sounded, he headed for the main building. Patrick nervously combed through his curly black hair with his fingers and pushed open the office door to the management section of the factory.

"Can I help you?" asked a young man sitting behind a very cluttered desktop.

"Yes, please." Patrick spoke haltingly, wanting his English to be understood. "I must see Mr. Townsend. T's urgent."

"Do you have an appointment?" asked the secretary.

"No. T's urgent." Patrick started fidgeting from one foot to the next. He was out of his element in this fancy room with this well-dressed man behind the desk. He heard his voice getting louder.

"Amárach..." Patrick started in Irish but corrected himself. "Tomorrow will be too late."

Just then an inner office door opened and the boss himself looked out into the smaller office.

"What's going on out here? Why all this shouting?" His voice boomed into the room.

Patrick rushed over to Mr. Townsend.

"Sir. I must speak with you. *"Tá mé i mo chonai I Sligo."* He stopped talking when he realized he was speaking in Irish. 'Ts my sister, Katie. I…"

"Why don't you come into my office, young man? Tell me…what is troubling you so?"

Patrick followed Mr. Townsend into the most beautiful mahogany-paneled room he had ever seen. He spent no time gawking about, however, as he knew this would be his only chance to tell his story.

"Please sir. My sister, Katie. Me ma and me da…both dead. Katie's all alone and has nowhere to go. She is about fifteen years old and a hard worker. I want her here with me." His English came out haltingly, but certainly understandable.

Another Irishman with another problem, thought Townsend. "Slow down, fella. Where is your sister, Katie?" He looked directly at Patrick. "What kind of trouble is she in?"

Patrick, now more at ease, repeated his story about Katie, filling in the details about the death of his parents, that Katie was left an orphan and how he had to bring her from Sligo, Ireland, to New York City. It was his responsibility to take care of his baby sister.

"Sir, I will work double shifts, anything, to pay you back for a loan of money. I need to buy Katie her passage, a ticket to come to America. We have to live free of the oppression in Ireland." He raised his hands and let them drop again. He felt helpless but not hopeless.

Mr. Townsend looked at Patrick, so out of his element and uncomfortable. "For God's sake, young man, sit down." He pointed to the chair opposite his desk.

"What's your name?"

"Patrick McBride, sir."

"You say you work for me?"

"Yes, sir. I work in the foundry."

"What do you do for me that makes you think you could work extra shifts? Don't we work you enough now?"

Peter Townsend walked to his desk and pressed a buzzer, an intercom system.

"Richard, please come in and bring your stenographer's pad," he boomed. The door opened almost immediately, and Richard stepped into the room ready to take notes. The contrast in dress and in body shape was noticeable between the two young men. The muscular Irishman, dressed for his work in the foundry, looked out of place. Richard, whose ancestry was of English descent, seemed rather frail, dressed in a wool suit, a tight neck starched collar and tight-fitting trousers. He wore gold-rimmed pinch-nez eyeglasses.

"I need you to write a money draft to the White Star Shipping Line, after you find out the cost of a third class, one-way ticket from Belfast, Ireland, to New York City, America." He turned to Patrick.

"What is your sister's full name? Should the need arise, will she have proper identification?"

Patrick hastened to say, "Miss Katie McBride, sir. And...yes. She will have a birth certificate, and letters from me."

"Fine then. Richard, Miss Katie McBride is to be the name on the ticket. I want this done now." Townsend took a deep breath. "After securing the ticket, please come back in. I want to dictate a document for an indentured servant."

As soon as the door closed, Townsend walked behind his massive desk and spoke to Patrick.

"I hear you Irish are unhappy with your jobs and the working conditions inside my foundry. Is that so?"

This news startled Patrick, as he was not part of the rabble-rousers that kept trying to stir up trouble inside the factory. Patrick could not think. He had to translate all of the questions into the Irish, and it was hard for him to do it quickly. He stared at the plush burgundy carpet. Finally, recovered, he answered.

"I am not unhappy with my job, sir. I live in the tenements with my brothers. We all have some kind of work. One brother is only able to get day jobs, but he does not go hungry." Patrick closed his eyes in order to concentrate.

"An tseachtain seo caite"…last week…we all worked. We save money to bring over our sister, but we are out of time." Patrick ran out of breath. He hoped his English was clear enough so that he would not be passed off as an uneducated, stammering bloke with no future.

The silence in the room was deafening. Patrick heard only the steady tick-tock rhythm of the glass-encased clock sitting on Mr. Townsend's desk. He felt Mr. Townsend's eyes studying him. The Captain of Industry had not been given that title by chance. He understood and recognized loyalty and work ethic. He also knew it ran deep in the blood of the Irish.

"You come back at the end of your shift, son. Richard will have the ticket secured by then," said Mr. Townsend.

Patrick reached out his hand to shake Mr. Townsend's hand.

"I'll be here as soon as the horn sounds, sir." He started toward the closed door, but turned back. "Thank you, sir." He carefully shut the door and left the building the way he had come in.

Richard re-entered the room, pad and pencil in hand.

"I need a housemaid for my daughter who is returning soon from Europe," spoke Townsend. "I will approve the purchase of the ticket. Go and purchase it this afternoon and as soon as McBride comes back later today, show him into my office."

Patrick McBride nervously watched the clock all through the rest of his shift. He worked carefully, not wanting anything to interfere with his appointment with the boss. At the sound of the horn, he quickly washed, changed into the street clothes he had worn earlier and hurried to the main office of the Townsend Foundry.

"Well, McBride, did you give me a day's work for your wages?" Townsend asked.

"Yes sir! I always do." Patrick answered without hesitating.

"Here is the ticket for your sister, McBride." He handed him the ticket. "See that it gets mailed today, son." Townsend stood up from his desk.

"Katie will be indentured to the Townsend mansion until the ticket is paid back in full. No need for you to be working extra hours and penalizing yourself with possible injuries."

Patrick's hands shook with relief as he reached for the ticket. "Thank you, sir! Katie is a bright lass. She'll serve you well. I'll see to it."

The tension in the room, the sheer torture for Patrick to have to ask for a favor, passed and Patrick once again extended his enlarged, calloused, stained hand in appreciation. "Thank you, sir. I'll be forever in your debt meself." Patrick turned on his heel and left the room, careful to close the door behind him.

Townsend again buzzed his secretary. "Richard, I want that man's work record. His name is Patrick McBride. But first I want to dictate."

Townsend then proceeded to dictate the document sealing the fate and future life of a young Irish lass, Katie McBride, to that of an indentured servant for as many years as it would take to pay back the sum of the ticket. The document stated: *She will be given room and board and a small stipend for her personal needs. She will be given free time one evening a week after her evening chores are completed and one other half-day, possibly Sunday morning, so she may attend Mass. She will be tutored in English by his Irish cook Bridget and she will help Bridget wherever and whenever needed. She will be his daughter's, Miss Elizabeth Townsend, personal maid.*

Richard returned to his desk and opened the stenographer's pad. His fingers were soon clicking away at the new-fangled machine that allowed him to tap a key and type a letter of the alphabet. He had, with practice, become quite proficient at his job. His private goal was to perfect this typing machine before him by making it smaller, easier to use, and cheaper to build. Who knew? Maybe in 20 years his model would be the secretary's best friend. Stranger things had happened to those willing to dream big in America. He'd call his version the *"typewriter."*

Katie arrived that spring of 1852, her ship arrangements being uneventful and the crossing taking less time than originally planned. The day her brother's letter had reached her with the ticket enclosed, Katie set out on foot for the city of Belfast. She had found some coin in a potter's jar on a shelf in the kitchen and with that paltry sum, she made her way to the east coast and the docks.

She took nothing with her but her Irish grit and pride, and a gunnysack that held the family Bible, the important papers from the treasure box, her mother's precious hairbrush and combs, and a tin whistle. The Galway shawl she wore around her extremely thin shoulders for warmth covered her ragged dress. Only after boarding the ship and seeing her cramped quarters, did an unexpected sadness rush over her from head to toe. Gripped with the realization that she was never to see her homeland again, she wiped away the unwelcome tears.

As the ship left the shoreline, Katie turned her back to it. She was on her way to a new life. *No turning back now*, she thought. The days were dreary and long crossing the Atlantic Ocean. The noise of the engines and the swaying and dipping of the ship caused nausea among the passengers in her Class C section, the smell unbearable. Katie kept to herself as Patrick had advised, and the journey unfolded uneventfully.

She was eager to see her oldest brother, Patrick. She would be forever grateful to him for securing her ticket to come to New York City. She wondered what it had cost him to do so. Soon she would see him in person to talk about her good fortune.

I was twelve when Patrick left. I wonder if he will know me, she thought. She spotted her brother before he found her in the gray mass of passengers disembarking slowly but deliberately along the dock. She stood out in the crowd, as the late afternoon sun illuminated her flaming red hair.

"*Dearthàir!* Brother! Patrick, here I am!" she shouted, waving her ungloved, coarse hands into the air. She ran to her brother's open arms, and he crushed little Katie to his chest. He heard her sobs as her frail body shook in his arms.

"*Deirfiùr*. Little sister. Katie. Everything is all right now, you are safe with me."

Katie clung to him, afraid to let go. "It has been very hard these past few months, Patrick. Am I dreaming? Am I really in Amerikay?"

"You are awake, dear little one. Now, we'll go to your new home and meet people who will be good to you and help you with your new life. You're going to live in a castle. No Irish ghetto for you, little sister."

Patrick grabbed her hand, and together they started the long walk to the Townsend Mansion on Fifth Avenue. Katie gawked left and right, unbelieving what her eyes were seeing. She could not talk fast enough to Patrick, asking him about this magical place called New York City. When they approached the imposing mansion and Patrick unhooked the iron railing fence gate, Katie held back. He motioned her to step through. That symbolic act would remain with Katie forever. It was like stepping through a fantasy mirror. Katie wondered if she were dreaming.

"I am to live here?" A quiver rose in her throat as she looked into the well-manicured gardens.

They entered through the servants entrance at the rear of the house and stepped into the kitchen. Bridget, the housekeeper and cook, stared hard at the young girl.

"*Bfhuil Béarla agat?*" asked Bridget. Katie shook her head. No, she didn't speak English.

"*Nil Béarla agam,*" replied Katie.

"Well, that is going to be the first thing we do, get you a new language," said Bridget as she assumed her leadership role. "You must learn English very quickly if you are to work in this household."

And a bath and a decent dress, she thought to herself.

"*Suigh sios,*sit right here and drink this milk, child." Bridget poured her a glass of cool milk. She reached for the bread drawer and a serrated knife. She cut the loaf in half and handed a portion to Patrick.

"You need to eat, too, young man."

Katie sat as told and gulped down the food, grateful for its fresh taste.

Bridget had slipped into the study where Mr. Peter Townsend had been waiting for them.

"The Irish lass and her brother are here, sir."

"Send them in now," he ordered.

"Katie, Patrick…please follow me to the study," said Bridget after she made a hasty retreat to the kitchen.

"*Cé hé sin?* Who is he?" Katie asked in Irish.

"He is Peter Townsend, your employer," answered Patrick, also in Irish.

When they were seated around the huge, ornate desk, Mr. Townsend produced the document for Katie's signature.

"Mr. Townsend, this is my sister, Katie McBride, from Sligo, Ireland, as promised, sir." Katie stood up in her rags, no sign of shyness about her.

She's got grit, I like her already, he thought.

"Welcome to America, Katie. Welcome to New York City, and welcome to my home." Mr. Townsend spoke the words solemnly to Katie.

"Katie, this is our agreement. Can you sign your name?" He looked to Patrick to act as an interpreter, and Patrick told Katie what she had to do. Looking a bit bewildered, Katie signed her name. She remembered how hard her Mum had worked with charcoal by candlelight after the chores were done and the dinner cleared away, to teach Katie the scratch marks. Then Mr. Townsend passed the pen to each person in the room, asking them to sign their names as witnesses to Katie's and his signatures. Mr. Townsend then turned to Katie.

"You will live here and work for me until you have paid me back the price of your ticket to New York City. Your brother will see to it that you do." He looked to Patrick, waiting for him to interpret what he had just told Katie.

How awkward, Townsend thought. But he continued, giving Katie all the details of her new employment.

"Bridget will teach you the ways of the Townsend household, and in turn you will be in the kitchen with whatever chores she needs help with." Again, Townsend paused, waiting for Patrick to catch up.

"I will give you room and board in the maid's quarters upstairs in the mansion…and, I will pay you a small stipend for your personal needs."

Bridget raised her eyebrows at that. Normally, Mr. Townsend was not so generous with newly hired help, although he had always been so with her. She had enjoyed being in this household, coming herself as a naive, simple girl from Galway, Ireland. Bridget looked at Mr. Townsend.

"Sir, if I might be so bold. Katie will need clothes. With your permission, I am sure I can find castoffs in Miss Elizabeth's wardrobe."

Mr. Townsend nodded his approval and continued to read out loud the rest of the document.

"You will be allowed Sunday mornings to attend Mass. You will be given one evening a week for your own free time and, if you are not needed on Sunday afternoon, you may consider that your free time, also. You will, however, sleep and live under my roof every night. Understood?"

Patrick spoke to Katie in their mother tongue. Katie's deep jade green eyes grew round as she listened to the contract. She nodded her head in agreement, telling Patrick that she understood fully. She could not believe her good fortune. Her brother had just told her she had her own room, her own bed, her own clothes, food every day, and for working hard, she would be given money for her own use. Life was good.

Before anyone could stop her, Katie jumped up and ran around the side of the desk. She threw her arms around Mr. Townsend's neck.

"Go raibh míle maith agat," she said. Her actions made the Irish "thank you" perfectly understandable. Bridget froze, her mouth agape. Patrick grabbed Katie by the back of her shawl and pulled her away.

"Har-r-um-mph!" said Mr. Townsend. "Please explain to Katie that she is not to be familiar and impulsive again in this house." Townsend spoke gruffly to Patrick.

"Yes sir! I will explain it all to her, sir." Patrick said, uneasy now in the confined surroundings.

"Then DO it!" shouted Townsend. The two Irish siblings practically ran over each other in their mad scramble to escape the study, out the kitchen door and into the street. They did not stop running until they came to a small neighborhood park at the corner of the block. Had they looked back, they would have seen Mr. Townsend, standing in the window, smiling at them.

"Stop! I am out of breath," said Katie as she fell to the grass. "He doesn't scare me." With a defiant tip of her chin, Katie bid her brother goodbye.

"Today is Monday, Patrick. Please come for me on Wednesday night after my evening chores are done. I'll make that night be my night off. Tell my brothers I am eager to see them." With that request, Katie marched back up the street into the kitchen. She picked up her gunnysack, asked Bridget where the stairs were to her room and without a backward glance, ascended to the third floor. She opened the door to the tiny, neat room tucked under the eaves of this huge Fifth Avenue mansion and settled in.

"So this is to be my new home," she whispered. "I'm home."

Bridget had left the girl alone for a couple of hours. She used that time to check through Elizabeth's wardrobe and found two dresses she knew were outdated and no longer a part of the Townsend woman's trousseau.

She took underwear, stockings, a sleeping gown and robe, a good, sturdy pair of shoes, the dresses, and some bathroom toiletries up the stairs to the third floor maid's quarters. Bridget knocked softly and was not surprised to find Katie sound asleep on the top of the single bed.

"Katie. Dear...I have things for you." She spoke softly, but loud enough to wake the teenager. Katie lifted herself off the bed and took the clothes from Bridget. She tried on one of the dresses, only to find it way too large. Katie looked longingly at the two colorful cotton summer dresses.

"I know how to sew, and I can make these fit me," she said, and she reached for the shoes. "Shoes and underwear." She spoke of her happiness in Irish to Bridget, only to be rebuffed.

"Katie, *An dtuigeann tú?* Do you understand? I will not answer you in Irish. You must learn English. The Townsend's are very important people, and they entertain at the mansion all the time. Elizabeth is scheduled to return in just a week, and she will not want to bother with a girl she cannot give orders to. So pay attention. No more Irish.

Katie nodded her head to Bridget, afraid to open her mouth. She began to set out the objects she carried in the gunnysack all the way from Sligo. She placed the family Bible, along with her mother's hair combs and brush, on the top of the doily on the dressing table. She placed her hand to rest on the Bible's cover. Her new life was beginning, but her past would be with her, too.

©Watercolor, Ellen K. Murphy 2005

CHAPTER 7

▼

SUMMER IN THE CATSKILLS

The Catskills proved to be a wonderful adventure for Katie. The very fact that the Townsend entourage planned to spend the entire summer in their cottage brought the gossipers and the speculators together. Eligible bachelors flocked around Elizabeth. Some cast glances Katie's way as well, wondering about her status in the family. The rich and famous from New York City came to play, and the summer passed quickly enough.

I love watching Katie blossom, thought Elizabeth. *It will be interesting to see how she re-adjusts to her household chores when we do return to the city.*

Elizabeth knew she was being lenient with Katie, letting her take time away from her mother and her, allowing her to go off with young people to swim, play tennis and lawn croquet. To hear her Irish laughter, so robust and full, gave Elizabeth pleasure.

The young girl had never been on a vacation, never been allowed to be away overnight from the Townsend mansion. Katie now took every opportunity to go off with her new friends. She was amazed at the gossip and stories they told freely about events and incidents that happened inside their places of employment. Katie would never reveal personal anecdotes to strangers. Bridget would skin her alive if the news ever got back to her. No, Katie was good at keeping her own counsel about things. In fact, it wasn't even an effort. Secrecy about family matters was second nature to her.

Inevitably, Katie quickly made friends with similarly situated indentured servants, vacationing with their "families" in the Catskills.

The other maids, when they first met Katie, crowded about her. "We are housekeepers, or upstairs maids. What are your duties in the Townsend house?" they would ask as they went off to the clubhouse. Katie was suddenly thrust into a new level of the social standings in New York City.

"I am the upstairs maid to Miss Elizabeth Townsend, and I shop with her for her clothes and supplies." Katie wanted to appear just a bit more important to this group who obviously had similar jobs as her own.

Every morning, before planning her own day's adventures, Katie saw to it that her chores were completed and that lunch and dinner were fully prepared. She was taking no chances of being sent back to the sweltering city before fall. On the second day at the cottage, she had overheard Elizabeth and her mother talking about her.

"Elizabeth, did you bring any sewing and handiwork for Katie to complete?" asked Mrs. Townsend. "You know I don't want her traipsing all over the compound, making a nuisance of herself."

Mrs. Townsend, an unassuming woman of social standing, kept a quiet profile and did the wishes of her husband. She was not unhappy with the extended stay requested of her in the letter that she had received in the mail on the same day Elizabeth and Katie arrived. Her husband Peter wrote:

> My dear,
> Please keep Elizabeth and Katie in the Catskills
> until September at least. You can tell her you need
> the mountain air. Anything you want, but keep her away
> from New York City. I want her to meet some men of her own
> social class and have her better prepared for the season beginning
> soon. She is developing old maid tendencies of wanting to become

involved in causes, and I will not allow that. No daughter of mine
will do public charity work in the tenements.
Affectionately,
Peter

Katie kept herself in the good graces of Mrs. Townsend. She was always polite, asked her for permission to leave, questioned what time she should return and inquired if Mrs. Townsend had any special needs for the day.

Mrs. Townsend, however, had a much more pressing concern in observing her daughter's conduct. Silently, she watched Elizabeth become more quiet and withdrawn; she saw her restlessness and her unease at being at the summer resort. Mrs. Townsend and Elizabeth did not have much to share as the days wore on. Elizabeth had refused any courting or invitations to dine or accompany the young people for boat rides on the lake. Tearing a page from a daily calendar appeared to be the only thing Elizabeth looked forward to each morning. The days turned into weeks for the sad young lady.

What on earth happened at home between Elizabeth and Peter? thought Mrs. Townsend. Elizabeth failed to communicate with her about anything other than the polite answering of questions when asked.

Despite her own summer of discovery, one day Katie noticed Elizabeth's puffy eyes. Elizabeth had not eaten her usual breakfast, and when Katie asked if she wanted to walk in the gardens, she heard sadness in Elizabeth's answer. "No."

Katie boldly approached Elizabeth. "Miss Elizabeth, may I visit with you?" Before Elizabeth could answer her, Katie sat in a wooden outdoor chair.

The two sat in a comfortable silence on a patio outside the cottage door, sitting in the shade so as to not damage their delicate complexions. Despite the obvious vulnerability of her Irish translucent, pale skin, Katie had not been attentive to it, and she failed to remember to carry her umbrella while out in the sun. However, Elizabeth and her mother, if they ventured out in the daytime, reminded each other of the need for one.

Katie could only hope that Elizabeth would open up to her. After all, they spent so much time together and shared secrets. Eventually, Elizabeth turned to Katie and spoke.

"Katie, will you teach me some Irish?" asked Elizabeth. "I want to be able to understand the women when I go into the tenements. I have been thinking this fall I might volunteer some time down there." Absentmindedly, she wound her dress sash around her wrist, let it unwind, only to repeat the action all over again.

This new development of wanting to perform a public service in the tenements surprised Katie.

"You would do well to carefully think out any plans you might have to go into the tenements. There are no ladies of your station down there." Katie paused and looked out toward the tennis courts. "Things happen down there, you know?"

"But you go there every week to visit your family."

Katie leaned forward and took Elizabeth's hands.

"That is what I am trying to tell you. I can come and go, because I am Patrick's little sister and because I have a reason to be in the tenements. I am one of them. Respectfully speaking, you, Miss Elizabeth, are not." Katie spoke the truth.

Elizabeth pulled away. "Will you or won't you teach me Irish."

"Of course I will, Miss Elizabeth. If you want to learn the language, then I'll be happy to teach you. We'll start right now. When I go to visit my family, we still speak in our mother tongue." She caught herself and said, "but mostly we speak the English."

Elizabeth perked up. "I fully realize the plight of your siblings, Katie. And, I have been studying the conditions of the various ghettos in the city. I've been attending meetings held by Mr. Meagher." Elizabeth smiled at the mention of his name.

"I don't understand, Miss Elizabeth. I desperately want *my* brothers to have a good life, away from the tenements, and you want me to take you there."

Distracted by the pounding of the tennis balls being struck and passed back and forth, Katie let her gaze stray again to the tennis courts where a match was under way between two young men who had been attentive to Katie.

"It hurts my heart to watch those two at play while my brothers are sweltering in the heat carrying hod." She sat up straighter in her lawn chair.

"But Patrick is making better wages, and Mr. Townsend has given him a title now. He is a foreman in the foundry, and we are very proud of him. He speaks English as well as I do, and he has the respect of the men." Katie shyly added, "And he has a girlfriend who thinks Patrick walks on water." This made both women giggle.

'Katie, that is wonderful. I am happy to hear my father is paying attention to the needs of the workers in his employ." She sighed deeply and spoke from her heart. Her next sentence took Katie off guard.

"Father means well, I know, but he was wrong to send me here." Elizabeth sipped her lemonade. "When we return to the city, it will be the fall season and the balls and operas will be in full tilt. I am wondering what father has planned for me then."

Katie was pleased that Elizabeth confided in her. She knew her heart was breaking at the thought of being separated from her new beau. To Katie, having Elizabeth on the arm of Thomas Francis Meagher, the famous Irish orator, was a wonderful and exciting thing. He could certainly support Elizabeth financially; maybe not as majestically as her father, but his financial status would change and develop as he aged.

My goodness, thought Katie. Mr. *Meagher is a lawyer in Tammany Hall politics. He certainly has plans and dreams, not only for the Irish but also for development and improvement of the City.* She wondered why Mr. Townsend would hire Irish to work in his factories and mines and employ them for domestic hire, but would not want his daughter to become involved in any way with their culture.

The women were silent for a moment, then Libby spoke.

"Katie, I've been thinking. You must bring your brothers to the house. We have never met them. I will invite them myself after the housecleaning projects are completed this fall." Elizabeth, sincere in her offer, wanted more than ever to meet these proud, hard-working, God-fearing people.

"That I will do, Miss Elizabeth. Thank you." Katie fidgeted. "Well, for now, let's start your Irish lesson by saying *dia dhuit* which means 'hello.' You will have to listen and try to get the sounds. *"Dee a gwit."* She smiled at Elizabeth. "Now you say it, *Dee a gwit."*

Elizabeth struggled at first but as the words became familiar, the sounds did not seem hard to make, and she actually enjoyed Katie's teaching style. By the end of the hour, Elizabeth had memorized several phrases that would let other Irish-speaking people know she was sincere in her intent to learn.

"It's hard," she whined. "I never realized how difficult it would be." Elizabeth looked over at Katie. "How in the world did you ever learn to speak English so well? I am very proud of you, Katie.

"I am going to tell you a little secret. I heard father talking to Bridget about you. He is pleased with your progress. Bridget has nothing but good things to say about how hard you work, how you do things before she tells you to, and that you are a very clever young woman."

Katie beamed. She tried her best and was grateful for the life she had because of the generosity of Mr. Townsend. She wanted to bring her indentured time closer to an end every year, and wondered how much longer she would be considered indentured to Mr. Townsend. She dared not ask, however, as the man, gruff and powerful, never showed much interest in Katie's activities about the house. Mr. Townsend seldom talked to her, or asked her how she was doing.

The women, tired of their studies, decided to take a walk in the garden after all. Mrs. Townsend heard their laughter. *Katie is good for my Elizabeth*, she thought, and she returned to her needlepoint that would, by summer's end, be a pillow cover in the parlor.

Eventually, the summer did draw to a close. Unannounced, Jack Frost had visited the Catskills, changing colors on deciduous tree leaves to spectacular hues of gold, orange, red, and burgundy, while hydrangeas and geraniums wilted in their pots. The caretakers methodically went about shuttering the windows as the cottages were vacated.

Upon arrival back in New York City, fall cleaning would occupy the four women and the butler in the Townsend household for several weeks.

The house would need a thorough overhaul, and it would take all of them to do the odd jobs most likely accumulated on a long list by Bridget.

Elizabeth was happy to be home. She ran into the kitchen to greet Bridget.

"Dia dhuit, Bridget." Elizabeth was so pleased with herself and couldn't stop grinning at the shocked look on Bridget's face. "Katie spent all summer teaching me Irish phrases. Isn't that wonderful?"

Then she ran into the parlor to check for any mail that might have been posted to her. She sorted through the recognizable stacks of envelopes, all announcements and invitations to balls and concerts for the social whirl that was about to begin. But the beautiful hand-scrolled, white envelope that she longed to see and hold in her hands was not there.

Disappointed, Elizabeth slowly climbed the front stairs to her comfortable bedroom chambers to change out of her traveling suit and to rest after the long ride home.

CHAPTER 8

▼

AUTUMN BALL

Autumn in New York City makes up for the unbearable and relentless heat of July as balmy breezes blow in off the Atlantic Ocean. Elms, maples, chestnuts, oak, and hickory trees shed their umbrellas of rust, gold, red, green, and tan leaves. The sensual night air feels unusually warm, and ladies attending special events need only a wrap to ward off any wind-chills coming forth in the later hours of the evening.

The social whirl of 1854 was about to begin. For the past two months, invitations had piled up on a sterling silver platter set on the foyer table. Elizabeth looked forward to each and every event, whether it was to a Sunday lawn social, the latest high tea sponsored by the Episcopal Church, or a private ball in the home of one of the rich and famous of New York City. This was her coming out year. She was now an adult, and her name had been officially added to the social register. Invitations would come directly to Elizabeth. No longer would she be Mr. and Mrs. Peter Townsend's tag-along daughter.

This early October night found the Townsend's carriage waiting third in line to enter the graveled circle in front of the Astor Mansion. Every window in the mansion held a soft glow of haloed candlelight shielded with a hurricane lantern glass cover. The heavy, gold-swirled tapestry drapes were pulled open to reveal the arriving guests, who appeared through the windows as colorful figures milling through the various rooms. Women were leaving their cloaks on the outstretched arms of hired maids, dressed in long black skirts with white weskits; the men relinquished their top hats and gloves and canes to tuxedo-clad menservants.

Elizabeth stared in awe at the gas lit lamps lining the grass bordering the front veranda. Footmen waited curbside to lower the carriage steps and open the carriage doors. They were there to help the ladies make a graceful entrance onto the walkway. One footman, dressed in a black tuxedo with long tails, white shirt and black tie, reached into the Townsend carriage and offered his arm to Elizabeth. As if in slow motion, she floated to the ground and then began the promenade.

Strains of a familiar waltz filled her senses as she caught her first glimpse of the Astor Mansion's interior rooms. Taken aback by the opulence, Elizabeth could only stop and stare.

"Are you all right, Miss?" asked the footman.

"I need a moment," said Elizabeth. She put her right hand to her throat and opened the cape strings. "I'm fine now," she said softly and flashed a genuine smile at the young man.

He backed away, eager to escort another beautifully dressed and coifed woman through the circles of light that shone down on the walk.

Her mother and father followed right behind Elizabeth. Her father gave her a gentle nudge, moving her further inside the mansion foyer.

"Come Elizabeth, give me your cape. I'll take care of it and your mother's."

Elizabeth couldn't stop staring. She looked from one antique piece to another. She and her mother moved into the main room and waited there for her father to return.

"There you are," said a familiar voice to Mrs. Townsend. "Welcome to my home." Mrs. Astor led the two women deeper into the room and nearer to the punch bowl. Elizabeth accepted two of the little punch cups and handed one to her mother.

"Caroline," gushed Mrs. Astor. "We have a very special surprise tonight. Our orchestra is to entertain us with a new Brahms sonata for the violin." Mrs. Astor clasped her hands together and gave an almost child-like clap. "The piece is called *Frei Aber Einsom*, which translates from the German to mean *Free, yet lonely.*"

Elizabeth's thoughts flew immediately to Thomas Francis Meagher. *He is free, yet lonely.* She heard. *Now why did he pop into my head?*

"It looks like *everyone* is here this evening," Mr. Townsend said as he rejoined his wife and daughter. "I see some of our friends, Caroline. Let's wander over to them and greet them. Elizabeth, there are other young people in the dining area, you'll be all right?" She could only nod her head.

Standing in the shadows unbeknownst to Elizabeth stood a well-dressed gentleman, enamored by the sight of Elizabeth as she floated up the driveway and entered the house.

"My *anam cara*," he whispered. It had been several months since he had seen Elizabeth. He felt himself going weak in the knees at the sight of her. Quickly, he turned on his heel and raced to the servant's entrance of the mansion, hoping to avoid introductions and delays. His mission was to reach Elizabeth before any other man in the room could stake a claim on her for the evening. He startled the kitchen maid who hurried over to him and spoke in a cockney accent.

"Good evening to you, sir. Can I help you? Are you lost?" She gave him a good long look from head to toe. "You're not crashing this wing ding of a party are you?"

The man paused and flashed a seductive smile at her. He pulled out his invitation from an inner pocket and held it up for her to read. Then he put his index finger to his lips. He placed that finger on the lips of the maid. His unexpected gesture pleased the maid.

"Please, don't expose me. I am playing a trick on one of the guests." She shook her head agreeing to the silence he wanted.

He paused at the closed kitchen door only long enough to take a deep breath. He plunged through to find himself on the opposite side of the room from Elizabeth who now was engaged in conversation with two young women she had met during her summer vacation in the Catskills. Her laugh reached his ears and gave him courage to approach.

The light from the crystal chandeliers showered down on Elizabeth. Her full-skirted dress, copper silk, set off her auburn hair. He noticed she wore a very large, clear amber topaz stone that balanced perfectly just above her cleavage showing seductively through the off-the-shoulder dress. The bodice, decorated with exquisite, tiny, handmade leaves of copper silk, spilled from her shoulder, continued across the waistline, and extended to the floor. When she moved, the leaves fluttered as if a gentle breeze followed her every turn.

The gentleman saw that other women were looking at Elizabeth with just a bit of jealousy as if their own creation were lacking. But Miss Townsend remained innocent of the stir her gown created. They would never know that this gown was not the latest Paris fashion, but was in fact, hand-sewn by Elizabeth's maid, Katie McBride. For the past several months Katie had been happily designing creations for Elizabeth. Her dresses for this season's social events would continue to raise the curiosity of other women.

The music played from the ballroom on the third floor, and many couples were making their way toward the grand staircase. Others milled about the wine table, lifting stemmed glasses filled with deep red wines, while still others were viewing the tables laden with platters filled with shrimp, fresh fruits, cheeses and breads, and roasted beef and turkey. Waiters mingled among the guests holding trays filled with flutes of expensive champagne.

Everything sparkled and glittered from the gaslights wired into the crystal chandeliers. To take it all in at one time was overwhelmingly impossible. Elizabeth tried to not be so obvious in her awe of the furnishings, but everywhere she looked she found another unique object to gaze upon. The spectacular house was filled with treasures from around the world.

To compare her father's house to this mansion was not fair. The Astor's traveled worldwide, and every stop found them freighting home another antique statue or bowl, or a piece of furniture. In contrast, her father's house stayed the same, comfortable and peaceful, and Elizabeth always had felt secure living there.

The gentleman strode across the room and very gently put his hand on Elizabeth's arm. She turned slightly at the touch.

"*Dia dhuit*, Miss Townsend." The handsomely dressed gentleman bowed from the waist.

"Why! Good evening, Mr. Meagher. How nice to see you again." Elizabeth felt her cheeks getting warm, and she knew she was blushing.

"May I have the honor of this dance?" he asked as he held out his arm.

Elizabeth graciously set down her empty punch cup on the table and took the arm of Thomas Francis Meagher. She had never felt more feminine in her life as she walked in step with him across the floor and ascended the staircase to the ballroom. Heads turned as the handsome couple made their way to the dance arena. Her mother and father were seated along the edge near the orchestra when they came into view. Mr. Townsend reached for his wife's hand.

"That man with our Elizabeth is Thomas Francis Meagher, the man I was keeping her from seeing this past summer." He tightened his grip. Seeing the two together, eyes for no one else, dancing so gracefully and completely as one to an Austrian waltz, Townsend knew his efforts were futile. The die was cast, and the courting had begun. There was no chance of contriving any further kind of separation between the couple.

Mrs. Townsend, watching her daughter in the arms of such a handsome man, could only smile the way women do when they recognize the budding romance of love.

"Care to dance at least once tonight with an old man, Caroline?"

Mrs. Townsend smiled, and stood up. She took her lifetime mate's hand and led him to the dance floor. "Yes, I do want to dance, but not with an old man." She smiled lovingly at Peter. "I'll only dance with you, my dear."

CHAPTER 9

▼

THE ASTOR BALL

Thomas and Elizabeth easily fell into step and danced as if they had been doing so forever. When she had placed her left hand on his right shoulder, he sensed her trembling and he deliberately held her at a proper distance. Elizabeth felt his hand warm on her back. Her heart had raced in her chest, and she was sure everyone in the room could see it beating wildly. She placed the tips of her fingers into his left hand and he swirled her into the music. The room began spinning with colors blending and melding, while Elizabeth kept the beat of the rhythmic count of the waltz.

Elizabeth's exquisite dress swayed and flowed as it circled around Thomas's black trousers, his highly shined boots catching the light on every turn. Caught in the moment, she secretly hoped the music would never end; Thomas on the other hand, felt the music just beginning.

He noticed a side door leading away from the ballroom. He guided Elizabeth toward that space just as the music came to an end.

"Why thank you, sir. You are a wonderful dancer. I enjoyed it very much."

"Miss Townsend, Townsend, I'll find a waiter. I'll find a waiter. We need a bit of refreshment. Whew! I haven't danced in a while, and I am warm." Thomas did not give her a chance to respond. He skipped down the grand staircase and caught a waiter carrying a tray full of champagne in beautiful long-stemmed crystal flutes. Carefully, he made his way back to Elizabeth.

"Thank you for getting the champagne." She tipped the glass to his as if they were toasting each other.

Despite his best efforts to appear casual, Thomas couldn't keep from looking at her. He thought Elizabeth, standing next to him, to be the most beautiful woman in the room: the way she held her head, her easy manner. The luminous amber topaz necklace discreetly placed on her low-cut neckline caught every glimmer of light. It was as if the stone was hypnotizing him, drawing him into her very essence of woman. He wanted to spend the rest of the evening in her company. In order to accomplish that goal, he realized he'd have to sweep her away from the dance floor. Other men were looking her way.

"Miss Townsend, may I escort you outside on the veranda? It is very warm in here tonight, and I want to talk to you about last July." He offered his arm, and they descended the steps to the porch. The garden, illuminated by gas lamps, beckoned.

"Now this is much better." He stepped off the porch onto the grass, his feet crunching fallen leaves. There was magic in every movement as Elizabeth felt the electricity in the crisp fall air.

"Miss Townsend, look! The North Star!"

Elizabeth carefully made her way off the porch to reach Thomas out in the garden, and she followed his arm to see where he was pointing in the heavens. It seemed as if every star in the universe was twinkling its brightest, and she made a secret magic wish.

They started to walk down a lighted path flanked by bushes still in bloom with the last roses of summer. They came to a gazebo bathed in the lights from well-placed gas lamps. Thomas reached out his hand to Elizabeth, and she put hers, trustingly, into his. *I want to do this for the rest of my life*, she thought.

She looked down in surprise at their fingers. *I can't determine which fingers are mine intertwined like this.* Elizabeth tipped her head and realized he was staring directly at her. She started trembling. Thomas pulled her close to him as they stood in the center of the gazebo.

"Miss Townsend, you must be cold. Here, put on my jacket. I'm sorry. I didn't think about getting your wrap." In one swift movement, Meagher was out of his jacket and had it around her shaking shoulders. They both knew it was not the cold of the night that had her trembling but the nearness of their souls, finally coming together.

Thomas cupped Elizabeth's chin and tipped her head to look into her shining eyes. They both heard the waltz music wafting softly out of the ballroom into the night air.

"Miss Townsend, may I have this dance?"

Elizabeth smiled a gracious, open smile.

"Delighted, Mr. Meagher."

Her skin glowed and her eyes shimmered as she looked up at Thomas. Slowly, gracefully they began the dance.

Thomas wanted to crush her to him and never let go. He had never in his life experienced these feelings. He knew he had met his *anam cara,* and he hoped she felt the same way about him.

Go slow...you fool or she'll bolt, he warned himself.

"Miss Townsend, may I call you Elizabeth?"

"Yes, of course. I'd like you to, Mr. Meagher."

"Oh! How I hate that Mr. Meagher formality. I left that name behind in the British Crown court. Please, please Elizabeth, call me Thomas." He smiled at her and, although Elizabeth knew it was only proper to address him by "Mister," she agreed to be more informal when greeting him in the future.

"Well, all right, then. Thomas it will be."

Elizabeth felt herself relax and enjoy the waltz. The hanging gas lamps made soft golden spots on the floor as they danced into and out of them. It was delightful to step from the shadows to be swirled into the soft glow and then back into the shadows.

Thomas stopped dancing when the music ended, but he did not let her go. Instead, he twirled her around one more time, hoping to hear her laugh.

"Elizabeth. Eliza…Beth, hhhmmm. May I call you Libby? Yes, I want to call you Libby." The lilt in his voice was so Irish, so captivating and happy.

"Then please do," said Elizabeth. "Libby…I rather like that myself."

Standing in that sacred time, neither was aware that guests were starting to leave the Astor's mansion. Mr. Townsend had gone to retrieve his wife's and Elizabeth's capes. He saw movement in the garden and walked through the open French doors to catch a closer look.

Why, that's Elizabeth and that Irishman. He watched the couple standing close in the gazebo. He stood on the veranda, in the shadows. With a sad heart, he realized who his future son-in-law was to be.

God help us all, thought Townsend. *He's everything I'm not. He's an Irishman, a Catholic, a charismatic figurehead, a lawyer, and a crusader for the Irish cause.* Well, he'd see to it that Meagher kept his daughter in the fashion to which she was accustomed, or there would be hell to pay.

He could partially hear their conversation and he was surprised at his daughter's boldness.

"Please come tomorrow for dinner…on Sunday, we eat our main meal at two o'clock, and it would be an honor to have you take a meal with us, Mr. Meagh…Thom…Thomas," Elizabeth shyly whispered, as she backed away from him. She flashed him a beautiful smile, and without notice, she ran back alone into the mansion, not waiting for his answer.

Mr. Townsend watched his daughter run from the gazebo, up the back steps and into the Astor parlor. Her face looked excited and flushed. Should he confront this *Meagher of the Sword* tonight? He thought better of it. *There will be chances soon enough.*

Thomas Francis Meagher stood in the garden breathing in the perfume of the night-scented roses. He was smiling at his good fortune. He watched Libby hurry back into the Mansion to disappear from his view, swallowed up in the color and movement he saw through the lighted windows. Completely captivated by this woman, he enjoyed the beauty of the female, the beauty of the night, the beauty and truth that welled up inside him. For the first time since the death of his beloved Catherine, the sadness he carried like an albatross around his neck was gone. He'd rediscovered the love that was missing from his heart, soul and body. The tiger was awakening within. On this wonderful night he didn't notice, as he left the Astor's garden to walk the many blocks to his suite at the Metropolitan Hotel, that he did not have on his coat.

CHAPTER 10

▼

THE COURTING BEGINS

"Good morning, ladies," sang a very happy Elizabeth. "Katie, I am so glad you have not left for Mass yet. Would it be possible for you to come back home after church?" She smiled a rather mysterious smile. "We are having unexpected company for dinner this afternoon and Bridget is going to need your help."

Katie and Bridget turned in surprise at the sound of Elizabeth's voice in the kitchen so early on this morning. The Ball at the Astor mansion had been last night and the Townsend's were rather late in returning home from that gala event.

"Oh! Miss Elizabeth. You startled us," said Bridget. "And just who am I cooking for today?"

"Mr. Meagher will be our guest."

Katie jumped up from the stool and ran over to Elizabeth. "Oh! Miss Elizabeth, come sit over here and tell us about the evening. He was there? Did he ask you to dance? Did you? You looked so beautiful...." Katie couldn't stop talking as usual, but suddenly her whole body froze.

"Miss Elizabeth. Did you forget about today?"

"Forget? What did I forget?"

"Me brothers are arriving at two o'clock today also. You invited them last week to come for dinner this very day." Katie put her hands over her mouth in dismay.

Bridget slammed the oven door and looked at Katie, then at Elizabeth.

"Have you both lost your senses? I am not aware of *any* company coming today and you are telling me we will be having four extra people for dinner at two o'clock?" She walked over to the kitchen table where Katie and Elizabeth were staring at each other.

"Oh! My! What a predicament." Elizabeth said unconvincingly. She looked at Bridget and smiled that mysterious smile again. "I don't see any problem. We will just have a table full of Irishmen in an Englishman's house." She laughed. "Father and Mother will just have to start getting used to it and today is the day."

"Bridget, we are cooking ham today and there will be more than enough if we make more potatoes and vegetables," said Katie. "I'll leave now for the earliest Mass and be back in plenty of time to help you. You've already made a dessert, Bridget. I can smell your wonderful upside down cake that is in the oven now." She started for the servant's entrance. "I hope you didn't make it fall when you slammed the oven door a few minutes ago."

"Just wait until me brothers see who they will be eatin' with this day." She giggled. "I'm not goin' to tell them before-hand, either."

"One more thing, before you leave, Katie, and Bridget, I want you to hear this, also." Elizabeth stood up from the wooden kitchen chair, pulled her morning wrap closer around her and spoke in a clear, energetic voice. "I now have a new name and I am going to use it the rest of my life. Please from now on, call me 'Libby'."

Bridget caught the edge of the kitchen counter. "Do your parents know of this name change?" she asked.

"Yes, they do, Bridget. I told them on the way home from the Astor Ball. Father just raised his bushy eyebrows, and said 'Harr-umph!' in that gruff voice he gets when he is totally confused." Elizabeth's eyes sparkled.

Katie and Bridget both moved closer to Libby. "We like your new name, don't we, Katie." Katie nodded her head and repeated, "Miss Libby,

Miss Libby." I really do like your new name. Why do you have a new name?"

Libby smiled, collecting her thoughts. "Mr. Meagher, and by the way, I am to call him "Thomas" gave me my new name last night."

"Miss Libby. Tell us. What happened?" Katie was beside herself with curiosity. "Tell us. Pl-e-e-a-a-s-e."

"As you know, Katie, I had not heard from Mr. Meagher…Thomas…all summer, but he was at the ball last night. He melted my heart when he came over and asked me to dance. I started blushing right off, but he didn't seem to notice. Bridget, could I have a cup of coffee, please?"

"Of course, Miss," said Bridget as she walked to the cupboard to get a cup for Libby. She filled it with steaming hot coffee and set the cup in front of Libby. Katie never left her side.

"We danced, and had a glass of champagne, then we went out onto the porch…you know what a glorious night it was last night…and we danced under the stars, and…" Elizabeth looked at the two women and was surprised at the expressions she saw on their faces.

"Don't stop now, Miss Libby, did he kiss you?"

"Katie, dare ye be so bold," said Bridget. "Excuse her, Miss Libby."

Katie just laughed. She knew Miss Libby would not be offended by the questions.

"Well, no, he didn't kiss me, but I thought I would die when he held me close while dancing. He gave me his coat when we were outside, and I forgot to give it back to him. Father took it from me right away when he presented me with my cape after I went back inside the Astor mansion." Libby once again smiled at the memory.

"Father brought the coat home." She sighed. "I fear Mr. Meagher is going to have to retrieve his property through my father's study." The three women laughed at the thought of it.

In the doorway, unannounced and certainly unexpected at such an early hour, stood Mr. Townsend. Just how much of the conversation he had taken in would be his secret. The three women jumped when they heard the familiar "har-umph" at the kitchen door. As so often happened, when

Mr. Townsend wanted to make his presence known, he would har-umph. He could instantly transform a room in this quaint, but effective manner.

Katie ran for the kitchen door, off to Mass; Bridget smoothed her hands on her apron and asked Mr. Townsend if he was ready for his breakfast, and Libby, remaining noncommittal, sipped her cup of coffee.

CHAPTER 11

▼

DINNER AT THE MANSION

Katie and Libby worked for an hour polishing the silver platters and bowls. Now the silver gleamed atop the beautiful lace doilies on the sideboard. The women spread out a freshly ironed linen tablecloth to cover the exquisitely carved mahogany table, and monogrammed plates were set in exactly the right place. Katie set sterling silverware to mark the places guests would sit for the meal. Off-white beeswax hand-dipped candles, set in a three-tiered silver holder, graced the center of the table, and a swag of greenery attached easily to the candlestick base. The chairs had been dusted and placed around the table.

"I must go upstairs and make myself presentable," said Libby. "Katie, will you stop fussing? The napkins look lovely folded in that mitered cap style, and the stemware is sparkling from your rubbing with the tea towel." Everything was ready for the guests with less than an hour to spare.

Katie closed the sliding doors to the dining room and entered the spotlessly clean hallway. She was happy that after all this time, at last, her brothers Connell, Patrick, Damien and Jimmy McBride were coming to dinner at the Townsend Mansion.

They are going to be so surprised, she thought. True to her word, she did not tell the brothers about the afternoon plans. *It will be great fun, and*

Lord knows, we need some excitement in our routine once in a while. To share dinner with the respected orator, Thomas Francis Meagher, would be a dream come true. When they had all lived in Ireland, her brothers had looked up to Meagher as their country's hero.

Her brothers were definitely not in the same class as the orator. *Meagher of the Sword* had had every opportunity for education, class, position and wealth, while the McBride's worked hard to eke out a living on their small farm. Coming to America was the only saving grace for her family. In fact, it was the common thread that would prevail at dinner today. All of the assembled men had come to America seeking a better life. All had, to varying degrees, succeeded in that quest.

From this day on, Katie predicted, *we will all be linked into our futures.*

Patrick worked in the Townsend foundry, putting in long, hard underpaid shifts. Connell, who had a head for numbers, had a position as a bookkeeper at a local bank, Jimmy spent his early hours in a bakery, while Damien, the youngest brother, remained the least successful, working day jobs found by standing in the street begging for work. He never knew what backbreaking work each day offered him. Weekends were no exception.

Katie was pleased all four brothers would soon be walking through the servants entrance and taking dinner with the Townsend family. Libby had invited her to sit at the table, but Katie knew her place. She would serve, help Bridget, clean the dishes from the table, wash dishes in the kitchen, and try to keep up with the conversation in between her trips to the kitchen. Milton would carve the meat, pour coffee and, when the men had retired to the parlor, serve brandy and cigars.

Katie watched the kitchen wall clock. It seemed to her the hands had not moved one second since the last time she checked. But, suddenly, she saw the four men walking up to the front door.

"Oh, horrors! They can't do that," she murmured. And she ran to the front hallway just in time to collide with Milton who was answering the knock. *"Oh! No! Milton. No one told him we are having guests today,"* she thought.

Milton continued toward the front door.

"Miss," he said. "Please stay back." He waited for the third knock, and then opened the front door. There stood four handsome Irishmen, dressed in their tattered best clothes, all smiling up at Milton, who looked aghast.

"May I help you?" he asked. "Are you expected this Sunday afternoon?" He looked from man to man, and then he glanced over at Katie who was standing by his side. She was smiling as if nothing was amiss.

"We are here for dinner and to see our sister, Katie," said Patrick, as he stared into the hallway.

"*Deirfiúr*. Sister. There you are." He sidestepped Milton and walked toward Katie.

The other three men followed suit. But to Katie's amazement, one of the men hung back, hat in hand.

"Katie, I hope it is all right with you, but Damien couldn't make it today. He got a day job with the city." Patrick waved his hand toward the extra young man. "I invited Seán Daly here to come in his place. No sense wasting that good food, now is there?"

Katie was mortified. She felt herself turning beet red. How would she explain this to her employer? Should she lie and pass him off as her brother? Secretly, she was happy to see Seán, the man of her dreams; she hoped to one day to marry this Irishman from Waterford.

"Seán, how nice to see you. Yes, do come in." Katie extended her hand and Seán took it into his. He stepped inside the hallway.

"Patrick said it would be okay if I came, Katie. I did want to see you today, too, and when you left Mass early, right after the distribution of the communion, I didn't have a chance to talk to you."

Katie took control of the situation. "Follow me to the parlor," she said, as she led the parade of grown Irishmen down the hallway and into the room. As she marched them past the open study doors, she felt Mr. Townsend's eyes following the group, but she did not slow her step. Waiting in the parlor were Mrs. Townsend and Libby.

"Mrs. Townsend...Libby. These are my brothers, Patrick, Jimmy and Connell. Damien can't come...so...Seán Daly has come in his place." Katie wanted to make a good impression on Seán. She wanted him to see her at her best. Libby sensed her unease and started a conversation with the young men.

"Please sit down," Libby offered. "Dinner will be ready in a few minutes." Her mind, however, was on other things. *What is happening to Thomas?* She wondered.

To add to the confusion, Thomas had also arrived and was standing just inside the doorframe, waiting to be admitted properly by Milton.

"I am also here for dinner," he said looking rather quizzically at Milton. "If you would be so kind as to announce me to Miss Townsend?"

Just then Meagher heard his name called out by Mr. Townsend. "Come into the study, Meagher. I want to talk to you. Milton bring him on back here."

Milton did as instructed, and Thomas followed him down the hallway. He knew his way to the study but stayed behind Milton.

Where is Libby? He thought.

"Come in, Meagher. Have a chair." Mr. Townsend pointed to the leather chair nearest the front window.

"Good afternoon, sir," said Meagher. "Thank you for the invitation for dinner today. I don't get home cooked meals often."

This attempt at casual conversation fell on deaf ears. He spotted his jacket slung over the back of a wooden chair in the corner of the room. Mr. Townsend noted Meagher's gaze.

"I believe I have something that belongs to you, do I not?"

"Yes, sir. That's my jacket. I put it around Libby's shoulders last evening when we were talking in the gazebo."

Mr. Townsend appreciated the honest, open answer from Meagher.

"That's another thing. What's with this name changing business? My daughter's name is Elizabeth. She may allow you to change her name, but she will remain Elizabeth to me. Is that clear?"

"Yes sir." Meagher shifted in his chair. He didn't like the tone in the older man's voice. He wondered where this conversation was headed. "Please call me Thomas, sir."

"All right. Thomas. I will be blunt. Just what are your intentions towards my daughter?"

"With all due respect, sir. I have nothing but honorable intentions towards Libby…Elizabeth. I would ask her to marry me this very minute. We have not spoken of our affections toward each other." Meagher paused. "I intend to find out just where I stand with Libby. That is why I am here today, sir. I want to start courting her in the traditional way. Visiting on Sunday with you in the parlor."

"Har-umph!" said Mr. Townsend. "Well, you are indeed arrogant. What makes you think my daughter is interested in you? You have already been forward with her, taking her to a public place without a chaperone. My daughter is innocent and does not know the ways of men. I intend to see she stays that way. Do you understand me?" He looked up at Meagher from his chair behind his study desk. "If you are her choice for a husband, then you and I have got to find some mutual ground."

Meagher stood up. "Sir, the mutual ground is Libby. I will answer your questions about me, anything you want to know."

Peter Townsend lifted a pen from the ink blotter and set it back down.

"I know all about your politics, Meagher. I have had a detective checking on you for some months now." He looked squarely at Meagher. "I know all about your activities in Ireland and your being sent to Tasmania." He waved his hand in the air. "I have read the accounts of your escape and landing in New York City, living with the Irish in the slums."

Thomas Francis Meagher, proud of his heritage and contributions to his fellow men, stood tall in the study of Peter Townsend.

"Then there is nothing left for us to discuss, is there? I would assume Libby is waiting for me." He started to leave the room.

"Not so fast, young man. I have more." Peter Townsend read from a sheet of paper he'd placed on the desktop.

"Let us begin with the fact that you are already married! Your wife and son live in Ireland."

"Sir!" said Meagher, taken aback. "My wife is dead. My first son is dead, buried in Tasmania. Your detective only brought you part of the information." He started to pace in the small space. "Had you just asked, I would have told you all of this." He walked directly to the desk.

"Because of my allegiance to Ireland I was sentenced to death, but my father's influence saved my life. I was exiled forever from Ireland and sent to Tasmania." Meagher paused for a moment and looked out the window.

"Catherine Bennett came to me in marriage in Tasmania, on Van Diemen's Island, and we lived a lovely life together."

"I had the opportunity to escape, but by then Bennie was expecting our child. She begged me to go, to be free, and that she would follow on a regular passenger ship after the child was old enough to travel. I did escape, but my son only lived a few short weeks." Thomas sat down in the now familiar leather chair and put his hand to his forehead.

"After she could control her grief, her father thought a sea voyage to join me would be healing. Bennie sailed to Waterford and lived with my family for a few weeks. Then she and me da finished the voyage together. She came to me to begin again our married life, but she could not take New York City's extreme heat. She suffered from arthritis and was in constant pain. So, when she became with child again, it was decided she would have a better life in Ireland. She and my father returned to his home in Waterford."

"I was heartbroken to see her leave. To say goodbye once again to the woman I loved…it was painful." Meagher was reliving that dreary day at the dock when he said goodbye to his beloved young wife once again. "The plan was to bring the child back to New York City when Bennie was able to travel safely." Meagher looked at the rows of books in Mr. Townsend's study.

"I was notified that my son was born and all was well. Then a few days later I received a letter that Bennie was dead. My God! Mr. Townsend, she was only twenty-one years old. He put his hand to his chest, covering his heart. "I have no joy, sir."

Mr. Townsend sat very still, taking in what he was hearing for the first time. *So much suffering in one so young*, he thought.

"Does Elizabeth know any of this?" he asked, barely above a whisper.

"Not from me, she doesn't." Meagher talked slowly. "We have not discussed intimate details of our lives, but I intend to tell her."

"I am thirty years old. I lecture on a traveling circuit, and I live in a suite in a hotel." Meagher dropped his hands to his sides in a signal of despair. "I am an exile. How was I to take care of an infant? Me da and his sisters decided it best for the baby to stay with them and be raised as an Irishman in Waterford. These same two aunts had raised me after me mum's death when I was just a lad. They promised to provide a good life for the child, my namesake." Meagher looked directly at Mr. Townsend.

"There was nothing I could do. My Irish friends here in the city took me in, kept me from extreme depression, and fed me. Eventually, the pain subsided, and I am again able to pursue my lawyer certificate and a legal position with Tammany Hall. I am in the process of becoming a naturalized United States citizen." Meagher paused, wondering if he should disclose everything, then decided to continue.

"My father sends me an allowance from the family holdings. I have part ownership in the family farm near Tipperary. Also, I *am* a successful orator. I can support a wife in the proper manner, sir. Maybe not as well as you, sir, but eventually my financial situation will change into a more secure position. I have opened my law office on Alice Street, and a few clients are coming."

Mr. Townsend raised his eyebrows at this information. He rose and came around the desk and walked over to Thomas. He put a steady hand on the younger man's shoulder.

"I had no idea."

The two men, one standing, the other now sitting, remained silhouetted for a few minutes against the afternoon light pouring through the lace-curtained window. An invisible bond formed between them: the ties that would bind them being the love they both shared for the same beautiful young woman.

Townsend stood back from Meagher.

"I'll not interfere with your courting my daughter."

He reached into his vest pocket, pulled out his fancy gold watch and flipped open the lid. The face of his beloved wife, Caroline, smiled back at him.

"Son, I think the women of the house are probably waiting dinner on us. Shall we make our way to the dining room?" He offered Meagher his hand and as the two men shook hands, an understanding passed between them.

When Mr. Townsend opened the study door, both men were smiling. *Now to face this meal with all these rough Irishmen sitting at my table*, he thought. *My whole house has gone absolutely mad this day."*

Peter Townsend and Thomas Francis Meagher walked to the parlor where Libby and her mother sat graciously visiting with the McBride brothers and Seán Daly. Libby smiled brightly at Thomas and quickly stepped over to his side.

"When do we eat around this house?" boomed Mr. Townsend.

Just then Katie opened the dining room doors, where the gaslights from the sconces on the walls illuminated the silver platter of ham, garnished with fresh pineapple slices. Libby was pleased to see the added touch. Bridget, whenever she could, used the traditional pineapple, the sign of welcome.

Beneath the flaming candlesticks were two vegetable dishes, one held steaming potatoes, heaped up in a rounded white mound with a large square of creamy yellow butter in the center. The other bowl held freshly shelled green peas, and the aroma of hot bread right from Bridget's oven lured them across the hall and into the well-placed chairs.

CHAPTER 12

▼

CHRISTMAS SHOPPING

Libby pulled her cloak tighter as the icy wind blew around her hooded wrap. She was grateful for her lined gloves and the extra scarf she'd tossed around her neck before leaving with Katie to go Christmas shopping. They had spent the afternoon looking in storefront windows and making just the right purchases for the family. Now, loaded with packages, they made their way across Fifth Avenue.

"Katie," she shouted above the wind. "Let's stop at a little tea shop. I'm exhausted from all the shopping we've done today. A cup of tea will warm us up, too."

The women did not hesitate to find shelter from the storm and they stopped at the first restaurant that they happened upon. Libby smiled when the tinkling bell alerted the male waiter that they had entered his establishment. They were the only customers this late in the day. She chose a small round table and pulled out a wooden ladder-backed style chair featuring wooden dragons carved out on the top rung. Katie piled all of her packages neatly on the floor and sat in a duplicate chair.

"OOHH!" Katie rubbed at her hands. "My hands are cold. I never do remember to wear my mittens," she complained.

Looking about the room, Libby noticed the counter with scones and sweet breads behind the glass. "Would you like a scone and some straw-berry jam, Katie? Umm, that would taste good with hot tea about now."

The waiter approached the two ladies and Libby placed their order.

"We will each have a scone with strawberry jam, and bring us a pot of hot tea…cream and sugar, also, if you will, please." The waiter joined his hands as if to pray and he bowed toward the two ladies before departing to fill their order.

"Our shopping excursion went really well, didn't it?" asked Libby when they were once again alone. Katie had dutifully carried the smaller pack-ages, wrapped in brown paper and string, but Libby had ordered the larger and heavier packages delivered to the Townsend mansion.

"I think your Mother will like that beautiful silk neck scarf. It looks so delicate and fragile, and the swirls in the design look Oriental." Katie picked up a long, slender shaped box. "This one is the fancy pencil box you purchased for Mr. Meagher. I believe it will blend perfectly on his office desk."

"I love the rich hues in the wood," said Libby. It is a handsome gift, and I can already see him placing it on his desk. It has a sense of solidness to it, and when I am with him I feel that from him as well."

The waiter returned. With another gracious bow from the waist, he spread out a large tablecloth tatted around the edges in a delicate lace floral pattern and gave them each a white linen napkin. He then picked up a tray already loaded with two china cups and saucers, a miniature silver knife, and the plate of scones along with a pot of strawberry jam. These he set in the center of the table. The teapot was a beautiful black glaze with a cloi-sonné fire-spitting 14 ct. gold dragon curling around the pot. The spout and handle were trimmed in the same gold. It was filled with steaming hot water, too hot to drink.

The waiter opened a special box filled with Ginseng tea leaves. Using miniature tongs, he dropped a clump of the tea leaves into the steaming water.

"This must steep."

With two swift slices from an elegant, black, bone-handled silver knife, the scones lay in four halves on the porcelain plate. He removed the jam pot lid and, using the same silver knife, he spread the strawberry jam.

"My wife, she make jam." Pride shone in his almond shaped eyes. "It very good. Not sweet."

Katie could not take her eyes off of the man as he continued his performance. He raised and lowered the teapot with his right hand, without making a splash as the golden liquid filled the cups.

Libby, in her hurry to get in out of the wind and cold, quite by chance had stepped into a Chinese Tea Shop. The waiter, an oriental from China, was dressed in a heavily embroidered, bright red long-sleeved satin jacket and black baggy pants. His black hair was pulled back into a braid, and an embroidered circular satin hat sat on his head.

"You like, I read your tea leaves when you finished? Maybe the leaves reveal your questions about love in future?" He flashed a friendly smile, then bowed, the ceremony coming to an end.

Katie's eyes were bright with the excitement of the afternoon. Early in the morning Libby had deliberately taken her to see Toyland at Saks Fifth Avenue Toy Store. Never in her life had she seen such beautiful dolls and games, blocks and books, and painting sets. They shopped for Libby's niece and nephew and other family members and friends.

It had been a memorable excursion into the wonderland of Christmas time in New York City. However, when Katie first spotted the dolls, she stood rooted to the floor. Her eyes, big and round, took in the magic of it all.

What particularly stunned Katie was the "Bru," an eighteen-inch, chiseled beauty dressed in the latest Paris fashion. The Bru was actually a miniature dress mannequin. New York City ladies could select their various sizes and colors and have dresses made for the upcoming fashion season. Once the ordering season ended, however, the doll was then sent to the toy department, to be sold as a toy, usually just before Christmas. To Katie's eye, she was the most beautiful doll she had ever seen.

Libby had walked to the clerk and discreetly engaged him in a private conversation. She told him to deliver the Bru, along with other purchases they would be making, to the Townsend mansion. She made it clear she did not want him to remove the doll from the window until after she and Katie had left the store.

"Yes, Ma'am," said the clerk. He took down her address and started a running tab. Come over here, Katie," Libby called out to her. "Look at these water color paint sets and puzzles." Katie crooned goodbye ever so softly to the dolls in the window display, then joined Libby.

"Did you have a doll in Ireland?"

"No, Miss. There was never money for toys…but we did have Christmas. We went to Mass on Christmas Day if a priest was in the neighboring town, and we sometimes joined our dinner with the next farm, but presents were not heard of." She looked around her at the myriad toys that fit all descriptions of wants and desires and dreams.

"Me mum did make me a rag dolly when I was very young. I don't know what happened to her, though. She probably just wore out."

Libby's heart couldn't take much more of this story, told so innocently and in truth, made beautiful in the telling.

They chose a rocking horse, some children's storybooks, a cradle and a baby doll, two paint sets and paper pads, the list growing, much to the delight of the store clerk. One of the paint sets would be Libby's gift to Katie. She had seen some doodling Katie had left on scraps of paper and thought she might have a hidden talent in art. Libby smiled knowing she would complete the gift by including a note telling Katie they would be going together to visit art museums in the spring.

Libby had signed the tab, and the two women had continued on their way. If Katie had taken one more glance back to look at the Bru in the window, her heart would have shattered. The doll no longer stood on display.

As the afternoon progressed, the shopping soon grew tiresome.

Katie had hoped to buy Miss Libby a gift. She had been saving her money, but it seemed everything was out of her price range. Katie, as a surprise for Miss Libby, was working on a delicate lace, shimmering thread shawl. If she worked hard, she'd finish it in plenty of time to place a wrapped package under the tree by Christmas morning.

For weeks now, Katie had been tatting in the evening hours. Sometimes she knitted in the parlor on other projects with Mrs. Townsend and Libby but she always went to her room and worked in private on the present for her mistress. She wanted it to be just perfect and had agonized over what thread to purchase to make it as delicate as her stubby fingers would allow. She finally had settled on a brilliant sapphire blue color.

As the tea simmered, Libby and Katie sat in silence for a moment, looking around the teashop.

"Christmas in America is so different from Ireland," a rather pensive Katie spoke slowly, and softly. "We made Christmas bread, but presents...well, that is all new to me. America has so much." She looked away to hide the start of a tear. This was not the place to remember her past life in Ireland and to think of her mum and da.

"Katie, what are you giving your brothers?" asked Libby, pretending not to notice the change in Katie's face.

"I've been knitting them heavy, warm socks, and Bridget promised me we will make Christmas bread like we did in Ireland." She glanced up at Libby. "It will be fun to give Patrick a gift. He saved my life by getting me to New York City."

"What about Seán Daly? Does he get a pair of socks made with love from your hands, too?" teased Libby.

Katie whipped her head back. "He gets nothin' from me. Why would I make him socks?" But then she grinned. "I do want to make him a loaf of Christmas bread with extra raisins and fruits and nuts in it." Katie cared for Seán and hoped someday he would see her as a grown woman and not Patrick's little sister.

"Did Mr. Meagher invite you to Midnight Mass?" asked Katie. "I certainly hope so. It would be good for straight-backed Milton to have to chaperone you two to church." She giggled at the scene she envisioned.

"Oh! I hadn't thought of that!" said Libby. "What an imposition that would be for Milton to have to sit through the service just to drive us to and from church." She thought a moment. "Maybe Father could allow you to be my chaperone that night. I'll ask him. You could ride in the carriage with Mr. Meagher and me. It would be perfectly respectable." Libby winked at Katie.

The waiter had been watching the women and when the last of the scones disappeared from the plate he used this opening to approach their table.

"Now we see your future. What do the leaves have to tell you? He lifted Katie's cup first and swirled the leaves.

"You be married in two springs. Man already know this. He waiting for you." The waiter smiled when he saw Katie start to giggle.

"Now read Miss Libby's," said Katie.

Libby handed him her teacup. They watched in silence as he swirled around her leaves. He looked, swirled again.

"Marriage for you. Next November."

Libby blushed. "You saw something else, didn't you?"

He grabbed Libby's hand. "Much happiness...much sadness."

A shiver passed through his hand and Libby pulled away from the electric tingle.

"Thank you, sir. We must be on our way. Come, Katie." Without hesitating any longer, she stood to leave.

Katie clapped her hands. "We best be getting home, Miss Libby. It is going to be a cold walk and it's getting dark." She reached over and scooped up the packages.

Libby paid the bill, and they left the store the same way they had come in, the little bell again tinkling their departure. The waiter smiled as he felt the warmth that radiated from the two young women. *She forget what tea leaves say*, he hoped.

He walked to the window and watched them make their way up the avenue, the wind unmercifully whipping into their backs. *Looks like snow. I go now to my room and drink tea myself.* He swiftly turned the door lock, clicked out the lights and made his way to the rear of the teashop.

At the same time as the young women sipping tea, Mr. Peter Townsend had left his office, thinking he needed to do some Christmas shopping for his wife and two daughters. He was walking towards Tiffany's, New York City's finest jewelry store.

Caroline appreciated him and was a perfect wife for him. She kept his household running well, knew her place as his wife and loved him, even though there were times over the past thirty years when he wondered why. Buying for Caroline was an easy choice. She loved jewelry. He would select a fashion piece with the help of Mr. Tiffany.

He continued to buy gifts for his two daughters, even though they were now grown women. Alice had married well. Her husband Samuel Barlow, a railroad industrialist and an educated man, practiced law and was successful both financially and in social circles. Elizabeth remained single and seemingly was in no hurry to marry. At least that was her behavior before she became involved with the Irish hero.

Mr. Townsend enjoyed this annual shopping excursion to Tiffany's. He never failed to purchase a nice bauble to surprise the women in his life on Christmas Day when the family all gathered in his parlor. He considered himself a very lucky and happy man. To give the women he loved a present at Christmas brought him great pleasure; to see their faces light up expressing happiness at the gift was all the thanks he needed. The walk to Tiffany's warmed his heart in spite of the chilly winds whipping around him. *We are in for a real snowstorm by mid afternoon*, he thought.

As Mr. Townsend waited on the corner for a carriage to pass by, he caught sight of Thomas Francis Meagher on the other side of the street, walking briskly as if on a mission. Townsend decided to wait on the corner and see where the young fellow was headed. To his disappointment he saw Meagher enter Tiffany's.

Wait a minute, he thought. *I don't want to run into him in Tiffany's.* Then it dawned on him what Meagher was up to. He was probably purchasing a jewel for Elizabeth. A pain called jealousy ran through his system as Meagher's actions struck him full force. *Some other man is buying jewels for my baby Elizabeth,* he thought.

Mr. Townsend did not want Meagher to see him, especially not inside Tiffany's show room. He hailed a passing carriage, climbed inside and in a rather defeated voice said, "Take me to my home, 129 Fifth Avenue."

As the carriage made its way against the blustery wind, he saw two young women on the side of the road, fighting against the elements, their arms filled with packages. "Stop the horse," he shouted to the driver. "Those women need some assistance." He opened the carriage door and stepped out.

"Excuse me, ladies, can I offer you a lift out of this storm? I just live up the street." He waved them to come into the cab. "You can then take the carriage the rest of your way."

The two women looked at each other, startled for a moment.

"Why thank you sir. That is very thoughtful of you." Libby looked up and stared into the face of her father.

"Father!" She ran over to the cab. "Oh! Thank you for coming along when you did. Katie is not dressed properly for this walk, and she is shaking in this cold wind." Libby grabbed Katie's arm and pulled her toward the waiting warmth of the cab.

Chapter 13

More Christmas Plans

Bridget was busy in the kitchen while Milton sat in a wooden chair drinking a cup of very strong coffee. He looked harassed. Both turned when Libby stomped into the house through the servant's entrance, followed closely behind by Mr. Townsend and Katie.

"Where have you two been?" shouted Bridget. "I've been worried about you out in this storm...fine thing."

Libby walked Katie over to Bridget who took hold of both of Katie's hands. "You are frozen, child. Stick your hands into that bucket of cold water there on the dry sink." She pulled Katie's arms out of her wrap. "I know its got peelings in it, but it's cold and you need to stop the frost bite." Without hesitating, Katie stuck her hands into the water pail.

Bridget looked at Mr. Townsend. "Evening sir. Good thing you brought these two home." Not waiting for an answer, she turned back to Libby who stood silently looking at her feet.

Mr. Townsend was smiling at the very idea that his housekeeper could make his daughter answer to her.

"What have you two been up to this afternoon?" She motioned towards Milton. "Just look at Milton. He is worn to a frazzle having to answer the door knocker," scolded Bridget. "We were inundated with all kinds of service and trades people delivering packages on the orders of Miss Elizabeth Townsend." She looked over at Libby. "You certainly did a lot of Christmas shopping today, didn't you?"

"Yes, Ma'am, we did." Then Libby flashed Bridget one of her most dazzling smiles. "And we won't tell you what we bought, either, will we Katie?"

"Humph!" said Bridget as she turned to Mr. Townsend.

"Give me your overcoat, sir. The three of you smell like a drowned dog." She wrinkled up her nose. "Whew! Wet wool." She carried the three outer garments to the washroom just off the kitchen and hung them on pegs to dry. With a big sigh she composed herself and returned to the kitchen.

"Dinner is about ready, Katie. Get your apron on." Bridget walked to her oven and checked the roast slowly cooking in its own juices. She lifted pot lids with her long apron acting as a hand protection, and with a large wooden spoon she stirred the pot full of brown gravy.

Libby, standing along side of Katie, was amazed when Katie pulled her hands out of the water. They were pink, but they apparently didn't tingle any more when she wriggled her fingers as she reached for her apron.

Mr. Townsend crossed the hall to his study. *I need a drink*, he thought. A shot glass full of Scotch would help settle his nerves and warm him besides. He could smell the roasting beef and his stomach growled.

Libby, seeing her father go to his study, decided to approach him about her attending Midnight Mass on Christmas Eve with Thomas. She started walking down the hallway, but abruptly halted her steps when she heard voices coming from the study.

"Hello, Peter."

"Caroline. Why are you sitting in my study with no lamps lit? Are you ill?

"Actually, Peter, I was waiting for you to come home and I must have dozed off. I wanted to visit with you for a minute before we are called to dinner."

Libby, knowing she shouldn't eavesdrop, especially before Christmas when people are planning surprises, decided to listen anyway.

"As you know, dear Peter, Christmas is only a week away. Libby has already mentioned to me that she wants to attend Midnight Mass with Thomas. She paused. "I told her that it was fine with us, and it is…right?"

Libby held her breath, waiting for his answer.

"Dear, you know…well, if you approve, I will approve."

"Another thing," Caroline went on. "I don't want Milton out on Christmas Eve. He is getting too old to be staying up late and taking care of the horses. Katie can accompany Libby and Thomas. They are only going to church. Thomas can rent a carriage and driver to take them to the church and then to return them home after the service."

"Now, Caroline…." He stopped before finishing his sentence. This conversation was totally unexpected, but he knew his wife was right in her observations of Milton.

"When Libby comes and asks you for permission to accompany Mr. Meagher to Midnight Mass, I want you to be civil and give her your blessing on this matter." She paused…."Promise?"

Just then Libby heard Bridget coming from the kitchen, obviously getting ready to announce dinner. The last thing she needed was to get caught eavesdropping at her father's study door. She hurried up the front stairway, carrying the brown packages from the shopping spree. She entered her extravagantly decorated bedroom and carefully set the packages on the top of her small table. *Katie was so excited today in the stores*, she thought. *She must have suffered so much as a child in Ireland. Well, I'll see to it she never goes without again,* Libby promised herself.

Milton had placed the delivered boxes in the hallway outside her bedroom door. Libby pulled them into her room and began removing the string and the outer wrappers. The first box she opened held the French Bru fashion doll. Seeing it again made Libby smile. Santa Claus would find Katie McBride in America.

"Miss Libby," called Bridget as she tapped on the bedroom door. "Dinner is served."

Morning came early and Libby and Katie were excited as they helped Bridget make the promised Irish Christmas breads. Bridget was giving final instructions for preserving their labor of love.

"Never would I imagine all the bustle for a holiday," said Katie. "I can't sleep. I dream of how beautiful and perfect and magical everything is."

She looked at the stack of packages in the parlor across from the kitchen, and wondered if any of them had her name on them, too shy to take peeks, even when no one would see her.

"Katie, be sure you soak the cheesecloth in that bowl of rum there on the counter before you wrap up the breads," said Bridget. She cut the material into a perfect square and dropped it into the large stoneware bowl. She allowed the rum to filter through the cloth. Next, she carefully lifted one of the heavy loaves, filled with raisins, nuts and candied fruits, and wrapped it in the rum-soaked cloth, being careful to tuck in the ends. They had made six loaves, Katie needing four for gifts and two for her gift to the Townsend's open house buffet on Christmas Day.

Katie, while in the Catskills that past summer, had made a sturdy, flat-based wooden basket, using soft green willow branches; the breads wrapped in heavy brown paper, would rest in it, making it easy for her to hand the gifts over to her brothers at Christmas Eve Mass. She would include bread for Seán, knowing he would be at Mass with her brothers.

CHAPTER 14

▼

MIDNIGHT MASS

After some juggling of schedules, the arrangements for Midnight Mass were complete and everyone was happy with the outcome.

Milton was relieved of his late night chaperone duties; Thomas hired a carriage to take Libby, Katie and himself to the Cathedral; Bridget had her baking all done and wrapped, waiting for delivery, and Katie could hardly stay inside her skin she was so excited. Libby couldn't stop smiling. This was a very important outing for both her and Katie as neither had been inside the Cathedral of St. Patrick. The building towered over a whole city block, and thousands of people would be present for this special Mass. She was eager to be a part of it, to see for herself what the celebration of the birth of the Baby Jesus would be like.

"Hurry Katie. It's almost ten o'clock and Thomas will be here soon." Libby fussed with her fox fur hat, its diamond shape more decoration than a covering for warmth. She pulled her heavy wool cloak around her shoulders. She slid her hands through the slits and reached for the matching fur muff. She snapped the frog holdings down the front. She took one final glance at her image and, satisfied, quickly left the room.

Katie met her coming down the front hall stairway. She hurried into the kitchen to grab the basket full of Irish Christmas breads to give to her brothers and Seán Daly. The carefully wrapped packages of handmade stockings were stuffed around the breads. A piece of holly decorated the basket handle.

"Just look at the two of us. We look so festive." Katie twirled around and around in the hallway. She couldn't believe the present from Mr. and Mrs. Townsend. Only two days after the terrible storm, a beautiful wool, dark green cloak was left on her bed with a "Happy St. Stephen's Day" note attached.

"No member of my household staff will be seen out in the cold not properly attired," said Mr. Townsend. He spoke in his usual gruff voice when she sought him out to thank him personally. Katie started to give him a hug in her excitement at having such a beautiful garment, but restrained herself and pulled back. Now here she was ready to go out to Mass and show off her fine present.

"Miss, your carriage has arrived." Milton still could not be cordial to Thomas. His English background forbidding such a friendship, no matter if he desired it or not. Even though Mr. Townsend was beginning to see a favorable side to the Irish orator, for Milton toleration would be the key word between the two men.

The light from the front porch spilled out onto the freshly fallen snow.

"Thomas! We are coming," shouted Libby. She walked with Katie out into the night. "Katie. Look up at the sky, see the stars, the moon." She sighed. "Isn't this just the most perfect night…and it isn't cold either."

The lamps were lit on the sides of the carriage and Thomas stood with the door open. The horse pawed the ground and in doing so, the bells attached to the head harness jingled, much to Katie's delight.

Thomas was filled with happiness. He had a few surprises planned for this memorable evening. He was counting on the miracles of Christmas to begin his and Libby's journey of discovering each other's heart.

Earlier in the week he had shopped for Libby and found the perfect gift in Tiffany's. After Mass, he planned to give it to Libby. He patted the pocket that held the black velvet square box, checking to be sure it was still there.

"Listen to the jingle bells. Thomas this is a wonderful surprise," said Libby as he tucked her under the huge, heavy buffalo robes. She had never looked lovelier to him. Her cheeks were glowing and her eyes sparkled up at him. "I don't want to miss a minute of this wonderful event. Let's not be late." Libby fussed a bit over Katie's robe. "Did you decide where you will meet Patrick?"

"We plan to meet at the west side entrance," said Katie. "That is where the carriages all empty out." Katie pulled her cloak up around her neck. She had chosen a lace scarf for a headpiece, knowing that a woman's hair had to be covered during church services. Her hands were covered in new, hand-knitted woolen mittens, a gift from Bridget given to her just for this occasion. She felt so special, thankful for so many things. First of all for the good fortune of being in America attending her first Midnight Mass with her family, and secondly, knowing her employers and the household staff loved her. Seeing Seán Daly made her smile, too. He would be very happy to have her Irish Christmas bread, since it had been several years since he had been in Ireland. Life was good this wonderful night.

"Katie, you look absolutely glowing tonight in this invigorating air," said Meagher. And Katie giggled as she, too, snuggled deeper under the robes.

They arrived at the Cathedral parking area and Meagher left the carriage first. "Katie, I want to talk to you. I have a secret. Wait for me by the horse's head," he whispered. Then he helped Libby out of the carriage. He walked to the driver, paid the man and instructed him to come back when the service was finished. Then he whispered something to the driver, who nodded in agreement.

Thomas quickly strode up to Katie. He kept his voice low.

"Katie, will you go home with your brother Patrick tonight? I want to be alone with Libby. Can I count on you to help me out?"

Katie smiled. "Will you make it worth me while?" she teased. Before he could answer, she said, "I'll have to see what plans Patrick has and let you know after Mass."

"Patrick already knows, Katie. I talked to him earlier about this arrangement."

Thomas hurried back to help Libby out of the carriage, leaving the warmth of the buffalo robes behind her on the bench. He put one woman on each side of himself, and they linked arms. Like three excited teenagers, they walked in a jaunty step up the drive to the huge double doors.

A blast of hot hair greeted them as the ushers pulled open the doors. "Merry Christmas to you all," they said in unison. One of the ushers recognized Thomas. "Mr. Meagher, how nice to see you at this Mass." From the red hair and freckles, it was easy to tell he was Irish. "How is your mum and da?" asked Thomas after recognizing the face. "The last time I spoke to your da, your mum was doing poorly." The usher's face grew pensive. "She is here tonight, sir. Thank you for asking. I'll tell her you asked about her. She still coughs a lot."

By now the line had formed behind the trio and Thomas moved them on into the vestibule. The fragrances of burning wax, pine and poinsettias greeted them and Libby sneezed. The huge pillars were swagged in pine boughs, and huge red ribbons were hanging from their centers. Everything was exquisitely decorated. Huge, ornately carved wooden candlesticks held four-inch based beeswax candles. Every corner and crevice inside the cavernous Cathedral was illuminated.

Even though thousands of people were spilling into the pews, there was a sacred hush in the building. Thomas escorted his guests to his rented pew in the front section near the main altar. They would be able to see and hear everything. Libby noticed most of the congregation was older men and women; no small infants or children were present. *It must be because of the late hour and that Santa Claus will be coming soon to their homes*, she thought.

Katie looked around for her brothers and spotted Patrick toward the rear, but the processional had already started to form, and Katie could not leave her place. *This is a better view anyway, and I'll greet him after the service*, she thought, and didn't worry about it again. The basket of presents she placed squarely on the floor in front of her. She was excited about being asked to help Mr. Meagher with his Christmas wish and would do whatever he suggested.

Libby looked up at Thomas. "This is my first time inside this building," she said. "I hope it is all right if I look around?" She was sitting primly next to Thomas.

"Here, let me help you out of that heavy cloak. You will get too warm," he offered. When he saw Libby's sapphire-blue satin gown with the pneumonia blouse insert, he held his breath. *She is like a china doll,* he thought.

Libby noticed a life-size Nativity crèche set up in the corner in the right wing. "Katie, look at that crèche," she whispered across Thomas' chest, and pointed Katie's gaze in the right direction. "The baby Jesus is missing from the manger."

By now the choir had assembled in the rear of the church. The organist had been entertaining with beautiful Christmas hymns, but suddenly, as if mighty trumpets were sounding, the organ burst forth, shaking the floor. The 100-year-old song, *Adeste Fidelis, Laeti Triumphantes,* filled every listening heart. Libby felt a shiver of pure delight tingle through her body.

The procession slowly wound its way through the levels of pews. The well rehearsed, vested men's and boy's choir accompanied a young girl dressed in a white cotton robe with a gold rope sash. She had wings attached to the back of the robe. In her arms she carried the baby Jesus. They made their way to the Nativity Crèche. She gently placed the statue in the manger, its raised arms reaching out to everyone. Libby could see the pride in the little girl's face. The honor of carrying the Christ child to the manger must have been a blessing to her and her family.

Acolytes carrying long wooden poles with swinging candles surrounded by glass hurricane type covers came next. They proceeded up into the main altar area, then turned and faced the congregation. Libby mentally sang along, *joyful and triumphant, Oh come, ye, oh come ye, to Bethlehem.*

Next, resplendent in gold-thread embroidered robes, came six priests guarding the celebrant of the Mass: the Archbishop himself, John Hughes, the giant for the Irish cause in New York City. When he saw Thomas, he gave a bow in his direction. Little did Libby know what part this man would play in her future. She looked at Thomas's face and saw the peace in his eyes. *This is his church,* she thought. *I wonder what makes it so very important to him?*

Finally, the entourage all assembled, the organist ended the processional hymn. One of the priests, in Latin, welcomed the parishioners. Thomas responded, much to Libby's surprise. *So he speaks Latin along with English, Gaelic, German, French, Spanish, and Italian,* she thought. *Thomas, you are a very complicated, and interesting man. I could spend a lifetime getting to know you.*

Suddenly handballs trilled as an altar boy shook his hand and arm. Something special was about to happen. "Sanctus, Sanctus, Sanctus," sang out one of the priests. "Holy, holy, holy," Libby heard. Thomas was whispering in her ear. Whatever Thomas did, Libby followed his actions.

When the congregation knelt, Libby did also. She could have sat back, but she wanted to be a full participant in this ancient ritual of Mass. Each step of the Mass was completed in proper order. Archbishop Hughes had delivered a memorable sermon about the true meaning of Christ's birth. The theme had focused on Mary, the Mother. The question he raised had been, "What if Mary had said no to the angel?" The assisting priests had read Bible verses from Matthew and Luke. Holy communion wafers were distributed to the waiting lines of parishioners. No one hurried the process and beneath it all, the organist kept a lullaby of music ever so softly playing in the background.

The choir had retreated to the rear choir loft and their next selection, another very old Christmas hymn sung in German, *Silent night, Holy night*, wafted out over their heads. The strains of violins filled her soul. A strange sensation washed over her, leaving Libby with an unexplained desire for more of this beautiful service. But to her dismay, the priests were following the acolytes to the rear of the church. People were dressing in their cloaks.

"Miss Libby?" spoke Katie. "I am going to go find Patrick now. I am going to go with him, and he will see that I get home safely." She paused only long enough to pick up her basket, then said, *"Ádh mór ort!* Miss Libby."

Before Libby could stop her, Katie was gone, mixed into the massive crowd of bodies. Libby was dumbfounded that Katie would do something like this. She took Thomas' arm, and together they walked out into the beautiful peaceful night, the beginning of Christmas Day. While they were inside the Cathedral, snow had fallen, and the streets were covered with deep, clean, white snow. Their city was clean, if only for a few hours, on the most joyous of holidays.

Thomas hailed their waiting driver and to Libby's surprise, he pulled up in a wooden sleigh, the two horses decked out in pine bows with bright red ribbons and jingle bells intertwined in their manes and tails.

"Hurry, Libby, I don't want you to get cold," said Thomas. He again tucked the buffalo robes around her. All that he could see were her shining eyes and a grinning face peeking out from under the heavy robe. *This is perfect*, he thought. He gave the driver the directions, asking him to take a long route home, and the driver tipped his hat in understanding. Thomas climbed in, sitting next to Libby instead of across from her as he had done earlier in the evening.

"What do you suppose Katie is up to?" asked Libby. "She said something to me in Irish. It sounded like "*admere moror et.*" Was she wishing me a Merry Christmas?"

Thomas mouthed the words that Libby had said. "HHMMM. I don't…" Then he tossed back his head and roared with laughter. "Aahh, Libby. Your little maid just wished you *good luck*," he said.

"Oh! My!" Said an embarrassed Libby. But then, seeing the look in Thomas' eyes, she realized he had put Katie up to abandoning her, and she joined in the laughter. It mingled perfectly with the clip-clop sounds and the jingling bells. All was well in the heavens and on earth this night.

Thomas reached into his coat pocket and extracted the small black velvet box. "Merry Christmas in Irish sounds like this Libby. *Nollaig Shona.*" He took her hand out of her muff and dropped the little box into her open palm.

Libby removed her other hand and delicately ran her fingers over the top of the box. TIFFANY was stamped on the lid in gold embossing. She wanted to savor this minute. Her very first present from the man she knew she was in love with was a gift from Tiffany's. "Aren't you going to open it?" asked a surprised Thomas.

She kissed the box lid and then lifted it. "OOH! Thomas! What have you done?" She picked up the chain and held it closer to her eyes to see it better in the darkness. His gift to her was a beautiful brooch: black onyx background with a carved ivory open rose in the center, circled with nine freshwater pearls. A pure gold casing held it all together. The gold chain was attached for when she wanted to wear it nestled against her skin, and it had a pin on the back for attaching it to her blouse at the neck.

Libby thought her breath had stopped. The brooch was the prettiest piece she had ever seen. She was speechless at first and could only stare at the piece in her hand. Then she gathered her wits about her.

"Oh, Thomas, how beautiful! It is so delicate and fragile yet has the sense of forever, a timelessness, about it." She looked up at this fine gentleman beside her. "Thank you for such a precious gift." She put the piece of jewelry back inside the box and snapped the lid tight. "I will keep it always." She smiled. "Merry Christmas, Thomas. *Nollaig Shona* to you."

Without thinking, she reached up and gently touched his cheek. Thomas took her hand and kissed the palm. He tipped her head back to look into her eyes. He lost himself in the joy and wonder he saw shining there. Libby did not resist as he put his cloaked arm around her shoulder and drew her to him.

"My *Anam Cara*," he whispered so softly only she could hear.

Snowflakes drifted from the heavens to land on the buffalo robes. Neither noticed, for Thomas, very gently and lovingly, had sealed their love with a kiss.

Libby lingered in the shelter of his comforting arms, not wanting to let the magic of this night come to an end.

"Libby, I love you."

Just then the sleigh runners slid abruptly to the curbing and the driver called out that they were at the address requested. With a laugh, the two jumped from the robes, and Thomas helped Libby to the ground.

"Wait for me, driver," said Thomas as he helped Libby up the snow covered walkway. One light shone from the Townsend mansion, and Libby noted it was her parents' bedroom.

CHAPTER 15

▼

CHRISTMAS AT THE TOWNSEND'S

Thomas worked his way up the slippery walkway first, kicking a path through the freshly fallen snow for Libby. Suddenly he stopped, put his hand back to stop Libby and whispered, "Shhh! There's something moving by the door."

"Mr. Meagher, it's us...me and Patrick." Shouted out Katie in a stage whisper. "We just got here ourselves; we walked up the other street."

Thomas continued with his path making, while Libby waited behind him. She didn't know whether to scold Katie for her misbehaving or thank her, but there was no need to discuss it here in the cold.

Patrick was stamping his heavy work boots, anxious to get in out of the cold.

"Come inside, all of you," she waved her hand toward the door. "Katie can brew us a pot of hot Chamomile tea." Patrick and Thomas both smiled at that. Tea was not what they had in mind to warm them.

"Patrick, there is no need for you to tramp all the way back to Orange Street. Why don't you just stay in our extra bedroom tonight?" offered Libby.

"Why, Miss Libby, thank you for the offer, but I can not accept it." He winked at her. "My brothers would be missing me, you know?"

Thomas joined in. "I have the sleigh waiting for us, Patrick. The driver will take you back home." Thomas looked longingly at Libby. "Until tomorrow, my dear." He reached out and planted a quick kiss on her cheek.

"Goodnight, Thomas. Thank you again for the most wonderful night of my life." She smiled, and Thomas felt warmth swirling inside his body.

Katie and Patrick stared at the two lovebirds, oblivious to anyone else in the yard. "Dinner is at two o'clock, love." Libby spoke in a low voice.

Then she turned her body to better see the McBride siblings. "Goodnight to you, Patrick. Apparently, I have you and Katie to thank for making this holiday such a special one. Merry Christmas."

Patrick and Thomas retreated to the warmth of the buffalo robes while Katie and Libby stood in the silence of the night until the last sleigh bell's jangle could be heard, carried on the still, crisp early morning air.

"Katie, let's go into the kitchen and have a cup of tea before we retire. I am not ready to have this magical night end, are you?" She opened the servant's entrance door and led the way into a darkened kitchen. "By the way, Katie, thank you for your excellent job of chaperoning tonight. I am sure Mr. Meagher will be calling on you to act in that capacity again very soon." Libby giggled and Katie sighed a big sigh of relief to know she was not in trouble for her high jinks.

"Miss Libby, there is light coming from the parlor," said Katie.

"Now, Katie, maybe Santa Claus is in there. We are up late, and we might just catch him leaving packages." Libby laughed. "Let's go see what's going on."

Earlier in the day, Libby had given her mother the Bru doll and had asked her to put it under the tree while she and Katie were gone to Mass. Unbeknownst to Libby, Caroline had convinced Peter to stay up. She had prepared a little speech to try it on him as he was retiring for the night.

"Peter, this might be our last Christmas with just our family. Please dear, drop the traditions and let us have a surprise for the girls when they return." She continued. "I want us to light the candles, set out presents and milk and cookies, and sing the new Christmas song." He looked at her quizzically.

"Sing Christmas songs? Do you know the words?" But instead of saying "no" to Caroline's request, he donned his dressing robe and followed his wife out of their bedroom and down the stairs. Before leaving the bedroom, he stopped to remove two small boxes from his dresser drawer and slipped them into the pocket of his robe.

Peter and Caroline were sitting in the parlor, enjoying the quiet of the night and the glow from the fire Peter had started for Caroline. They wanted to surprise the two women.

Libby had led the way and opened the parlor doors. She never expected to see such a glorious sight. The tree was lit up from floor to ceiling with little wax candles and strung with popcorn chains, and delicate German ornaments in wonderful shapes. She spied the popular glass pickle ornament hidden inside the tree branches hung to remind the Townsend's that their pantry was full. It was the prettiest tree Libby could remember seeing in the corner place of honor in the Towsend parlor. The fireplace glowed and reflected on the faces of her dear parents.

"Mother! Father, what are you doing up? What a wonderful surprise!" Libby walked to her parents and kissed them. She could not remember a happier Christmas. Her heart beat full in her breast.

"Miss Libby, look!" Katie dropped to her knees in front of the tree to better see the Bru. "That's the doll we saw shopping." She reached for the dangling tag. "It has my name on it." Katie jumped to her feet and danced around the room hugging the doll. Mr. and Mrs. Townsend, sitting on the horsehair couch, touched hands. The innocence of their little maid brought to them the joy of Christmas giving. Libby was right in purchasing the doll. Caroline had thought it a bit frivolous when she first heard about it. But now, seeing Katie and the joy that the Bru brought to the child/woman, she was happy for Katie.

Bridget, asleep in her room off the kitchen, was awakened by the noise in the parlor. She slipped into her slippers and left her warm bed to investigate. She kept a fireplace poker by her bed, and she reached for it as she padded across the darkened kitchen. She walked quietly to the re-closed parlor doors and threw them open.

"Well, now what are you two up to?" She scolded. Then she saw Peter and Caroline.

"Welcome, Bridget. It's about time you woke up and joined us," said Caroline. We are having our Christmas now. Why don't you put on the kettle, and we'll dive into your cookies, or maybe some of that Irish Christmas bread we have been hearing about for the past week."

Bridget joined right in the festivities. "I'll be right back," she said. She hurried off to her room, pulled out her gifts to the family and placed them at the base of the tree. Then she went to the kitchen to make tea. Somewhere along the way, she started humming, singing the new Christmas song for 1854. *Good King Wenceslas looked out, on the feast of Steven. When the snow lay round the ground....* Bridget continued through the stanzas of the song until she came to the last line, *You who now will bless the poor shall yourselves find blessing.*

"Bless you Mr. and Mrs. Townsend for making a poor waif from Ireland the happiest child in New York City," said Bridget out loud as she stood near the stove in the well-prepared kitchen. It warmed her to hear laughter coming from the parlor at two-thirty in the morning. *We certainly have broken from tradition this Christmas,* she thought as she prepared a tray laden with goodies and teacups and the teapot.

"Mother, here is a present for you," said Libby. "And one for you, too, Father." She found her gift for Katie and handed it to her. Katie could not believe there was more for her. She ripped open the package to reveal the paint and drawing set. "Never would I believe such fine supplies would be for me." She ran to Libby and threw her arms around her neck. "Thank you Miss Libby. I'll paint you a special picture soon."

They thanked each other for the gifts as each one was opened. Libby put Katie's beautifully tatted shawl around her shoulders. "I'll show this off at dinner tomorrow, Katie. When did you ever find the time to work on it?"

The tea and breads and cookies fit their party mood, and no one noticed that the grandfather clock in the hallway had chimed three times.

The house was full of warmth and love and sharing. Time, as if frozen, marked the scene.

Mrs. Townsend looked at her daughter's face and instinctively knew she had done the right thing by planning this impromptu celebration. Without asking her, Caroline knew her daughter was in love with Thomas Francis Meagher. *So be it,* she thought.

"Libby, did you receive a gift from Thomas this evening?" asked Caroline.

"I have to show you, mother…all of you, my beautiful brooch." Libby jumped up and untied the opening inside her muff where she had placed the tiny box on the ride home. "Here is my Christmas gift from Thomas." She opened the Tiffany box lid, and her parents peered down on the lovely piece of jewelry.

"Doesn't he have good taste, father?" asked Libby. She saw a sad look in her father's eyes. Not wanting anything to spoil this evening for any of them, she snapped the box shut. "Father, don't you have your traditional gift for mother and me? Are you going to make us wait until dinner? Please, let's open them now." Libby walked over to her father and put her hand on his arm.

"How can I not give in? My entire household has gone completely mad this night, or should I say morning?" He reached into the pocket of his dressing gown and pulled out the two black boxes, each stamped with the now familiar gold embossed TIFFANY. He handed one to his wife and the other box to Libby.

"Merry Christmas to both of you," he said. Caroline slid over to him on the couch and kissed him full on the lips. "Harrumph!" he said, and the room exploded in laughter.

Caroline's gift from her husband was a pair of pearl earrings. "Mr. Tiffany told me earrings are the latest fashion adornment for you ladies this year," he said.

They all turned to Libby. "Now it is your turn, daughter."

Libby savored the moment, realizing the importance of the gift from her father. He had never once faltered in giving her a piece of exquisite jewelry for Christmas every year since she was born. She still had the tiny baby spoon with her month's birth stone embedded in it. Carefully, she opened the lid. There, sparkling back was the largest cut diamond Libby had ever seen. It was not set, but lay loose on the black velvet pad. Libby blinked, then stared.

"I know you are very soon going to be entering a new stage in your life, Elizabeth," said her father. "This diamond is an investment stone and is for your future." He smiled. "It is pretty obvious you have another man to buy you trinkets and baubles."

Libby walked over to her father. She put her arms around his shoulders and laid her head on his ample chest. There was no need for words, nor did any come to her.

Bridget broke the silence. "Come along now…bedtime. We have a big dinner to prepare for tomorrow. Your grandchildren will be here looking for their toys and gifts." She made clucking sounds and started picking up the wrappings. Mr. Townsend walked to the tree and, one-by-one, he pinched out the wax candles still sparkling in the glow of the fireplace. The glow was now dimmer as the logs burned slowly in a red-gold ember.

"Merry Christmas, everyone," said Katie as she left the room, carrying her precious doll and the other gifts.

"Merry Christmas, Mother and Father," said Libby. She carried her two little black boxes as she left the room.

"Merry Christmas, Peter. Thank you for this wonderful night. There will not be another quite like it ever again, I predict."

"Merry Christmas to you, too, Caroline. Your prediction is probably accurate," said Peter to his wife. He walked over to her and arm-in-arm they left the parlor to walk the stairway together up to their bedroom.

Bridget, left alone in the hallway, watched them all disappear from her sight. *"Nollaig shona,"* Merry Christmas, she whispered.

Once again a peaceful quiet settled over the Townsend Mansion. Bridget looked out the window before returning to her little room. The moon was high, and a silvery light had settled across the lawn and garden that was now buried in the beauty of the white, clean snow. She started humming, *Silent Night, Holy Night* as she shut the door to her room.

CHAPTER 16

▼

THE LOVE LETTER

Thomas Francis Meagher slept fitfully, finally giving up the effort. *I might as well get up,* he thought as he rolled off the large, comfortable feather-stuffed mattress. He lit a lamp at his desk in his hotel suite. He opened a desk drawer and extracted several sheets of pure white paper, and uncapped his ink well. He was about to write the most important letter of his life before the sun came up.

He had set his Christmas present from Libby, a handsome wooden pencil box, on his desk, and seeing it now, he picked it up and rubbed the side of it. *I must remember to pack it when I leave for the tour,* he thought. It was the only thing he had to remind him of Libby.

He was leaving the following week for St. Louis, St. Paul, San Francisco, and the newly incorporated city called Los Angeles on the West Coast. It would be more than six months before he'd return to New York City. The lecture circuit promotional had been a huge success and now Thomas was committed to making the tour. He looked forward to it in many ways. This was his opportunity to enlighten the Irish-Americans of what was continuing to happen politically in Ireland, and for that matter, all of Europe. It would strengthen him financially also, and if his Irish luck held out, he planned to be a married man before the year's end.

St. Paul, and San Francisco, both held much promise for Thomas, financially as well as politically. Large contingents of Irish had accumulated to those fine cities and were expecting him to spend several days with different groups. His law office he'd leave in capable hands with his partners looking after his clients. He was ready to leave the city for the excitement of the tour, but there was one drawback. He'd not see Libby for months.

This letter would have to be a worthwhile substitute for him and he would struggle to get it just right. There was so much he wanted her to know. For the first time in his life, Thomas Francis Meagher of the Sword, the famous orator fighting for Irish cause, was at a loss for words.

He dipped his pen into the ink well, and with a flourish, he began:

Metropolitan Hotel,
New York, Jan. 2, 1855

My dear, dear, Miss Townsend,

I am very unwilling to leave for the South without placing in your hand the fullest expression, which written words can give, of the feelings with which I bid you, for a time, an affectionate farewell. No one can faithfully express, in spoken syllables, what the heart feels, and the thoughts by which the mind is crowded, when, as with me at this moment, both heart and mind are deeply moved. Nor is it alone what I now feel—what I now think, and hope, and promise—that I wish to place forever in your keeping. I have, before this, spoken to you like one suddenly waking from a dream. Breath and utterance almost were wanting. My words, heretofore, have barely told you the secret of my heart. They have fallen, here and there, shapeless, colourless, in disorder—leaves, stricken by the sun or wind, and whispering to the generous breast on which they lie, no story of the fresh life from which they sprung. Yet, it is well that men who are often times strong and confident elsewhere, and in the ruder circumstances of life, should be thus reminded of the weakness which is their portion, and which confesses itself inevitably, with humbleness and timidity, in the presence of great goodness, and a nobler nature. Thus instructed, the giddiest or the vainest of us retire, as from a sacrament, with a steadier, wiser, purer purpose. Thus instructed, and thus improved, do I feel myself to be ever since I made known to you my love, and the proud blessing which, in the promise and posession [sic] of your love, I sought for. I can, therefore, speak to you now more fearlessly and fully than I have hitherto done. The cowardice has fled. Heart, hand, and tongue—all are free. The story can be easily told. The more easily, since, if I mistake not, you know most of it already. You know I was a "rebel"—and you know I am an "exile." You know I was married and you know there has been left to me a little fellow, who knows not what a mother would have been. Of other events and aspects of my life, you may not be aware. But, familiar with those I have mentioned, you know the worst, and you know the best.

Why it was I became a "rebel"—that is, foreswore allegiance to the English Government, took up arms against it, and incited others to do the same, it is scarcely necessary for me to explain. The world knows what Ireland—the land of my birth and early home—has been. For years and years, a mere wreck upon the sea, she has had nothing but a long list of sorrows, ignominies, and martyrdom to contribute to the history of nations. Believing that such has been her fate through the culpable design of those who rule her, every generation has witnessed an effort made by her sons to redeem her sinking fortunes. That such efforts have been justified, and generous, and upright, and righteous in all respects, none save those who befriend the wrong, will question. The wisdom of them may, perhaps, be questionable. Success covers a multitude of infirmities and errors—nay, of vices. Adversity drives the gravest virtue out upon the world, like old King Lear, with folly to attend it.

In the last attempt of the kind in Ireland, it was my fate to be involved. The papers, I send you, explain all. Through much idle flattery and exaggerated colouring, the fact and the truth of my short course in public life are clear enough, and that there is nothing in it all—not a word, an act, a sentiment, from first to last—you would fear to own, or blush to own, I feel proudly satisfied.

Banished to an island in the South Pacific—sixteen thousand miles from home—compelled by the Government to move away into the very heart of the forest, and there to stay my weary feet—left alone with my memories, my thoughts, and the pale shadows that had once been hopes—I grew sad and sick of life. In the darkest hour of that sick life, a solitary star shone down upon me, making bright and beautiful the desolate waters of the mournful wild lake on the shore of which I lived in that wilderness. I met her who has left to me the poor child, for whom, as yet, I have no home, and who knows not the warmth of a mother's breast. She was the daughter of an honest, pious, venerable, poor old man, who, years before, had journeyed from Ireland to that distant land, and there built up, with thrifty and courageous industry, a sweet though humble home for the children who made the evening of his life vocal with the song, and crowned his grey hairs with the flowers, of hope.

I had not been four months married, when I saw that she had to share the privations and indignities to which her husband himself was subject. A prisoner myself, I had led another from the altar to share with me an odious captivity. This I could not bear. Without her, I might have hardened my heart, and so have stoutly borne the lot assigned me. But that she should have to drink from the bitter cup that was given to me to drink; that her days should come and pass away in solitude, and that to the brighter scenes and nobler cares of life she should be held there, in that dreary hermitage, a stranger;—this I could not bear. Hence I came to the determination of breaking loose from the trammels which bound me to that hateful soil, and, flying to another land, beckon her across the ocean to a home, the foundations of which in the midst of a free people, would be laid in joy. Sometime elapsed. At length she joined me—but to part again, and part forever. We were three years married. Of those three years, but eight months were we together—but six without a separation. It is a dream! I have been through the ocean in a troubled sleep—have seen through clouds a vision, beautiful and luminous, moving up from the waves to the stars, in the light of which it blended and was lost—and I awake beside you, to tell the dream. And thus I've told it. Told it not indelicately, I trust, for it was with the fond, fond feeling, that not even the secrets of the grave, of which I keep the key, should be withheld from you. Let us close the gates and over the grave to which I have led you for a moment, may flowers spring up, in the light and warmth of your consoling love, and make it as sweet and sacred spot forever!

And now that I have said so much about the past, let me say a word or two about the present time, and that which is yet to come.

In making known to you my love, and asking—as heaven knows I did with a throbbing heart—the honour of your hand and the proud blessing of your love, I told you that I had, from the first, been forcibly struck with the evidence of your mind and heart, and that I could not rest easy until I had made known to you how much I admired, and thought of, and loved you.

I begged of you, also, not to regard this declaration of love on my part as inconsiderate and premature—reminding you that, although our intercourse had been limited, still, having had many, many opportunities of seeing and knowing others, I could not be considered as acting with haste or thoughtlessness in pledging myself to you. I now, deliberately, seriously, with a full conviction and impression of its intent and obligation, repeat this pledge and declaration—deeply and thoroughly convinced my judgment often errs—my instincts, my intuition, my inspiration, never that heart and intellect—all that can bestow happiness—all that can adorn and sanctify a home—all that can kindle in man a noble pride, and prompt him to a generous and chivalrous activity, whilst it purifies his thoughts and renders his affections, his sympathies, his passions, holy and intense—have been given to you in rich abundance, and that with you—with you, as my noble wife and the mother of my little boy—life to me would be joyous beyond utterance—with you, all my duties, aims, and hopes—all my future labours, achievements, honours—all would be the loftier, and the prouder, and more perfect.

I know not whether you observed it or not, but the moment I was introduced to you, I was overcome with this consciousness—with this belief. And until I met you again—until, indeed, I revealed to you the secret with which my heart was throbbing, almost breaking, this consciousness, this belief, was to me a torture. I could not—dare not—hope for such a wife. I felt, however, it would be a relief to me, even though my love was not returned, to let you know I loved, and deeply loved you. And when I broke the seal—opened to you my heart, and made you the favourite owner of its inmost secret—there came upon me a delicious joy, like dews and sunshine,—a joy which, for many a day, I have not known. But when I heard from you, that "you could deeply love me," there passed through me a wild delight which made my pulse beat quick, and my brain reel, and a thousand suns to flash in the giddy air about me. Oh! I felt—I felt myself a generous, guileless, joyous, bounding, loving, hopeful boy again—felt the heart, that had been bruised and wounded, filled with a fresh and glowing life, and all its chords vibrating with a hymn of love and gratitude to her who had come to lead me from the Valley of Shadows—from beneath the cypress and the yew, and from the broken pillar and the funeral urn—to a beautiful and cheerful garden, as it were, sparkling with fountains, and full of melody and fragrance.

But these are idle words. Idle, where my look, my hand, my lips, my heart, have told you all, and your noble trust, so prompt and fearless, in my pledged affection, will conceive and understand what words, however fruitful, cannot impart.

That there would be—that there will be—objections to our union, I foresaw, and yet foresee. I had learned little of the world, if to these objections I had been blind. I saw them; the moment I looked upon and loved you. In the bloom and pride, and the genial glorious dawn of womanhood—stationed in the highest social rank, in a community the wealthiest in the world—the eldest unmarried daughter of a family, affluent in its circumstances, and by long descent and residence in the country rendered most noticeable and attractive—I was fully sensible, that, in claiming the honour to be your husband, I should have to meet no slight contradictions and rebuke. For, I have no fortune—at least, nothing that I know of. I never asked my father a single question on the subject. I have fought my own way through the world, and will fight it to the end. I am, as I have already told you, a homeless exile—dependant [sic] on my own good name and labour for a fortune. I am not yet an American citizen, and have not, therefore, a recognized standing in this country. I am here alone. Family, old friends, the familiar interest which sustains, the honours which naturally attend on one in the land of his birth and boyhood—I parted from, to be true to my convictions, my conscience, and my cause. To be thus true, I broke from, and bid farewell to the honours and endearments of a happy and honorable home. But, in doing so, I did no more than many a hearty and gallant young American did for the honour of his flag, in the war of 1812, and the other day in the war with Mexico. I did no more—indeed, [I have] done far less—than many a young nobleman and high-bred gentleman of England has done this day before the guns and walls of Sebastapool [sic], for the historic credit and glory of the country, the lustre of whose ancient crest and arms it is his perilous and fatal duty to preserve and perpetuate.

Would to God I had a wound to show! but I have nothing to show—nothing to give you—nothing to promise you—nothing but "a true heart" you will remember the words "and a willing hand."

And that heart you shall have, with the fullest measure of it's love, to the last beat it gives. And that hand, with all the strength and industry, and pride of manhood that is in it, you shall have—loyally and bravely to serve and guard you—until death has struck it down forever.

Of other objections, I shall not speak. When they are mentioned, I shall be prepared as I am now, to meet and answer them for your sake—to be united to you at once—to press you to my heart, and look proudly in your eyes, and feel we were never on this earth to part—oh! how I wish to Heaven I had mines, and rivers, and fleets, and warehouses—yachts and carriages, and palaces! Had I these, the world—the world!—would have little to say against me.

You are aware I have declared my intentions and purpose becoming a citizen of America. For some time past, I had been thinking of going to Calafornia [sic], and there permanently settling. But, from the moment I first saw you, this purpose began to waver;—and now, that I have had the assurance of your love—now that I am to act, and live, and die for you—I shall remain here—in the city of New York—and practice at the bar.

To win distinction in this profession, shall be my study and ambition—that so, I may, to some extent, reflect honour on the noble girl, who, in giving her hand and heart to one so humble and so downcast, conferred upon him a dignity higher and more precious than even the citizenship to which it has been his glory to aspire.

However, with regard to this, and other matters, I am ready joyously to accept, and promptly to obey all suggestions and desires. Your will, in all such matters, shall be my sole guide and law.

This brings me to the end of what I have, and had, to write. But I cannot close this letter, without renewing the request I have already made, that you will never, never hesitate to question me concerning anything which interests you, painfully or otherwise, in my regard.

Rest assured, I shall ever prove to you most truthful, frank, and upright, and shall forever remain, as now, with fondest, deepest esteem and love,

Your devoted and betrothed,

Thomas Francis Meagher

(Permission given from the Montana State Historical Society, Helena, Montana)

CHAPTER 17

▼

THE WEDDING PROPOSAL

Meagher left the city of New York by steamship. This mode of travel created a stir in him and he found it rather tolerable. His tour-speaking schedule was to begin in the southern states, then west to St. Paul, Minnesota; his final destination, California.

The Irish orator's arrangements were in place, made by a group of Irish fighting men called Fenians. They had set up their headquarters in St. Paul, and to them to have *Thomas Francis Meagher of the Sword* from Waterford, Ireland as their main speaker for several days in a row was a real coup. The parade that greeted Meagher had been totally unexpected and it pleased him.

I wish Libby were here to see this, he thought. He smiled and waved at the gathered street-lined crowd. The carriage waiting for him from the dock had been decorated with flowers and the horse sported ribbons braided into his mane. The whole atmosphere was one of festivities, and as they paraded up the street toward the Fenian Hall, flags, both Irish and American greeted him, along with shouts of "hooray!" that swelled up from the men, anxious to hear him speak.

However, Libby had her own agenda. The last night she and Thomas were together he had proposed. As was the custom, they had retired to the parlor after the main Sunday meal. A roaring fire warmed the room as Libby set a newly acquired Ming vase, a Christmas present from her mother, on the mantle piece. When she turned around, he surprised her by dropping to one knee and taking both of her delicate hands into his larger ones. "Libby, *ta me i ngra leat. An bPósfaibh tú mé?* And not waiting for a translation, Libby said, "Yes." The only discord would be their separation due to the schedule Thomas had set for his lecture tour for at least the next six months.

Now, in his absence, she found herself very busy making plans for their future life together. When she heard Thomas professing his love for her and proposing in Irish, it was music coming from his soul to hers. The arrival of the love letter the next day, cemented her commitment and future to the only man she would ever love.

At Thomas's insistence, her first visit was to Archbishop Hughes. It was in his office she discovered his magnetic qualities. After being properly introduced, their conversation turned to why she was there, that Thomas had proposed, and she needed information as to the wedding. Since she was not a Catholic, certain arrangements would have to be made.

"It is nice to meet you Miss Townsend." He pointed to a lovely green wingback chair. "Please sit down. I recollect seeing you with Thomas at Midnight Mass," he said. "Thomas is eligible for full Catholic sacramental blessings my dear. His first wife died, therefore he is free of any encumbrances."

He smiled at the lovely Miss Townsend, dressed so proper in her winter cloak and hat. "You cannot be married at Mass or at the altar, but we will arrange for you to be married in the rectory of my home, if that is satisfactory with you," he said. "You have not been married before have you?"

Libby laughed as if she had just heard a joke. "No, I am very much a virgin bride, Father."

She wondered if she should bring up the matter of joining the church and decided to ask.

"I am considering taking instruction in the Catholic faith, but I will not join until after we are married out of respect for my parents," she said.

Father Hughes gave a knowing smile. "Good idea, Miss Townsend."

"Oh, please father...Call me Libby."

"Libby it is. Do you have a date in mind? I'll look on my calendar."

"I would like a very small, family only, November wedding." Libby said. "I need some time to prepare for it, and I also want to give Thomas the summer to grieve for Bennie." She looked directly at the priest. "Another problem area is whom to invite. Thomas knows so many people I don't think St. Patrick's Cathedral would hold all the guests if we opened it to everyone to attend." They both laughed at that.

Libby dropped her eyelids and voiced a grave concern. "Thomas would like his father present, but it is doubtful he will make the crossing. He has hopes of seeing his father and his son." She looked at the priest.

"And Mr. Meagher, Sr. is not happy that Thomas is marrying so soon after Bennie's death. To add insult to injury, he is also going to marry a non-Catholic, and as if that weren't enough, I am not Irish." Libby was not smiling now, but showed a deep concern for this sour note for the beginning of her married life.

He smiled at this beautiful young woman now standing before him. She obviously was in love with Thomas Francis Meagher, and it did him good to meet her. She would be the woman behind the man, and Lord knew Thomas needed a good woman to keep him on course.

"How about November 14, 1855."

"We will hold the ceremony here in my rectory. Good luck on how you handle the invitations." He wrote notes in his scheduled appointments book.

"Thank you so much, Father Hughes." She turned to leave the office but stopped. "Father, I would like to start taking instruction whenever you have a class."

"My dear, I will instruct you myself." He returned to his desk to look at his scheduled appointments book. "I have an open hour at two o'clock on Wednesday afternoons, starting the first Wednesday of next month."

"I'll be here." Libby walked over to the priest and extended her hand. They shook hands and then Father Hughes walked her to the front door of his rectory. He stood in the doorframe watching Elizabeth Townsend as she returned to the waiting carriage.

"Meagher is one lucky son of an Irishman," he thought, as he shut the door and returned to his study.

The large white envelope in the familiar scroll of his son's hand sat waiting to be opened on the table in the Meagher study in Waterford, Ireland. Thomas Meagher, Sr. had just met the postman at the gate. It was obvious the postman wanted to hear about Thomas Francis in New York City, but the older gentleman was not about to share the letter with him. He would leave the letter unopened until his sister returned from her shopping. The toddler, asleep in the next room would not be disturbed this cold February day and besides he was wanting a tumbler filled with some good old Irish sipping whiskey in it.

When his sister finally arrived back home, Meagher, Sr. scowled at her and took another swallow of whiskey, rolling it around on his tongue, savoring every taste. He waved the white envelope in front of her. Meagher, Sr. sat near the table, his Blackthorn walking stick leaning against his leg, his pipe stuck in the corner of his mouth. Quickly she pulled off her woolen wrap and sat in the chair across from her brother.

"Open it for God's sake man," she said. "What news does it bring this house?"

Meagher, Sr's. hand trembled as he slit the end open and extracted the two white sheets of paper. His eyes scanned the Irish words.

"It is too soon!" shouted the man. His hand hit flat upon the smooth tabletop. "I'll not bless this union. Bennie is hardly cold in her grave."

He put the letter back on the table and gently shoved it across the surface to his sister. She read the letter and frowned.

"Surely, he can't want the child, not now, with a new bride, would you think?" She wondered what was to become of the little tyke; both she and her sister were very grandmotherly toward the little guy. They all loved little Thomas. He had a gentle, unspoiled personality, was sharp for his age, and he got along with everybody. His massive curly red hair took on a carrot-top color in the afternoon sunlight.

The loud voices coming from the other room woke him and with sleep still in his eyes, he rubbed them with his chubby little fists as he waddled out into the room. Losing his balance, he flopped onto his butt. There he happily played on the hand hooked rug, sitting in his nappy, trying to figure out how to catch the sleeping cat's tail.

"I'll not attend and that's that." He rocked back and forth, back and forth, the runners making a squeaking noise on the waxed floor's surface. Smoke curled from his pipe, making a distinct halo wreathing his head, floating towards the ceiling, unnoticed. The sister stared at her opinionated brother.

"Mr. Meagher, you can be a mighty stubborn man," she scolded. "At least sit down and write him a letter and wish him well. How long did you think it would be before he sent for his son, your grandson?" She held up her hands in supplication.

"Thomas says he is marrying Miss Elizabeth Townsend, an American Industrialist's daughter. She is not Catholic…and is interested in Irish causes just like he is." Meagher paused. "My son is a fool. I am going to cut off his allowance upon his wedding day."

With that surprising decision, he got up and walked across the room to the fireplace. With one swift movement he tossed the invitation and the letter into the fire. Meagher, Sr. watched the corners curl and burn. With a flu-up sound, the flames consumed the very important information that Thomas had carefully penned.

He would write back to his son, but not until he was sure it would arrive too late for any chance of hope that he would be in attendance.

"America has changed him," he said.

Meagher, Sr. felt a bit bewildered as he thought of the future for his grandson. *The wee lad does need a mother*, he thought. But this was just another facet of an inner conflict the senior man had been struggling with the whole time the letter lay open on the table.

History was repeating itself. His own beloved wife had died, leaving him Thomas Francis to raise. *Why without the help of my sisters back then*…he let his thoughts drift. Then Bennie, whom he had grown to love as his own, died leaving him the responsibility of Thomas Francis III.

By God, this child will be raised an Irishman, and I'll see he has a proper life and upbringing. If I failed with my son Thomas, I shall not fail with his!

No, he thought, *my mind is made up. I'll not go to New York City. If he wants to see his son, let him come here.*

Knowing that his exiled son would never set foot in his homeland again, the old man smiled for the first time that day.

CHAPTER 18

▼

MORE WEDDING PLANS

Bridget and Katie were delighted. The announcement last night at dinner that Thomas and Libby were to marry in November came as no surprise to either of them. Now in the early morning hours, the two were gossiping in the kitchen.

"About a year ago you predicted a wedding in the Townsend household, Katie, dear," said Bridget. "Soon enough, November will be here and it will be up to you and me to prepare a reception." Bridget pulled several cookbooks from the shelf and started thumbing through them. She shoved a book toward Katie. "Have a look see young lady. We will be having to chose and soon."

Katie opened one book and saw a beautiful cake. "Look, here, Bridget. A Matrimonial Wedding Cake, made from that new white flour. Can we make this?" She read the ingredients to Bridget.

1 cup flour

½ teas baking soda

¼ teas salt

1 cup butter or lard

1 cup brown sugar

2 cups rolled oats

Filling
1 lb. Dates
1 tablespoon brown sugar
¾ cup water. Boil together
Put ½ of top ingredients in pan and press.
Spread filling and then cover with rest of ingredients.
Bake 350 degrees for 45 minutes in oven. Let cool.
Top off cooled cake with powdered sugar dust and chopped walnuts.

The two were studying the recipe when Libby walked into the kitchen.

"Good morning. Why do you have your heads together so early in the day?" Libby glanced over Katie's shoulder. "Oh! I see…you are busy already with cookbooks. Care if I take a peak?" With a sigh, she said, "Now remember you two this is going to be kept to a *small* family wedding."

Katie giggled. "Miss Libby, do you remember the Chinese man who read our tea leaves last winter? He predicted you'd marry in November."

Libby looked rather puzzled at Katie. "Oh! I'd forgotten all about that. Well so he did, so he did."

Bridget smiled knowingly. "Miss Libby, would you be in agreement to making an Irish groom's cake for Thomas and his Irish friends? I know he will be wantin' to invite his office partners and a few of the families he is close to."

"Patrick and me brothers will be comin' for sure," interrupted Katie. "Patrick's girlfriend would like to play the Irish harp if you say it is okay, Miss Libby. We can set her in the corner of the larger guest-receiving parlor. She plays some beautiful airs and ballads, Irish tunes." Katie looked at Libby. "I've heard her and she is very, very good at playin' the strings. She would add a bit of class to the affair, I am thinkin'."

"Why, that would be wonderful, Katie. Please tell her I would be honored to have her play at our reception. Tell her to come here to the house and set up early before the ceremony if she would like." Then as an afterthought, Libby continued. "Be sure to give me her name and address so I can send her an official invitation, Katie. I want her to be a guest as well."

I wonder where the girl ever found such a fine instrument as the harp among people in the tenements, thought Libby. *Maybe she works for someone who owns the instrument and allows her to practice on it?*

The ways of the Irish community would remain forever a mystery to Libby. Their resiliency and faith amazed her, and kept her curious about their existence and their future. One thing she did know, her Thomas would be fighting for the Irish cause in Tammany Hall. He had been selected as one of the main lawyers. Already his name carried weight among the cases he had won.

For some time Libby had it in mind to work toward a public health system that would make sanitary conditions better in the tenements. While Thomas was away on his speaking-lecture series, Libby planned to spend time learning what was needed in health care. If nothing else, she could use her name and social influence to raise public awareness to the plight of hundreds of thousands of men, women and children, who because of no fault of their own, came into the country ill-prepared to face a life of hardship and degradation. Few immigrants spoke English upon their arrival to America. The Germans, Scandinavians, Yugoslavians, French and Italians came with craftsmen skills: masons, carpenters, artists, furniture builders, gardeners and cooks. The Irish escaped Ireland with nothing but their beating hearts, their sense of humor and their love of their music.

Fundraisers were Libby's main idea at the moment. She could arrange for summer band concerts in the city parks. Families would come for the Sunday outings and bring their picnic lunches. With the ten cent coin per family charge, the tenement leaders could hire lawyers to force the heartless landlords to clean up the slums, get better sewage control, and have a community tenement nurse's station. The need was great for someone who could help with the birthing of babies, and be able to dispense cough medicine to those suffering with croup and colds. A teacher could be hired to explain about lice and treat rat bites on infants' toes and fingers.

This fund could buy yarn for women to knit caps, scarves, socks and mittens to save children from frostbite. A cottage industry would allow women to work in their own homes and tend to their children, but be able to work at their own speed and have piecework to sell. The local stores could be their selling outlets. There were many ways and means for help to reach the tenements and Libby expected to take a lead part in these changes. The women knew how to knit. Their problem was that they had no money to purchase yarn. The program had merit. It would be easy to control and with proper leadership would provide much needed money for food and rent. The women could knit even if their husbands could not find work, especially in the winter months.

Over the months Libby had been questioning Katie about the tenements. When she told her of the pecking order of the tenements Libby was appalled. Five different levels of poverty, the worst being Orange Street, closeted away the immigrants from Ireland. Raw sewage, both animal and human, ran in the streets spreading disease.

The flats, overrun with rats and fleas, held as many humans as the walls could hold. Landlords unscrupulously charged outrageous rent. Women hid their newborns from the landlord to keep the cost of rent from changing.

There was no money to be giving it to lawyers to fight the system. With the raised funds, some of that poverty could end. *Millions of people live in New York City, and have not been exposed to the slum areas of New York, including me,* thought Libby.

When Patrick McBride first arrived in New York City, he had slept many a night in an open park searching for a place to lay his head. Eventually, a buddy from Ireland took pity on Patrick and secretly let him move into his one room flat with him, his wife and their three children. They had no running water, no toilet save for a shed out back, no reliable room heat, and only a small wood burning stove for cooking. Fire reigned as the biggest threat and fear to the tenement dwellers. Thousands were left with nothing and were put on the street when a tenement section went up like a tinderbox.

After the three brothers were once again united, they pooled their resources, and with hard work and good luck and time, they were going to be moving soon into a decent apartment on the edge of the tenements.

They were making pretty good money; the problem was that there was no housing to move into.

That was about to change. The visionaries had started discussions about building apartments in different sections of the city. The industrial giants would finance the construction of nicer tenement buildings and in turn profit from the higher rent.

Summer targeted the actual construction start up plans. The need for skilled help and laborers was advertised, offering better wages for those landing the coveted new jobs. Men stood in line and around the block at the construction sites, hoping to put their "X" on the hiring/employment rolls. Attitudes that only a few months before had been low now held a promise of hope.

Patrick had applied for two apartments, one for his brothers and one for him and his bride. He was involved in the making of his own Irish wedding probably in December, but he had not told Katie his good news yet.

It was an exciting time for Libby. Very quickly it turned into February, and good planning weather for the many different journeys she now found herself embarking upon. She had been to the rectory and met with Archbishop Hughes who would perform the ceremony in his rectory chapel; she had spoken to him about her taking instructions in the Catholic faith, and she had a solid charitable plan to unveil very soon.

Over the next months she planned to draw the Archbishop into the execution of her welfare plans. He'd be able to open doors for her in the Irish community and they, in turn, would find the right people to help make her program work. She needed to be connected with women from his parish who would organize the knitting projects, and keep track of the sales.

"Katie, are you willing to try something very daring with me?" asked Libby one day early in March. "Will you go with me to *Old House at Home Pub* on 15 East Seventh Street? on St. Patrick's Day night?

Katie's head jerked up. She was stunned by this request.

"What? Why? Well…sure," she said. "You do know that *Old House at Home* is a man's bar for Irishmen only? What's the reason for us to go there?"

"I need to sit there and listen to the men talk. The women don't trust me yet, and they do not tell me about the things I need to know in order to help them and their families." Libby sighed. "Thomas told me that is where he goes when he needs information about a case he might be working on, and I know that is where a lot of his clients meet him." But Libby knew Thomas would never take her into a man's pub. It was a matter of honor among Irishmen to keep this pub strictly as their own meeting hall. It was inside these walls grave matters of life and death were often discussed over a pint of Guinness or a boilermaker.

Katie sat very still listening to her mistress.

"I have an idea," she said. "Maybe me brothers will loan us some clothes and we can dress like men. We'd need caps and scarves. St. Patrick's Day revelers will be pushing the walls." Katie started to smile. "I'll be seeing me brothers this Wednesday and I'll shanghai what we'll need." Now both women were intrigued with their outlandish plans.

"Should we let Patrick in on our plans? Do you think he would stand guard for us and help us out if we get caught?" asked Libby.

"I think he'll protect us from the men, but if we get caught we're on our own," Katie said.

"Miss Libby, you will need some Irish phrases to use in the bar, like 'I need a pint," or "Hey! That's my chair," she said.

Katie already knows what these pubs are like, thought Libby. *She leads a much freer life than I do.*

"You do know if you get caught your name will make the front page of the *New York Times*," said Katie. "I can read it now." She held up her hands in a square in front of her face as if she were reading a newspaper.

Libby Townsend, daughter of Industrial Giant Peter Townsend, and engaged to Mr. Thomas Francis Meagher of the Sword, caught drinking with Irish riffraff in Old House at Home Pub.

"Father would never forgive Thomas if it is in the paper," said Libby with a lilt in her voice. "He'd find a way to make it be Thomas's idea that I was down there in the first place." Libby paused and sat back in her chair. "Thomas would be furious if my name were in the paper for doing such an outrageous thing as dressing up in men's clothes and sneaking into a men's pub." She looked at Katie's face. "Let's do it, anyway."

"How do you propose we be out of the house? And where will we stash the clothes until we need to wear them?" Katie asked.

"I am going to leave those details up to you." Libby stood up and winked at Katie. "I trust you will find a quick solution to this problem, my dear." Libby left the front receiving parlor the way she had found it, with Katie dusting the knick-knack shelf.

Nothing out of the ordinary happened in the *Old House at Home*; Libby and Katie sat in a corner very much protected by Patrick. Conversations on this St. Patrick's Day evening were not focused on their terrible plight but centered on the positive things in their lives. The men toasted their health in song, to their good fortune at being in New York City, and they raised a glass to the "ole sod" and to their dear families left behind. Libby wondered if Patrick would tell Thomas about this escapade and she decided that he would.

Katie ordered them a Guinness and when three pints came, she told Libby to not say anything to the waiter.

"It is the custom here to always serve an extra beer. No one really knows why, but I think it is because he wants to share his good fortune with those left behind or who have died trying to get to New York City."

Katie took a good gulp and grinned. She knew she had the priest's collar on her lips. "Libby, did you know that the white band of foam has to be a certain depth? Yes, really. It represents the priest's collar and is put on every glass of Guinness since time began makin' the stuff."

Libby snorted. "How do you know these things, Katie?"

"I am not joking, Libby. Now you better drink up like a man."

Katie motioned to Patrick to take the extra pint for himself.

CHAPTER 19

▼

THE WEDDING AND
RECEPTION

The carriages lined the horseshoe-shaped driveway in front of Archbishop Hughes' home and rectory. The invited guests were assembled to witness the wedding of two very popular people in New York City's social circle. The drivers had gathered into the largest carriage to visit and keep warm under the buffalo robes. Thomas Francis Meagher and Elizabeth M. Townsend eagerly looked forward to this day, November 14, 1855. At last the vows would be spoken for everlasting love. This was their cherished wedding day.

Libby had deliberately kept the invitation list to close family and friends, and even in doing so, that number was fifty quests.

Thomas and the groomsman were sequestered in the library, while Libby and her sister completely took over the space in one of the Archbishop's many bedrooms. The plan laid out by the Archbishop's house-keeper worked well. Libby would descend the grand stairway with Thomas waiting for her at the little chapel altar at the end of the hallway. Her father, Peter Townsend, would escort her to that space. Happily, Thomas would be able to see his bride as she descended the stairway and make her way to him.

The church pianist sat stiff and prim, ready to do her part to get this wedding underway. When she saw Libby at the top of the staircase, she struck a resounding chord. All heads turned toward Libby.

"Oh! Doesn't she look splendid?" said Bridget. But Katie was speechless.

She had never seen a more beautiful bride in her life and to think she was wearing a creation from Katie's hands. The white satin fitted waist covered with seed pearls shimmered in the light from the large stained glass window at the top of the stairs. The fingertip veil was held in place on her head by the headpiece that Libby's mother, Caroline, had worn on her wedding day years before. Even with her face shielded by the sheer veil, it did not filter out the spiritual essence that emanated from Libby. She looked ethereal in her stunning beauty. Libby carried one long-stemmed Calla Lily tied with a white satin ribbon.

She is so beautiful. Thomas could only stare at Elizabeth. The strand of white pearls, his gift to her at a family gathering the night before, gleamed around her neck. *Am I dreaming? Can she really be coming for me to love her?* For Thomas, it was like watching a cloud of white loveliness floating effortlessly toward him. Libby smiled graciously as she met her father at the base of the stairway. Peter took his daughter's arm, and giving in to an impulse, leaned over and kissed her cheek through the lace veil. "Be happy, my daughter," he whispered. He had a tear in the corner of his eye, but he knew it was not visible to anyone, other than perhaps Caroline who was happily standing next to a groomsman.

The groomsman escorted Caroline into the little chapel and helped her to a chair. Then the guests stood and turned toward the doorway to watch the groom enter and take his place. Archbishop Hughes, already at the altar, gave Thomas a quick "over here" type of wave and Thomas came out of his stupor to follow the instructions. Next, the best man and matron of honor entered together and walked to the front of the altar.

Now the pianist gave her all as Libby stepped down the hallway. It was a memorable occasion for everyone, elegant in its simplicity. Archbishop

Hughes had instructed Libby over the summer months in the Catholic traditions, and he was sure this was a match made in heaven.

"Good afternoon Thomas and Elizabeth." He motioned for the guests to sit down. When Thomas pulled back Libby's veil he looked deep into her happily shining eyes and knew without a doubt that she loved him. The couple repeated their vows and exchanged rings of bands of gold. When Archbishop Hughes announced them "man and wife," Thomas could wait no longer. He pulled Libby to him and kissed her tenderly. The guests, taken by surprise at this gesture, applauded.

The reception was scheduled to follow at 3:00 p.m. at the Townsend Mansion, only a few blocks away from the church.

"At last," said Mr. Townsend's driver, "here comes the bride and groom." He stood as the couple hurried down the walkway. Elizabeth's head was tilted back and she was laughing and smiling as if the sun was shining only on her.

"Katie, get your apron on, hurry!" Bridget and Katie had Milton drive them home from the rectory in record time. Milton was positioned at the front door. He opened the door with a great flourish for the bride and groom who swept into the foyer gracefully.

"Your cloak madam," he winked at Libby and she smiled back.

"Bridget, my parents are slipping in the backdoor. Guests are arriving now. What do we do next?"

Bridget came to her rescue. She took Libby and Thomas by their elbows and together she placed them in a line in the front parlor. Harp music filled the room with a soft, happy, heavenly sound. Patrick's fiancé looked queenly sitting with the harp, her red hair spilling over her shoulders and breasts, giving the Irish woman an angelic pose. Her fingers deftly plucked the strings, harmoniously blending the musical rhythms.

"Here come Alice and Sam." Libby put her arms around her sister's neck. "Thank you for being my matron of honor, Alice." Then she took Sam's hand. "You made a perfect attendant, Sam." Sam smiled and moved on down the line. He clasped Thomas' hand. "Well, she's all yours now, my man."

Guests filed into the mansion. For the Irish guests it was their first visit. Curious, they allowed themselves the privilege of looking around. Others made a beeline to the punch table. Hired servants took orders for drinks and scotch and water, a favorite drink of the elite. Ladies took delicate crystal cups filled with a sweet non-alcoholic punch.

On one table the matrimonial cakes were cut and folded into tiny white boxes, tied with a green ribbon. Thomas laughed at the pretty young girls, giggling when they took their prize cake to put under their pillows.

"My mama told me I'll dream about the man I am going to marry," said one young girl to Thomas. "I want to dream of you!" she blushed at her boldness but didn't run away when Thomas reached down and gave her a special bear hug.

"Come and cut the traditional wedding cake, Libby…Thomas," called out Caroline. She was enjoying the festivities. "Peter, keep the groups conversing," she whispered to her husband. "The Irish group looks rather uncomfortable." "We can not have them feel unwelcome."

Peter introduced himself to Meagher's friends, Dan Devlin, Michael Doheny, Richard O'Gorman, John Blake Dillon, John O'Mahony, Pat Smyth, and their watchful wives. Archbishop Hughes also joined the celebration.

Bridget looked on with pride as Libby and Thomas cut out a small piece of cake for each other to taste. She had stayed up late for the past two nights working on the final touches of decorations. Miss Libby wanted white cake, white frosting and tiny green shamrocks all over the cake. On the top stood a very elegant bride and groom.

"Libby and Thomas come here," instructed Caroline. "Peter and I have a surprise for you." Peter held up a large key decorated with a red ribbon bow. He said, "Thomas, this key opens your own front door. We have remodeled the west wing to the mansion while you were on tour. You have your own entrance and carriage house." Thomas looked at Libby in total surprise. "There is no need for Elizabeth to live in a hotel suite. Your plans will have you two moving around in the next few years, and there is plenty of room in this big old mansion."

Peter turned to Caroline. "Now it is your turn. Go on," he said.

"Libby, we released Katie as our wedding gift to you…" she held up her hands. "Now wait, there is more. We have hired Katie to be your house-keeper." She turned to Katie. "Thank you, young lady, for keeping our secret."

Libby was stunned. She moved to stand by her parents.

"Thank you, father and mother. That is a generous gift." She gave her dad a peck on his cheek. The guests were silent as Thomas strode over to his father-in-law. "That is very generous of you, sir. Thank you."

"Katie, get Libby some punch," spoke Caroline, breaking the moment.

Katie wiped a tear of joy from her eyes and poured the punch. She was a little self-conscious because Seán Daly was still mixing with the guests, but she knew he was watching her.

She decided to visit with him and Patrick and Patrick's girlfriend.

"Katie, come here to me," said Patrick. He put his arm around Mary Margaret's waist. "I have something to tell you. Mary Margaret and I are engaged and plan to be married before Christmas."

Katie clapped her hands in surprise. "*Comhghairdeas! Go maire tu!* Congratulations! I am happy for you two. "We'll have a good time dancing at your wedding."

Libby slipped out into the hallway. She noticed her father had left the room, and she was concerned about him. A noise in her father's study caused her to pause. Her father stood near the stick table that held the oversized family Bible, pen in hand, his back to Libby. Libby smiled, for her dear father had recorded this day, her wedding day into the Book of Life, the Townsend family records of all births and marriages and deaths for several generations. He gently closed the book.

"It is now recorded." He turned. There he saw his beautiful daughter and he came out to her.

"Are you happy today, my Dear?"

"Father, this is the day I'll never forget. My wedding day." She smiled at her father. "Thomas is generous and kind Father, we'll be happy. God will lead us." She lowered her eyes and her voice so that only Peter could hear her.

"The only shadow over this day is the absence of Mr. Meagher, Sr. Thomas had so wanted his son to join us today,"

"Father, something is going to have to happen to bring Thomas and his son together." She clasped her hands together. "Maybe next year I'll have to travel to Ireland and spend some time with the Meagher clan. I want Thomas's son in our life to make us complete."

Before her father could respond, they heard voices coming into the hallway. Guests were leaving and the maids were dispensing coats.

Just then Thomas appeared in the hallway.

"Here you are." He put his arms around Libby's waist and pulled her to him. "Our guests are leaving, dear." They shook hands as each guest departed the Townsend mansion's front door.

At six o'clock, Bridget served a roast turkey with all the trimmings, creating one of her sumptuous meals for the family and wedding party. Archbishop Hughes also stayed for the feast.

By eight o'clock Thomas was getting nervous. He found Libby in the kitchen. He watched her as she gently gave Katie and Bridget each a hug and a kiss. "Thank you both for everything. You made this day so special for Thomas and I. I'll never forget it, ever." She turned and saw Thomas standing in the doorway.

"It's time for us to leave, Libby."

Libby looked at Katie and they both hurried up the front stairway. Mr. Townsend saw the commotion and joined Thomas in the kitchen.

"Sir, I promise you I'll make Libby happy and I'll cherish her and love her always."

"See that you do, son. You have a future in America. When you return from your honeymoon, I want to visit with you about that future. Now that you have passed the bar, Sam and I can use your lawyer skills in our conglomeration of railroads, mines, lands, travel." He shrugged. "Come in as soon as you can, son."

CHAPTER 20

▼

THE WEDDING NIGHT

Thomas surprised Libby by taking her to his hotel suite at the Metropolitan Hotel. Earlier in the day he had made arrangements for several bouquets of flowers to be delivered and placed in the rooms. On a romantic impulse, he had also tipped a hotel maid who promised to light candles throughout the suite, illuminating the marriage bed. She would see to it that a bottle of the best champagne would be chilled and waiting for the bride and groom. The maid agreed to be out of the room by eight o'clock.

With the click of the key in the lock, Thomas pushed open the large hotel room door. Libby could only stare at the luminous fairyland scene that greeted her.

"Welcome Libby."

"Thomas, it's...." She swept into the room. "It's so beautiful!" She reached for his arm and slid into his waiting embrace.

As he slowly waltzed with her, humming into her ear, like the night outside the Astor mansion, Libby felt herself meld to his body.

The stars are surrounding us, she thought.

She opened her mouth but remained silent, captive in the gentle embrace. Thomas held Libby close, and he could feel her heart pressing against his heart. Soon two hearts would beat as one.

His mouth found her eager lips and they clung to each other.

"I love you Libby. Everything I am or will be belongs to only you. You are my *anam cara* forever."

"This is the happiest day of my life, Thomas. I *am* your *anam cara* forever."

They sealed their precious covenant of love to each other and became one.

Thomas released Libby's lustrous tresses and his eyes followed the fluidness of the curls as they tumbled around her bare shoulders and back.

"I've waited so long for this night," he said. "From the moment I first saw you, I knew we were meant for each other." He stroked her glowing cheeks with the backside of his fingers.

Libby smiled, her eyes and body showing contentment with their lovemaking. She felt complete.

"Thomas, I knew I was in love with you when you so boldly invited me to dinner two summers ago. Why did we wait so long?" She lay, stretched and relaxed next to his body, basking in the candlelight surrounding them. "May this deep and abiding love and affection be with us all our lives. We will have a wonderful life together and..."

Libby never finished her sentence. She had drifted off into a comfortable sleep cradled in the arms of her lover.

One of us has to blow out the candles, thought Thomas. He pulled himself from the marriage bed, a complete and whole man again. He walked around the rooms of the hotel suite blowing out the candles, noting daylight was showing a thin gray line at the edges of the closed heavy velvet drapes.

He'd called this suite of rooms "home" for several years. *Funny*, he thought, *I'll not miss it.*

With the last candle extinguished, Thomas returned to his bed. He looked down at Libby sleeping so trustfully and deeply. A lightbeam filtered through a slit in the drapery and had illuminated a spot on the edge of her pillow. "I'm a fortunate man," he barely whispered. Thomas slept soundly next to his wife.

CHAPTER 21

▼

LIFE TOGETHER

Thomas and Libby spent several days honeymooning as was the custom. While they were gone, Peter Townsend oversaw the removal of Thomas's things from the hotel suite. Hired men packed his belongings and books and carted them by horse and wagon to the remodeled section of the Townsend Mansion at 129 Fifth Avenue. The newlyweds would set up housekeeping in a cheerful atmosphere. Thomas was comfortable with the arrangement, as he knew he would be touring come spring, and he didn't want to leave Libby alone.

A freezing cold spell fell over New York City. The slum dwellers were in terrible conditions. Water froze in buckets inside the tenement houses, and humans huddled together for warmth under rags for blankets. It was Katie who brought the conditions to Libby's attention.

"Isn't there something we can do?" she asked. "My heart reaches out in pity and in shame for these people." She pleaded with Libby to come forward with some aid. "We have so much," she said.

Thomas sent sleigh loads of wood, food, bread, milk, blankets and coal into the area. He worked through Patrick for distribution to those most in need. Thomas, now hired as a Tammany Hall lawyer, spoke out for the need of public assistance. "Health and jobs need immediate attention," he wrote in Letters to-the-Editor to the *New York Times* and other newspapers. "People are dying from these debilitating conditions. We must act now." People responded by donating food and clothes and wood through their church groups.

Libby used her influence to hire nurses to go into the slum sections and help mothers deal with children coughing and burning with fevers. She taught these women the importance of keeping records on their patients, and soon a sort of public health system was in place. The crisis was averted for that winter.

"Thomas, I like working with the women in the tenement sections. I'd like to continue doing so, getting some kind of a public health program in place," said Libby. "Katie will help me to get the people to trust me."

This took many months of dedicated work. Most slum dwellers would not give out the important and necessary information for fear something bad, like eviction would occur. However, gradually the work started to show some direction, and responsible women were offering their services on a volunteer basis. Libby worked through Archbishop Hughes. He put her in touch with the Catholic Ladies Altar Society, and from that group came the needed volunteers with foodstuffs and manpower hours.

One evening in July, Thomas called Libby to the carriage house.

"Let's go for a buggy ride, Libby. I want to show you something." They went uptown to the top of the slum area and Thomas pulled over and set the buggy brake.

'See that slum section, Libby?"

She nodded, curious as to what Thomas was trying to show her and tell her.

"I've been working on a project that is now out of the dream stage." He waved his arms around, and said, "This is going to be a grand park very soon. My law firm has been working with the city government and with upstanding and wealthy businessmen to clean out these shanties and this despicable Irish slum area." He shut his eyes concentrating on his words.

"Libby, we are going to see new, clean and affordable tenement sections rise up, and this area in front of us will be destroyed forever. No more wild pigs running through the streets. We hope to be able to control some of the gangs that congregate in this part of town from all the different nationalities." He looked at Libby. "It will be called Central Park. By this time next year, it will be open for everyone to use. Why, we will come here for grand evenings with picnics and concerts, and they are planning a wonderful play area for children." He pointed to the right. "The plans call for a lovely lake for canoe rides, right here…and over there, tennis courts."

Libby loved to hear the excitement in her husband's voice. She knew he was happy working as a lawyer achieving things for the Irish community. "This is absolutely astounding, Thomas. We certainly are living in New York City at the right time. Just think of all the growth in the last year that you have been involved in also. The Irish have you to thank for a good many changes, and all for their betterment, Thomas."

The horse pulled at the buggy wagon tongue. "Let's take a spin around the city," she said, not wanting to go back to the house just yet.

CHAPTER 22

▼

LIBBY IN IRELAND

Libby waited patiently for Thomas to arrive from his law office on Alice Street where he had shared space with other lawyers for several years now.

Tonight we discuss my plans to sail to Ireland, she thought as she stood looking out at the solid, dirty mounds of snow piled high against the carriage house. She watched her well-dressed husband as he skirted the distance from the curved drive for the carriages and the walkway to their front door. He was determined to keep his shoes dry.

"Here you are at last." She opened the door for Thomas and once inside, she gave him a warm, inviting kiss.

"How I love to come home to you," Thomas said. He put his cold hands around her neck and Libby squealed.

"Katie has made us a special dinner tonight. We've been married one year today, my dear." Thomas feigned surprise, "Only one year? No, can't be. It seems like years and years."

Her frown turned to smiles as he pulled out the familiar black box from Tiffany's. Playfully he handed it to Libby. "Go ahead. Open it."

Inside the velvet lined box, Libby saw a ladies gold watch on a chain. It looked so feminine and delicate. Intricately engraved on the backside, Libby read the inscription. *"To my anam cara."*

"It is just what I need," Libby said, as she reached up to kiss her hand-some mate once again. "My other timepiece shattered apart when I bumped it off the dresser top a couple of weeks ago." She looked at the sheepish grin on Thomas's face. "Oh! Katie must have told you."

Libby snapped the now empty black velvet box shut and set it on the hall table next to a silver platter that collected both incoming and outgoing mail. She immediately clipped the chain to the top blouse button and slid the timepiece into a hidden pocket in her bodice near her waistline.

"Your gift is a welcome and pleasant surprise. Every time I look at it I'll be thinking of you," she said.

They ate the lovely meal that Katie had prepared and had moved to the parlor to enjoy a robust Irish tea, when Libby became very pensive.

"Thomas, I want to discuss something with you tonight. I know you were unhappy that your father did not travel to America for our wedding," she paused to look at him. "The real reason he did not come, I think, is because of me."

Thomas sat still, listening to his love speak what was on her mind.

"You need your son here. I know it is a cloud over you, and I have decided something that I want your approval and blessing." She swallowed some tea.

"Dear, I want to leave next March for Waterford. Your father needs to meet me, and if I stayed a few weeks I could win him over, I know. He apparently grew very fond of Bennie and now he is raising your son. It is time we raise your son, don't you agree?"

Thomas sat back in his chair and stared at Libby. "What on earth? Yes, of course I want my son, but to be separated from you? I can't bear that thought." He got up and left the room.

The boat left New York City on a beautiful spring morning in March. Libby waved from the first class passenger deck. Katie stood at her side. She was going home again. In a few weeks she'd see her beloved Ireland.

Thomas felt empty and alone and even a little scared to watch the huge transatlantic ship leave the dock, carrying Libby out to sea. "Come back to me, Libby," he shouted hoping she heard it. All the arrangements had been made: letters sent to and from Ireland, dates for travel set, and trunks packed. There was nothing for Thomas to do now but go home and muddle through each day until she returned.

Mr. Townsend, however, had plans for Thomas. He had decided to wait until Libby was gone to tell him about sending him off to Costa Rica on a business venture.

The crossing went smoothly and good winds carried them, making the journey about a six-week cruise. Libby and Katie were on deck when they heard the cry from the crow's nest.

"Land ahead!" shouted the sailor.

The two women crowded the edge of the bow and peered into the endless ocean, seeing nothing. Then Katie grabbed Libby's arm, "There! Libby. Look over there. We'll be in Waterford City within the day. We must get packed." Katie scurried toward their cabin door. Libby lingered for a while longer, savoring the site of Ireland's shore once again.

Her thoughts roamed to Thomas and his exile from his beloved homeland. *How cruel it is that you can never see this site again, my love. Someday, maybe things will change in your sentence and you will once again come to your roots that you love so very much. Oh, how you must miss this, and you never speak of it.* Libby turned from the railing and followed Katie's lead to the cabin they shared on this uneventful crossing of the Atlantic Ocean.

As the huge vessel arrived at the docks of Waterford City, Ireland, Libby hoped Mr. Meagher, Sr., would be on the quay to meet and accept her as his daughter-in-law.

"*Well, I'll find out soon enough,*" she thought. A shiver ran through her body with anticipation and she shut her eyes. "Dear God," she prayed. "*Help me to say the right words to Mr. Meagher. He is Thomas's dad, and he is raising Bennie's and Thomas's child.*"

Katie also held her hands in a prayer fold inside the cabin. She closed her eyes. "*God let us be accepted here in Waterford.*"

"Mrs. Elizabeth Townsend Meagher?"

"Yikes!" Katie jumped at the male voice.

Libby reacted first. "Yes? I am Mrs. Meagher."

"Come with me please." The man motioned for the two women to follow him off the boat and down the gangplank, and then up some stone steps to the dock along the quay. He walked briskly and it was difficult for Libby and Katie to keep astride with the young man.

"Excuse me, young man," spoke Libby. "Would you mind walking slower? We have sea legs don't you know?"

"Oh! Yes! Of course you do. I am sorry for being inconsiderate. It is just that I am following orders."

"Where are you taking us?" asked Libby.

The escort pointed to a narrow, block-long warehouse, activity bustling with wagons being unloaded inside the cavernous space.

"Mr. Meagher is in his office in that building. I have been checking every passenger ship for the last five days." He stopped at the edge of the quay. "Be careful, Mrs. Meagher. This is a dangerous stretch of road here, but we have to dart across." He took Libby's arm on one side and Katie's hand on the other and the three of them rather clumsily scurried between wagons and animals.

"Whew! That was some run young man. Please give us a moment to catch our breath. Whew!" Libby fanned at her face, having only her gloved hand to move the air.

"Mrs. Meagher, I presume?"

Libby turned and peered into the black cavernous warehouse space. Katie took a step forward. At the same time they both saw the silhouette of a man walking towards them, beckoning them to enter the cool, smelly building.

"*Dia Dhuit*, good afternoon. I am Thomas Meagher, Sr., your father-in-law."

Libby extended her hand. They faced each other for the first time and greeted each other in the Irish.

Thomas Meagher, Sr., impressed with the greeting, welcomed the ladies as he steered them toward his office. "Please, we can sit in my office and shut out some of the clamber of the street noises".

"My, it is warm here this afternoon," Libby spoke with ease. "We had a very easy crossing, and actually gained one full week."

"Mr. Meagher, sir, let me introduce my housemaid, Katie McBride."

Katie curtsied. "Sir, I am from a farm north of Sligo. My parents are both dead. Does England still own me da's farm?"

Mr. Meagher smiled at Katie and in Irish told the younger woman the bad news. England still ruled that section of Ireland.

The initial meeting went well. Instinctively, Libby knew to be cautious in both words and actions.

"Thomas sends his love," she began. "And some essays he has been working on." She handed him the packet of letters from his son and Libby looked into her father-in-law's eyes. "His heart will always belong to Ireland." She rubbed her arm without thinking. "He has told me so much about growing up here in Waterford."

"Yes, he did love it here as a youth," spoke the elder Meagher. "I am happy to hear he is well." He looked at Libby, really looked at her this time. "My son certainly has an eye for beauty. Well, I'll have my office boy gather your trunks and bring them to the house." He hit a buzzer and the young man re-entered the room.

"Donal, bring around my buggy and see that Mrs. Meagher and her maid are deposited at the house. Then I want you to return the buggy and find a wagon on the Quay and collect their baggage." He turned to Elizabeth. "May I have your claims tickets?" Libby reached into her purse and surrendered the necessary papers and receipts.

"Come Katie, we have kept Mr. Meagher long enough from his work day." She and Katie left the room and were happy to take in a breath of clean air. The warehouse reeked of fish and other odorous, unidentifiable smells.

The trip to the Meagher house was short. Libby noted the two-story square building, similar in design to an apartment house in New York City. The two mistresses of the house, Thomas's aunts, were expecting them. When the green front door opened, Libby was pleased. At least these women were smiling and greeted them with hugs and favorite Irish welcome greetings.

She had barely sat down in the flowered pattern chintz covered horsehair stuffed chair, when a bundle of energy burst into the room. A curly topped redheaded whirlwind ran over to his Auntie and grabbed her knee.

"*Cé hi sin?* Who is she?" he asked in Irish pointing to Libby.

Thank you, Katie, for teaching me some Irish, thought Libby.

"That's Libby. She came to meet you. She lives away across the ocean in America."

The boy stared hard, then he pointed to Katie.

"*Cé hi sin?* Who is she?"

"That's Katie. She came with Libby."

Libby fell in love with Thomas's son the second she saw him. "He looks just like Thomas," she said, awe in her voice. "I never expected an exact copy."

As if on queue, the boy was drawn to Libby. He walked in a straight line to stand in front of her.

"*Dia Dhuit.*" He bent at the waist, one arm behind his back, the other tucked in at his vest.

"*Dia Dhuit* back." Libby smiled. At that moment she knew in her heart that she would do everything in her power to bring the child back to Thomas.

Later that evening, in the privacy of their lovely spacious bedrooms, Libby confided to Katie. "If it is the last thing I do, Katie, the toddler must return to America with us. The child belongs with Thomas."

Libby attended daily Mass at the Catholic Church near the Waterford residence. Only a few months earlier, she had finished her studies with Archbishop Hughes and had announced her intentions to join the Catholic faith. A special baptism had been held in Waterbury, Connecticut, and Libby was given the spiritual name of Bridget. Thomas was very pleased with Libby's decision, and he presented her with a beautiful green crystal rosary made at one of the convents in Ireland. The rosary went everywhere with her. She carried it in a small pouch, hidden inside pockets sewn in the waistbands of her dresses.

She soon became good friends with the Waterford parish priest who recognized her spiritual depth. He was happy to meet the wife of the younger Thomas Meagher. But he also understood the tension in the Meagher household. Libby was not Bennie. Libby posed a serious threat for upheaval in the family. How long would it be before she spoke of her intentions to take the boy to his father? The priest wondered if he would be called in to help with the decision.

It was only a couple of weeks later when Libby spoke of her intentions. She found the elder Meagher seated in the bentwood rocker by the fireplace.

"Mr. Meagher, I would like to discuss a very delicate subject with you. I've spoken to your parish priest about my returning to New York City with Thomas's son. We want to be a family. Do you realize the sadness in Thomas's heart? He grieves the loss of Bennie and his first son. Now his namesake is growing up away from him." Libby stopped talking and the room became like a closed tomb.

The rocking chair had stopped moving.

"I suspected such." The man got up from the comfortable padded cushion, shuffled across the kitchen and left the room. *Why do the Meagher men all leave the room to hide their true emotions?* thought a very confused Libby.

On the other side of the Atlantic, in the office of Peter Townsend, that same wonderful spring day, Thomas, his brother-in-law, Sam Barlow, and his father-in-law Peter Townsend were discussing a sound financial investment.

Costa Rica needed a railroad. That country's landscape would easily lend itself to laying track. Their government wanted contracts. Townsend's factory would produce the rails and the engine and cars. Barlow's law firm would handle the legal work and Meagher would go to Costa Rica for at least a year to oversee the whole project. The men recognized the millions of dollars in profits to come their way.

"I'll wire Libby today," said Thomas. "I'll not be separated from her like I was Bennie. She'll want to travel with me." The three men toasted each other with a drink of Scotch in Townsend's downtown office.

"Katie, I am needed in New York City,' said Libby after reading the ocean liner's telegram. Thomas wants me back home in June.

"Do you want to go to Costa Rica?" She mentioned the trip so casually, Katie thought she heard wrong. "Where is Costa Rica? Why are we going there?" asked Katie.

"It seems my father wants Thomas to build him a railroad there."

Libby's thoughts were already returning to the important question at hand.

This letter changed things. The boy would have to remain in Waterford for at least another year or so. Costa Rica was not a country to take a small child to live. *One upheaval at a time,* thought Libby. She sought out Mr. Meagher, Sr., and told him of her need to return to America. Her planned few months in Ireland had been disrupted.

It broke her heart to sail away without the child. Libby stood on the ship's deck waving back to shore where she watched Thomas's little toddler son. The scene etched its way into her mind, and heart and soul.

To leave him behind was unthinkable, yet necessary, at least for now. Thomas had other plans for their financial future, and although Libby didn't fully understand it, she knew this was his chance to build prestige in her father's company. Knowing how important it was to Thomas to achieve financial success, she would not interfere with his decision.

She stared long and hard at the two figures on the dock. The little boy was standing, gripping the pant leg of his grandfather. Libby watched the carrot-topped head of hair blowing in the breeze.

Mr. Meagher stood very still as he watched the ship leave the dock. Only then would he breathe a sigh of relief. The child was to remain in his custody.

Buíochas le dia! Thank God.

A MAP OF
THE KINGDOM OF IRELAND

CHAPTER 23

▼

COSTA RICA BURSTS

The Costa Rica adventure proved financially sound. Comfortable housing greeted the Meaghers and Libby quickly picked up the language. Meagher already spoke Spanish and Portuguese fluently. The ease he possessed when dealing with the government officials brought well-founded business deals. Peter Townsend was pleased with the results. Nothing could stop this business venture. Tracks were ordered and crews hired.

However, overnight and for no apparent reason, things went sour in Costa Rica; revolutionaries took over the railroad construction and the whole project was abandoned. Meagher once again felt the wealth he sought slip away.

He plunged into a depression that deeply concerned Libby. Pneumonia ravaged his body and coughing spasms weakened him physically. There was nothing to do but return to New York City and their home on Fifth Avenue.

"Katie, what can we do?" Libby worried the winter away. "Everything Thomas enjoys is slipping away from him."

"I don't know, Miss Libby. He seems so tired." Katie, too, worried about him. She watched over him at breakfast, hoping to get him to eat a good meal.

"Don't you tell me you aren't hungry, Mister. You eat some scrambled eggs at least. How do you expect to get well?" But none of her cajoling perked up Thomas. Day after dreary day he left the table after only eating a few bites of toast, and drinking black tea.

Thomas worked at his office when his health would allow him to venture out. His lecture tours were sporadic and the *Irish News* was running smoothly without his input. There was still one star left in the heavens with Thomas's name written on it. That was his association with Tammany Hall. He had the responsibility of difficult cases dealing with the poverty and poor treatment of the Irish.

NINA (No Irish Need Apply) signs sat in the corners of store windows slapping the face of every immigrant believing in American freedom for all races and cultures and beliefs. Thomas worked for justice and jobs and health and housing for his Irish brethren. By spring Thomas was feeling healthy again. He found himself taking an interest in the problems facing this great nation.

Politically, there were rumors of unrest in the Southern portion of the country. Secession of states, and serious talk of a confederate government located in the South became imminent. Thomas read the newspaper headlines night after night to Libby as she sat working on a needlepoint design for a pillow.

"Libby, President Lincoln has stopped the Union states from trading with any state that secedes. Listen to me. We might have a war between the north and the south by the end of this year. Talk is getting heavier at the Hall."

Meagher read the signs of war. He recognized civil unrest. His longings erupted from days of his young Rebellions group in Ireland.

"Thomas you are keeping things from me," sighed Libby. "What's wrong? Tell me, what has you so depressed." She stood in a familiar stance with her hands on her hips. A worried frown made wrinkles appear at the bridge of her nose.

"It's the political climate, Libby. Nothing for you to worry about." But Thomas began to pace on the oriental carpet. He took measured steps, leading an imaginary group of soldiers, forward…turn…back…forward…turn…back.

Instinctively Libby put her hand to her throat. She touched her beloved brooch. "Thomas, talk to me. Are you scheming something to do with the impending war? You can't shield me from what I read in the newspapers. I know division is beginning in the Southern States." She walked in front of Thomas, forcing him to stop moving.

"Are we headed for a war? Are you thinking to become involved?" She grabbed his arm with both hands. "Tell me you are not thinking of getting into the mix of things?"

Meagher of the Sword didn't answer. He didn't look at his wife. His mind was focused on 1848, and the Young Rebellions in Ireland. Meagher's blood stirred at the very thought of him giving service to his recently adopted country.

"This war between the North and the South will build until Lincoln is forced to take up arms," he said. He avoided Libby and went to his desk.

Meagher's mind started racing. *I could build an Irish Brigade. All volunteer's to join up from the very beginning; three months assignments, uniforms, training, a payout to feed their family.*

"Perfect." He shouted and hit his hand on his desk. "Libby, I've got a plan that will help the Union army and will eventually save Ireland from the British Crown."

Using his orator's skills, Meagher soon had the Irish lads lining up to sign on with him to help save the Union. Abraham Lincoln had heard of Meagher's patriotism and loyalty. He summoned Meagher to his office. During that same meeting Lincoln gave Meagher the authority to recruit Irishmen for an Irish regiment. The Fighting 69th from New York City is recruiting right now," said Lincoln.

"The North will settle down the South," said Lincoln. "Can you imagine that Jefferson Davis fellow? He is calling himself President of the Confederate States." Lincoln stood, unfolding his long angular legs like one opening a jackknife. "Mark my words, Meagher. Not a shot will be fired from the Northern Union Army unless provoked."

"Meagher, your group will set up in Virginia for training. Three months and we'll have the South back in line. The latest news is that South Carolina has seceded. It's going to be a tough year." Lincoln poured two tumblers of whiskey and handed Meagher one.

"I predict with certainty that 1861 will remain one of the most important years in America's history. Drink up, man. You'll need every drop to keep your spirits high these next few months." A very sad expression crossed President Lincoln's face as if he had seen a horrible vision. "This *will* be settled through paper work and mediation." Both men hoped the other's predictions were correct.

Meagher smiled and drank from the glass. "We'll have a regiment, sir. New York City's finest fighting men. I'll help with recruiting and I know we can count on the Irish from the slums. They need the money, Mr. President. Their families live in the worst imaginable poverty and disease."

Meagher's men trained daily on a hillside in Virginia. The days of January, February and March were checked off the calendar. Soon Meagher would send his boys back to New York City.

"Extra! Extra! Read all about it!" *Irish News*! *Irish News*! Get your copy here! shouted young paperboys standing out on street corners all over the city. "Only two copper pennies. You can read all about it."

Every morning Milton collected from the front walkway a delivered copy of the *New York Times*. He'd take it to the kitchen where he could stay warm from Bridget's oven usually already baking bread and cinnamon rolls in its cavernous space. Milton looked around to see if anyone else was stirring about in the house this early. He heard nothing, but he realized Bridget had to have been up very early. Delicious smells of fresh baked bread filled the air in the kitchen.

God bless you Bridget, you keep an old man alive with your cooking, thought Milton. He thought about all the years of faithfulness she had given to the Townsend and Meagher families. *I wonder if she ever felt she was being treated like a slave?* He laughed at that thought. *And what about me? I've worked here for Mr. Townsend for over 30 years.* His chuckle was cut short and died in his throat. Milton stared hard at the headlines. *Fort Sumter Fired Upon.*

With a cannon ball manufactured in the Townsend Foundry, the explosion changed forever the face of America. The article predicted that by August Federal batteries and ships would bombard the Charlottesville harbor. But by early spring the Confederates intentions were well broadcast.

PART II

▼

THE CIVIL WAR
YEARS
1861–1865

If a statue in the park of a person on a horse has both front legs in the air, the person died in battle. If the horse has one front leg in the air, the person died as a result of wounds received in battle. If the horse has all four legs on the ground, the person died of natural causes.

—(Civil War statues)

CHAPTER 24

▼

KATIE ELOPES

"Miss Libby, I have something to show you," said Katie. She held up her left hand, and Libby spotted the heavy gold wedding band on Katie's ring finger.

Katie smiled the knowing smile of a woman in love.

"Seán and I. We eloped last night. Father Sullivan from St. Francis Xavier Church married us." She lowered her eyes.

"I wanted to tell you, Miss Libby. I hated keeping a secret from you, but Seán..." her voice trailed off. "Please forgive me, Miss Libby. I love him so much."

Libby hugged Katie close. "Oh! Child. You took me by surprise. Come sit here on the couch and tell me about it. Did you have your brothers there? Katie sat and now, knowing her secret was out and Libby did not chastise her, the words spilled from her very heart and soul. Her eyes sparkled with the telling.

"Yes, they were all there. Patrick stood up for Seán, and his new bride, the girl who played the harp at your wedding, stood up for me. It was a grand event. We kept the wedding party small. We went to their apartment for a light supper and the prettiest wedding cake. It was covered in fluffy white frosting and real garden flowers. I carried a bouquet of garden flowers and…Katie paused and looked over at Libby, now lost in the remembering of her own wedding five years ago. *Where does the time go?* Katie waited for Libby to speak again.

"Tell me, where is Seán now?"

"Seán joined Mr. Meagher's army, Miss Libby. He leaves with the unit for Virginia. He says the money will give us a nest egg to give us a home someday soon." Katie paused.

"I would like the rest of this day off, if I may? Seán wants me with him when he tells his father what we have done." Katie took a deep breath.

"The Judge will be all right with the news, I am thinking, but his mother…she will be unhappy with us. I am not the girl for her son, she will be thinkin'."

"What's done is done, Katie."

"I am not worried, at least not now. Three months will rush by and then we'll be together forever." Katie smiled, refusing to allow her fears to surface. "I'll still work here? That will not change? At least for now?"

Libby smiled at the younger woman.

"Katie, you know this is your home." She stood. "Be off with you, now." The day will be here soon enough and we will go together to watch our men as they march down the street." Libby turned back to Katie.

"Congratulations, Katie. Plan to bring Seán to dinner tonight. We need to toast you properly. Are you going to tell Bridget your news?"

"Later that evening, with open arms Libby welcomed Thomas to her bed. "Remember always, I love you, my *anam cara*." He sighed. "It is amazing how out of control this war is becoming. I am worried now about the involvement I have put our boys in, Libby, but I have to see this through. Thousands of men have signed on and I promised to lead them."

"Shhh, now. We'll talk of war later. Come here to me."

Slowly, deliberately they sealed their love for each other. Thomas combed his fingers through Libby's hair, an intimate act he had developed over the years. The gentle stroking always secured her heart, calming her fears, and she rested in the rhythm.

Her satin nightgown felt cool against his naked body. He liked lying alongside his *amam cara*.

"We leave from the docks at ten o'clock in the morning, Libby."

"I'll be there to see you off," she said. "Your uniform is ready. I finished sewing the braid yesterday. The green uniforms will certainly look sharp and be distinctive. I am proud of you, Thomas." She sat up and pulled on a robe.

"The flags are finished. I put an Irish harp in gold threads in the center. Gold braid finishes off the edges. The enemy will know they are facing the Fighting Irish from New York City, my love."

Libby, at first, did not want Thomas involved, but as the news became more ominous, she knew he would not stay away from the action. She decided to join him in his patriotism.

"I plan to be in Virginia…to be with you, Thomas."

Thomas started to protest, but she hushed him.

"Mrs. Lincoln and I plan to help in Virginia with the troops. We can write letters, and help care for the sick and wounded."

"Libby, there will not be any wounded. No shots have been fired and Army Intelligence says this will be settled in the White House and on paper."

Libby did not respond to his attempt at soothing her jangled nerves. Instead, she changed the subject.

"One more thing, my love. As you found out tonight at dinner, Seán Daly and Katie eloped."

"Well, that certainly came as no surprise, did it? Katie has been in love with him for years. About time they got married, is what I think."

Libby laughed softly. "I told her she can live with us while he is away. Seán joined up with your men. If you can, please keep an eye on him. For Katie, and for me too?"

Libby leaned over and pulled Thomas close to her once again. She did not want him to feel her shivering, but she could not stop. "Please don't be the hero, Thomas. This is not your war. Remember that." She wanted to give Thomas her full attention. This kiss would have to warm her for many weeks.

Bull Run. Death. Meagher's men bravely faced the enemy. Chaos and screaming and smoke and dead bodies lie scattered like rag dolls all over the proscribed battlefield. The battle hit with deadly force. Meagher felt the searing pain enter his body as the shot from the rifle held by the soldier boy in gray hit its mark. The heavy thud took the wind from his lungs as his body hit the ground, his horse dead, on top of him.

Libby! I need you. Libby, my Anam Cara. I...need...you. Like a curtain shade being lowered, the color behind his eyes rapidly faded from gray to black. He thought he heard Warblers in the branches of the nearby bushes. Then nothing.

General Thomas Francis Meagher of the Sword faded in and out of consciousness. The battle raged on. The confused men no longer had a bugler who would call out orders, nor a drummer to tell them to advance or go back. Their green flag with the harp that Libby had so painstakingly hand sewn, lay crumpled in the dirt.

CHAPTER 25

▼

SEÁN DALY

Seán Daly died at Bull Run. The son of Judge Daly, dead. The friend of
Patrick McBride, dead. The husband and soul mate of Katie, dead.
    The letter, addressed to Libby, was from Thomas.

> *My dearest Libby,*
> *I have to write you the most devastating news. Please sit*
> *down before you continue this missive.*
> *I'll come right to the point.*
> *The Battle of Bull Run created havoc and destruction*
> *and death so horrible for my men. Hundreds are dead and*
> *hundreds are injured and dying still.*
> *Seán Daly is among the dead.*
> *Libby, I swear we didn't see this coming until they were*
> *swarming over us. They let out their rebel call, and the hair*
> *stood up on my arms. You can tell Katie, if it's any consolation,*
> *Seán died a brave man. He did not run or hide, but kept*
> *advancing toward the enemy.*
> *My God! Libby! I'll never be able to erase this from my memory.*
> *May God have mercy on my soul.*
> *Faithfully yours,*
> *Thomas*

Libby, stunned, felt a surge of emotion rushing through her. Thomas was alive! But now she would have to tell Katie that Seán was dead. How could she do this? *Lord, help me. Give me the words,* she prayed.

Just then Katie came into the room, humming an Irish tune. She saw Libby, sitting stiff-backed on the edge of a wooden chair; a letter crushed in her lap.

"Why, Miss Libby. You don't look well. Is anything wrong?" Katie immediately tensed up when she saw the depth of sorrow and grief in her mistress' eyes.

She reached for the letter and started reading it to herself.

"Seán...Seán...No!" She began keening and twirling madly in the center of the room. "God...no! Not my Seán!" Katie crumpled to the floor at Libby's feet.

Libby ran to the intercom system and pulled the rope connecting the two sections of the mansion. "Bridget!" she screamed, "Bridget, I need you. Come now." She ran to the kitchen, found a towel, wet it, and placed it on Katie's forehead. It seemed an eternity before Bridget burst into the room.

"What is it, Miss Libby?"

Sad News

When Lilacs Last In the Door Yard Bloomed

Coffin that passes through lanes and streets,
Through day and night with the great cloud
Darkening the land,

With the pomp of the inloop'd flags with the
Cities draped in black,

With the show of the States themselves as of crepe-veiled
Women standing,
With processions long and winding, and the flambeaus of the night,
With the countless torches lit, with the silent sea of faces and the unbared
heads,
With the waiting depot, the arriving coffin, and the somber faces,
With dirges through the night, with the thousand voices
Rising strong and solemn,
With all the mournful voices of the dirges pour'd around the coffin,
The dim-lit churches and the shuddering organs—where
Amid these you journey,
With the tolling, trolling bells' perpetual clang,
Here, coffin that slowly passes,
I give you my sprig of lilac.

(Not for you, for one alone,
Blossoms and branches green to coffins all I bring
All over bouquets of roses,
O death, I cover you over with roses and early lilacs
But mostly and now the lilac the blooms the first,
Copious I break, I break the sprigs from the bushes,
With loaded arms I come, pouring for you,
For you and the coffins all of you O death.)
Walt Whitman, April 1865

CHAPTER 26

▼

LINCOLN'S ASSASSINATION
APRIL 1865

"Libby! Come here…Quickly!" Thomas stood up from his desk in the study, and folded over the early edition of the *New York Times*. He waited for Libby to enter his study.

"What? Thomas you are white, what's wrong?"

"Look!" He shoved the folded paper toward her.

"Read the headline." He started pacing the oriental carpet.

Libby turned the paper around and gasped.

"Lincoln's dead? Shot? How horrible."

She sat on the edge of a leather chair, and continued to skim the article.

"We all feared this might happen. Oh! Mary must be out of her mind. Thomas, you must go to the funeral." Thomas continued pacing as if in a trance.

"To think someone would be so bold as to shoot the President while he and Mary were watching a play in Ford's Theatre. What group would do such a thing?" Libby put the paper in her lap. "Will this take us into another war?"

Just then a knock at the front door brought Thomas to action. Standing there was a telegraph boy; in his hand he held an envelope edged in black.

"For you, sir." He handed over the envelope.

Thomas tore it open and read the message.

General Meagher, stop.

Lincoln assassinated, stop.

Need you in honor guard, stop.

Stay in the White House, stop.

Honor guard to accompany the body, stop.

Will ride train to Springfield, Illinois, stop.

Reply immediately, stop.

Thomas lowered the yellow piece of paper and saw the young lad still standing on the outer step.

"Come inside. I'll send an answer with you."

Thomas hurried back to his study and reached for his quill pen.

"Libby?"

"Go Thomas."

She turned from him and hurriedly left the room.

Thomas thought a moment. He needed just the right words for the reply to the telegram. He wrote on a clean sheet of paper.

White House, Washington, stop.

Leaving immediately, stop.

Arrive early evening, stop.

General Thomas Francis Meagher, stop.

He gave the boy his answer and some Union bills.

"Keep the change, son."

He shut the wood door and turned to see Libby standing by the front window, her hand pulling back the heavy drapery. She had been crying, but only her puffy eyes remained as a telltale sign.

"When will this madness end?" She rubbed her hands together and looked squarely at Thomas.

"Katie is pressing your uniform and will have your valise packed. Will you take the train to Washington tonight?" Libby's voice cracked.

Thomas pulled her to him. "The war is over, Libby." He held her tightly against his chest. She stood very still, deeply aware of the heaving sighs coming from her husband.

"Even though we were politically apart, most of the time, I had a deep respect for the man." In fact, Thomas had recently submitted his application hoping for a government position.

"The body will go by train to Springfield, Illinois, Libby. I'll be gone several weeks. Hhmm…I must get messages to my partners."

Within the hour Milton had delivered the necessary handwritten notes. Bridget had prepared a small wicker basket of food since eating on the train had not yet been restored. She put in a small jug of water, also. Katie had everything packed and ready.

The carriage team of horses was ready to transport the General and Libby to the train depot.

"Be safe, my love." They sat closely together and Thomas draped his arm over her shoulder. He slowly twirled his finger in her curls and smiled. The late afternoon setting sun cast a luminous golden glow upon Libby. *This picture of my anam cara will have to suffice me and remain in my heart,* he thought.

"I'll try to send you letters by train, Libby, but you might have to get details from the newspapers as to where I am daily." With a swift kiss, he left the carriage and hurried into the train station. Libby had to smile as she saw him struggling to carry the food basket, jug of water, and his large valise. *How handsome you look in that uniform,* she thought, as she dried a tear from the corner of her eyes.

"Let's go home, Milton." The clipity-clop of the horses' hooves on the pavement soothed Libby as the fancy black carriage smoothly carried her away from the train depot and him.

Immediately upon arrival in Washington, D.C., Meagher hailed a horse drawn carriage. He tossed his valise up to the driver who set it on a ledge on the roof.

"Take me to the White House," Meagher instructed. When he opened the door, he found it crowded. People scooted closer together to make room for the General. Immediately a Union soldier still in uniform started talking to him.

"Sir. "Are you here for President Lincoln? Will we go back to war?"

All heads turned to hear the General's answer.

"Yes, son, I am." He shifted the now empty food basket to place beneath his feet to make it a little less crowded. "The war is over." He heard a collective sigh.

The young soldier spoke again. "Well, what about Seward being stabbed in his neck…in his bed…in his house?"

Meagher went numb. "My God!" Meagher put his hand to his forehead. *I am on my way to the White House now. What am I walking into?"*

"What? What are you saying, lad. Tell me."

"Sir! A madman broke into Seward's house and killed five people, including Seward's son. He used a huge knife for a weapon."

"When?"

"While somebody was shooting the President at the theatre."

All the people in the cab nodded in agreement that this news was true.

"What about Vice President Johnson? Is he alive and safe?"

"Will he become President now?" anxiously asked the lone woman in the cab.

"Yes, ma'am. That is the chain of command." Meagher turned to the soldier sitting next to him.

"What else do you know, or have heard as a rumor? Are there any leads as to who is responsible for this reign of bloodshed?"

The soldier, now thinking he was important to Meagher, wished he had more to tell.

"Some are saying it's the Confederates. If they kill off our leaders we will be eight months without a President and they can take over Washington."

"Is Johnson alive?"

"As far as I know, sir."

Johnson, that drunken dolt, will be our next president. Meagher lost himself in thought. *What madness has gripped this country?*

The cab stopped at the White House front door and Meagher descended the cab. He paid the driver, caught his valise as it was pitched to him, and felt a tug on his hands at that same time. A White House guard was taking his valise.

"Your name sir?"

"General Thomas Francis Meagher. I have a telegram from the White House and I am to lodge here."

With the devastating news, springtime left the countryside and dark ominous clouds dropped heavy rain, as if even heaven were shedding tears. The eastern coastline was sent into a deep, shivering paralysis. However, the next day, as if on queue, the sun came out in the city of Washington.

Thousands of mourning citizens lined the Capitol walks to pass in a quiet file in the rotunda to view President Abraham Lincoln one last time as he lay on a bier draped in black velvet swags.

Lilac bushes burst into flowers overnight all over the city. Their captivating fragrance perfumed the air. Workers placed large bouquets of lilacs to cover the rotunda carpeting, softening the view. The poet of the day, Walt Whitman, penned he would never forget the fragrance of the lilacs. He wrote, "I find myself always reminded of the great tragedy of that day by the sight and odor of these blossoms. It never fails."

The funeral train cortege kept the oversized coffin covered in lilacs the whole arduous journey to its final destination, Springfield, Illinois. There the president's body would rest side-by-side with his favorite son, Willie, who had died three years earlier in the White House from typhoid.

Disbelief filled every conversation. Congress convened immediately and went into session to swear in Vice President Andrew Johnson to the highest office in the land. The government, of the people, for the people, and by the people, would remain intact. A committee was in place to conduct the funeral. Organization was returning. The sixteenth president, Abraham Lincoln, would be remembered as the first American president to die by an assassin's bullet.

Union generals formed the honor guard. They stood at the head and feet of the body, providing respect and dignity to the drama of the bier.

The body would be carried on a meandering train slowly winding its way, stopping at major cities and even at crossroads in rural America. The crowds would line the railroad tracks all along the route to view the cortege as it passed by. Meagher was one of the men chosen to carry out this duty. He would stand beside Civil War comrades once again. Sanity was slowly creeping back into the reality of the day's aftershocks.

Early in the morning, the now familiar guard took Thomas into the oval office where the former Vice-President Johnson sat behind the handsome desk. The men, tolerating each other's presence, shook hands and Johnson offered Meagher a cigar. He accepted the tobacco, but did not open the wrapper. Instead he put it into his breast coat pocket.

"Mr. President. It is good to see you are safe. I have seen hundreds of military guards stationed everywhere on my way from the train depot last night."

"Let's get right to business, Meagher." Thomas noted the lack of respect Johnson had for him by not calling him General.

"One of President Lincoln's last official works had your name on it, Meagher. Of course that has to be rescinded." He deliberately did not reveal what that position had been, and he waited for a response, but Meagher remained quiet.

Johnson knew he held the better hand this time. Yet he seemed nervous and paused a little too long. "Sidney Edgerton is the Montana Territorial Governor." Again he paused, but this time he looked directly into Meagher's eyes. "Edgerton has requested a secretary." Johnson puffed on his lit cigar. "Meagher, if you want to be the Secretary to the Governor of Montana Territory, the position is open. You need to be there before fall."

Meagher was deeply disappointed in this news. He had petitioned President Lincoln for a political position, but had not received an answer. Most generals were being given government assignments, with good pay and bonuses for their services during the War Between the States.

Meagher looked Johnson squarely in his eyes. He would not show his disappointment, nor give the other man any satisfaction at being disrespectful to him by assigning this lower level government position. He was obviously being sent away from the political scene in the East, but for what reason.

"I accept the position, sir. Thank you for the assignment."

The meeting obviously over, Meagher departed the oval office. Standing in wait at the door was the same White House guard.

"I want to visit with Mrs. Lincoln," requested Thomas.

The guard led him to Mary Lincoln. She was seated on a horsehair divan and appeared to be totally exhausted. Thomas walked to her and knelt down on one knee and took her hands. Neither spoke at first. Then Mary, holding a tear-soaked handkerchief clutched in her right hand, cried out.

"Thomas, Oh! Thomas. That evil man came right into our box and shot Mr. Lincoln. Why would he do that?" She clung to Thomas's hand. "He died in the house across the street. They wouldn't let me into his room. The doctor said I was too distraught." She slowed her speech as if it were an effort to finish her sentences. "Near the end I was allowed in. Such a darkness I have now." She rubbed her head above her eyes and looked directly at Thomas.

"Mary, I am so sorry." Thomas's throat went dry. The mighty orator had nothing to say.

Thomas's head was bursting from all the activities of this long day. He kept his thoughts on Libby. *As soon as I am in my room I must write Libby*, he thought. The same guard escorted him to his assigned bedroom. His first act was to write Libby.

> *"Dearest Libby,*
> *I have so much whirling in my mind. I met with Mary.*
> *I wish you were here. She is quite distraught, and sees nothing but darkness.*
> *The funeral plans are enormous but under control.*
> *President Johnson has called his cabinet together, and the*
> *Nation will find footing, both North and South.*
> *I have news for our future. It seems we will be moving west*
> *to Montana Territory. I have been assigned Secretary to Montana*
> *Territorial Governor Sidney T. Edgerton. I am disappointed, as you*
> *well know I would be.*

Libby, please have Katie and Milton fill my trunk and ready it to ship. Since I haven't a clue as to what to expect in Montana, such as housing arrangements, the winter weather, lawlessness, and even other citizens,

I feel it best that I go alone, with you to follow in the spring, if I am still there.

My darling Libby, I hate the idea of separation from you. I do not function well with you not at my side. But for me to take you to the Wild West with such an uncertainty in my future would not be wise or fair to you.

Your loving husband,
Thomas

CHAPTER 27

▼

GOING WEST

"Miss Libby, I can't stand watching you any longer. Every day you wait for a letter from Mr. Meagher and every day nothing comes." Katie moved toward the front window and watched the mailman as he passed by the house.

"You are so sad all the time. I know you miss him, but you will become ill if you don't change your ways." Katie stopped speaking. She knew she was near the edge of stepping over the line.

Libby could not bear the idea of spending the rest of this long winter without Thomas. His leaving for Montana Territory still stung deeply.

"Katie, I am so lonely." Libby looked at her housekeeper and dear friend. "Why did Thomas think I should stay behind? What are a few Indians and inconveniences of a small town? I've been in worse conditions with him." Libby paused for a moment as if trying to figure out the reason. "Surely he knows I would love to see the Wild West. He writes me he needs a secretary. Didn't I act as his secretary all through the war between the states?"

Katie remained silent. Everything Miss Libby said was true. She had accompanied him everywhere over the past ten years: to Costa Rica and to cities in the southern states while he was traveling on his lecture tours.

During the long, dragged out years of the Civil War, she camped with him at most of the battle sites.

Libby felt her depression. "Katie, I wasn't called the 'Darling of the Brigade' for nothing...you know? Didn't I help tend to the needs of the wounded soldiers?" Libby tugged at her apron front. "I nursed Thomas back to health after he was wounded and left for dead on the battlefield." Libby put her hands on her hips. "For heaven's sakes, now he is alone in the wilderness, and I am safe and lonely in this gilded cage of a mansion in New York City."

Suddenly, Libby stopped pacing. As if a bolt of lightning had hit her, she stood up straight, and looked at Katie.

"Katie, let's go to Montana Territory."

"Well, it's about time you said that, Miss Libby. I'm goin' to the attic right now to check on trunks. I think four of them would do it." Katie hurried toward the steps to the attic before Libby could stop her. "We are already on our way, Miss Libby. You write your Mister today and I'll go out and post it for you."

A very determined and excited Libby hurried through the west wing of the mansion to tell her parents of her decision to move west. She would not stay and discuss it with them, as she knew they would need time to digest her news. She did not want to hear their protests.

She would write Thomas this very afternoon. *He won't get this letter for at least three months. I'll make the arrangements and, whether he likes my decision or not, he can expect us in June,* thought Libby.

Libby's letter reached Virginia City during a time of confusion for Thomas. Things were not going well. He had made enemies of the political parties already established in the Territory, and he knew it. The contents of the letter both pleased him and scared him. He wanted Libby there by his side, and he missed loving her, but to put her in harm's way...he tried to dismiss that thought.

I should have brought her with me. Over and over I've regretted that decision to leave her in New York City, thought Thomas.

He knew from the tone of her letter that there was no stopping Libby from making the journey. He would write her immediately and welcome her to join him in his log cabin of a home in Virginia City, Montana Territory.

He would not write her of the problems and dangers he now found himself embroiled in politically and mentally and physically. Instead he would write to one of his loyal Irish Brigade soldiers from New York City and ask him to accompany Libby.

He was sure that Capt. Eamon Roberts would be up to the task. Meagher remembered that all Roberts could talk about during the war was his wanting to go out west, and claiming that is what kept him alive while his soldier-brothers died all around him. Meagher liked the young man and knew he would keep his Libby safe from all harm. That evening Thomas wrote two very specific letters and posted them himself.

"Katie! Thomas received my letter." Libby rushed to the kitchen where she found Katie busy making fresh bread. "I just received his answer." She skimmed over the white sheet of paper. "Thomas is elated that we are coming. He says he wintered well in Virginia City and thinks it will be an adventure for us to see the west. He hopes I receive this letter before my departure date."

Libby continued to read out loud. "Capt. Eamon Roberts, one of his men from the Brigade, is to escort us." Libby laughed at that. "As if we need an escort, indeed." Katie giggled at the thought, but said nothing.

"Katie, can you just imagine? We will be seeing the West! James Fennimore Cooper wrote about the West and all of the mysteries it holds in his *Leatherstocking Tales*. Why, Katie, for us to cross the Mississippi River is going to put us right into the hands of the Devil himself. Are you ready to fight off the Devil himself?" Again Libby laughed a full, happy laugh, and again, Katie giggled.

"Miss Libby, I am packing summer and winter outer garments of course, and several of your fancy ball gowns, and all of the shoes we own, and our every day dresses. We will easily fill the four trunks. Should we take cooking supplies as well?"

"I want to take herbs and medicinal supplies as I am sure they are in short supply. I doubt there is a doctor anywhere near Virginia City. Thomas did tell me they have something like 70 pubs and saloons in this little town, and a weekly newspaper, but no medical facilities or school for the children." Libby sighed.

"I know there is a Catholic church there." She turned to Katie. "Maybe my coming out west will have an influence on the community and we will bring some culture and social skills to the women already there." Libby thought for a moment.

"Oh! I want to pack my Bible, some classics and other good books, writing paper and ink, and music, too. I'll carry my jewelry. Will you sew pockets in my underskirt and the hem of my traveling suit? I'll be wearing the dark green one with the gold trim. Since we don't know how long we will be living in Montana, I really think it best to take everything we might anticipate a need for, don't you?"

"Dear Katie, are you sure you want to do this? You will be leaving your brothers and their wives and children behind for a very long time, maybe forever. I never even considered that you might not want to accompany me out West."

"Miss Libby, I have traveled with you all of these years. Do you think I want to miss the opportunity of a lifetime? Who knows what awaits us in the West? My mind is filled with curiosity about this untamed, lawless place you are draggin' me to. Me brothers will wish me well. After all, didn't they leave me in Ireland for a new life?" Katie continued with her bread making. "Sure and who can say? Maybe they will decide to pack up and move west themselves after I write telling them of the chances to get rich." She smiled at the thought of her family following her and becoming rich in the gold fields of Montana Territory.

A whirl of social goodbye dinner parties helped Libby to finish the worst part of the winter months. Hyacinths and tulips were already poking their heads through the last layer of snowdrifts near the house, promising that spring was near. Libby anticipated at least a three-month ordeal lay ahead for them. She and Katie were scheduled to leave by train to Chicago, then stagecoach to St. Louis, Missouri, and from there steam up the Missouri River to Fort Benton, Montana Territory, arriving in June 1866.

At last the departure date arrived. Caroline and Peter still opposed to their daughter going west, stood ramrod stiff at the train station. The trunks had been sent ahead and each woman was traveling with her personal valise and satchel.

"Libby, telegraph us whenever you can," said Peter. "Here are some extra gold coins. Greenbacks might not be accepted in some of the remote areas. Use this for emergencies…like delays along the route and illnesses or accidents." He handed Libby the pouch but did not look at his daughter. Libby took the leather bag and stuffed it into her valise.

"Father…Thank you. Mother…." Libby put her arms around her mother. She had not realized how frail her mother had become this past winter. "Mother, I must be with Thomas. You understand, don't you? I love him so much and a part of me dies inside when I am away from him." She let her mother go, slowly drawing back from her. Libby had no idea if she would ever see her parents again, but the drive to be with Thomas was her strongest desire.

"Goodbye my daughter, God speed." Caroline turned to Katie. "You watch out over my girl now, you hear?" She unashamedly allowed her falling tears.

Peter Townsend reached for Libby's gloved hands.

"Tell Thomas we expect you all to come back to visit. Unfortunately, we know the West is the place for Thomas to be. He will find himself in that new land. Have a happy life and be sure to write your mother."

He turned to Katie. "If you need anything at all, you write me. Maybe someday the West will be civilized and have telegraph lines, but you make sure we get news, Katie." He, too, allowed his tears to fall.

"Goodbye! Goodbye!" Another round of hugs and kisses and then Katie pulled Libby into the train station building. "We don't want to miss the train, now do we?" And with a rush, the two women hurried down the long corridor to start their new life. Both were rather giddy in their own dreams, expectations and curiosity of what lay ahead over the next few months.

As prearranged, and not wanting to barge in on the Townsend family goodbyes, Capt. Roberts and his recent bride, were to meet Libby and Katie at the ticket office. Capt. Roberts was excited to have the honor of accompanying the wife of his hero, General Thomas Francis Meagher, to the Territory.

Roberts had dreamed of moving West. When the opportunity presented itself out of the blue in the form of a letter from the Ex-General of the Irish Brigade, along with a letter of introduction for Roberts to present at the bank, Roberts did not hesitate. He talked to his bride about a visit to the Townsend mansion.

"Mary Margaret, come with me to meet Libby. She is a wonderful lady. I want you to be in on all the plans. Can you believe our dream is going to come true for us?" He put his arms around his bride's waist. "We will have a new start in Montana Territory. I know a job will be waiting for me. Maybe the General has plans for starting another militia to protect the settlers. And for me to be working with him again, why that is more than I could ever expect."

His instructions in the letter from Meagher were for Roberts to make a personal visit to Libby and explain his position in journeying west with her. That following Saturday, Roberts and his bride rang the doorbell of the Meagher wing. Katie hurried to answer it and showed the young couple to the front parlor. She waited until Libby came into the room before she went to the kitchen to make some tea and set out some refreshments.

"How nice of you to call, Capt. Roberts. She motioned for them to all sit down on the velvet couch. "Welcome to our home, Captain and?"

Roberts jumped up. "Oh! I forgot. This is my bride, Mary Margaret." He smiled fondly at the lovely Irish girl who looked rather embarrassed at his failure to introduce her to Libby.

"Don't fret, Mary Margaret. He couldn't remember important details while in the Irish Brigade, either." Libby smiled fondly at the young woman. "Welcome to you both this fine afternoon."

Katie returned carrying a tea tray and some of her delicious scones and strawberry jam. She had sugar and cream and lemon slices for the tea. It wasn't long before the four of them were busy making plans to leave for Fort Benton.

The Robert's would be packed and ready on the decided date, and they would meet at the train station. They would need to make their own "goodbyes" to their loved ones in the next few weeks. For Roberts that would not be difficult. He could see the good fortune and opportunities in making the decision to go west. However, Mary Margaret would have a harder time as she had family in New York City. Her family lived on Orange Street and there would be no extra money for visits.

"There they are." Katie spotted the Robert's and walked over to them. Libby followed. "Hello, you two," she said as she held out her hand to Roberts. "We are just in time."

A conductor had set down his stepstool and motioned to the group to board the train. The locomotive let out a rush of steam and hot air just as Libby walked by. She almost lost her ostrich-plumed traveling hat and it made her laugh. She slipped her gloved hand into the long brass bar and pulled herself up onto the steps.

"All aboard for points West," shouted the conductor.

PART III

▼

MONTANA TERRITORY
1865–1867

Níl aon éaló ón gcinniúint—
There's no escaping what's meant to be.
Irish Proverb

©Lenore mcKelvey Puhek 2005
Missouri River
Fort Benton, Montana

CHAPTER 28

▼

LIBBY ARRIVES IN FT. BENTON

"Hurry, Mary, here comes the *Ontario*; Libby's arriving today."

Acting Governor Thomas Francis Meagher, the guest of I.G. and Mary Baker, had spent the night with the Bakers. His darling Libby was finally on her way. The sternwheeler required 57 days to complete the journey from St. Louis to Fort Benton.

The trip, usually uneventful, had bothersome mosquitoes to torment the brave souls who'd ventured outside their cabin door. Indians had stood guard along the river's edge, confused and curious by the belching smoke from the stack on the boat that moved upstream. They had remained non-threatening. One passenger, Father Pierre J. DeSmet, also had noticed the Indians. He had been standing next to Libby at the deck railing.

"These poor creatures don't look like the men in the delegation who came to St. Louis to meet with me about bringing Christianity to their tribes." He sighed. "I really don't know what I expected, and I don't know what peril I might be putting my men's lives into. Hopefully, there will be peace and understanding among us when we meet in Benton's fort." He continued to stare out at the river's edge.

"You are undertaking a great adventure, Father," said Libby. I am sure my husband, Thomas Francis Meagher, who is serving as the territorial governor, will greet you warmly, and give you some type of protection. He is planning to provide a militia force for the homesteaders as soon as possible."

Brrrraaatt, brrraatt. The steamboat sounded its horn as Thomas ran out the kitchen door to cross the dirt street and stand on the dock. Mary and I.G. Baker ran right behind him, eager to meet Libby.

The Missouri River was high and deep. Boats arrived all hours of the day and night, and the noisy levee was a cacophony of sounds; men cursed and shouted at animals who felt the sting of the bullwhacker's whip tearing their hides.

The *Ontario* crew was no different. The air crackled with energy from dockworkers moving nonstop to unload the boat's hold. Farm equipment, tools, seeds, food, and mercantile items, like furniture, soon filled the space in front of the passenger platform.

One-by-one passengers began disembarking the boat. Each one shaking hands with the captain before taking the giant step from riverboat to the dock and eventually earth.

Thomas spotted Libby easily in the crowd. "Libby, Libby." He waved his hat in the air. "Over here." He ran to her side and in one swoop, he picked her up and twirled her around and around.

"At last! You are here!" Thomas laughed heartily. He crushed her to him and Libby clasped her hands around his waist.

"Thomas. Oh! My Thomas. At last! Don't you ever go off and leave me again." Libby kissed him and held him tightly to her. "I'm so happy to see you!" She reached up and kissed him again. All the other passengers walked around the two lovers. All accept one. Katie Daly stood patiently waiting.

"Katie, Oh! Forgive me." Thomas gave Katie a welcoming hug and she laughed as she grabbed for her hat that was about to fall off and into the river.

Finally, Thomas led Libby and Katie back to Mary Baker.

"Mary. Here she is. Meet my Libby," said Thomas.

"Welcome to Fort Benton, Libby. I trust you traveled well?"

"Hello, Mary. It is nice to meet you. Thank you for asking about the trip. The weather actually improved the farther up the river we went. When we entered Montana territory, the sky reflected such a brilliant blue, it was hard to look into it.

"Katie, is it?" asked Mary.

"Yes Ma'am." Katie curtsied.

"Come to the house across the street while you wait for your trunks. I've already prepared a meal," said Mary as she began to walk backwards toward the exit gate, motioning with her hands for the group to follow her. The June sun rising high in the sky silhouetted her. It was a perfect day for a family to be reunited after the dismal winter of 1865.

Thomas started to protest, to tell Libby he had made room reservations at the Cosmopolitan Hotel for all of them, but he saw Libby already walking with Mary. Libby easily maneuvered the dusty, rutted road. Thomas paused a moment just to look at his beautiful wife. He heard her lilting laugh. *Thank you God for Libby's safe delivery into Montana territory and my waiting arms,* he said in a quiet prayer.

The white picket fence gate swung easily as the three women crossed into the yard and disappeared inside the small house. The food would be fresh, and the conversation delightful. He would surprise Libby and Katie at lunch with the news that they would rest in soft, unmoving beds for a couple of nights here in Fort Benton before resuming their trek to Helena and ultimately Virginia City.

"General?"

Thomas turned around. "By God! There you are Captain Roberts." The two men saluted each other before falling into a tight hug. "Thank you for bringing Libby safely out west." Thomas couldn't stop smiling. "How good it is to see a familiar, faithful face." Thomas reached for the man's hand and shook it again. He noticed a beautiful young Irish woman standing back rather shyly, but obviously interested in this exchange between the two men.

"General, this is my wife of ten months, Mary Margaret." Roberts moved the woman into Thomas's line of sight.

"Well, congratulations to you both. What a pleasant surprise." Are you planning to continue with us to Helena and to Virginia City?"

"If we may accompany you sir, I think it would be safer. Is there a wagon available?

"My friend I.G. Baker will fix you up. I made reservations for everyone at the hotel there across the street. Plan to travel with us. I'd feel better about it myself as there are Indian uprisings in the area and the more banded together we are the safer we will be." Thomas slapped the younger man on the back. "It is so good to see you again, my friend. Let's go over to Mary's house for her lunch. We can talk over the details later."

A well-muscled dockworker approached.

"Sir, your wife's trunks. What do we do with them?"

Thomas couldn't believe his eyes. Before him were four steamer style trunks, two small valises and two satchels.

"I've a wagon!" Thomas stammered. He looked around for the man who had accompanied him to Fort Benton. Thomas himself had come on horseback and he had planned to put Libby and Katie on the stagecoach. To his dismay, he discovered the stage had left Fort Benton and would not return for several days. It would be Libby and Katie's fate to have to ride in the old buckboard of a wagon, at least until Helena.

"Meagher." Said a familiar male voice. "Hello."

Thomas turned to see Wilbur Fiske Sanders, a political enemy from Virginia City. It was a known fact there was no friendship between the two men. Sanders was a nephew of Sidney T. Edgerton, the man Meagher twice replaced as Acting Governor.

"Hello, Sanders." I'm here to welcome my wife to the territory. Looks like the Meaghers' are going to stay." They talked briefly about the politics of the day and soon parted paths.

I don't trust him, thought Meagher. He then turned his attention to the problem of the trunks.

He squinted into the sunlight, identified Sgt. Sullivan and motioned him to bring down the wagon to the dock. He was going to need help lifting the trunks. He also had ordered a 50-gallon oak-staved water barrel to keep the six of them from dehydrating as they crossed the prairie toward Helena. The horses would need water also, if they were forced to stop away from the known rest areas along the route. They would pick up the barrel, filled with cool well water, at the back door of Baker's store in a few days.

"Thank you for the lovely breakfast, Mary." Libby gave the other woman a hug. "Thomas says we must leave now, and we'll be camping out on the prairie for several nights with the Indians."

Mary smiled. "With you riding in a wagon, it might be a three day trail."

Libby's first look at Montana Territory might prove to be very exciting indeed. However, Thomas intended to make the stage line rest stops if the trip went according to plan.

"Let me help you ladies into your fine carriage," teased Thomas.

Katie and Libby sat primly on the wagon box. They both carried large umbrellas to shield their fair skin from the hot afternoon sun. Mary handed them a large basket filled with bread, a chunk of ham, boiled eggs, cheese, a jug of homemade wine, and cookies. She also had canteens full of water for each of them to drink. "You'll need this for sure later on today," she said. "Be sure to pick up a block of ice for the food when you get your water barrel, Thomas." She spoke to Katie. "Tuck the basket under your seat so it stays cooler in the shady side of the wagon. It looks like it is going to be a hot one today." With a final wave goodbye she backed away from the wagon.

"Thank you so much, Mary. If you and I.G. ever get to Virginia City, please be our guests," said Libby. "You have been so kind and thoughtful to us."

Union Army Sgt. Patrick Sullivan, a loyal follower of Meagher's brigade, clicked the reins and the wagon lurched forward. Thomas mounted his favorite horse, Champion, a white appaloosa-mix gelding. Libby's eyes shone as she stared at her husband, sitting so straight and strong on the animal's back.

"How handsome you look on a horse," said Libby as she grabbed the wagon box edge for balance. She laughed. "I think you will have a smoother ride than Katie and I."

Captain and Mrs. Roberts were fully outfitted at I. G. Baker's store. They were able to make a fine purchase of a spring-seated wagon and two strong workhorses. The plan kept them all together while crossing the long miles to the Prickly Pear Valley and Helena. Thomas wanted to discuss the plans for a Montana militia with Roberts, and he intended to offer Roberts a commission.

Seeing the territory from the eastern entrance had been an eye opener for Libby. She had nothing to compare this desert-landscape to, and the wide open space was frightening as well as awesome. Indians sitting or standing on the docks at the river's edge and at stops along the route for wood and food had always startled her.

Now, in the wagon, Libby thought about the romantic "Redskin" written in the newspapers by roving reporters looking for news after the Civil War. The Indians she had encountered so far did not fit that image. At fort and fuel stops along the river, Libby could see the poverty endured by the women and men, wrapped in Hudson Bay Company blankets, wearing eagle feathers in their long black braids. "Fort Injuns" is what the boat captain had called them.

Would they encounter Indians along this wagon route? She did not want to bother the men with her foolish questions, yet she felt uneasy as they seemed so vulnerable traveling in two wagons, alone on the prairie. Libby felt as if she had been swallowed up. *I must trust Thomas,* she thought. *People do this every day, and I have to get used to it. How primitive Fort Benton is. What is Helena and Virginia City going to be like? Was I too hasty in my decision to come out here? Was Thomas right in holding me back? Well, it's too late to turn back now,* she thought as she jostled from side to side in the slow, lumbering wagon.

The ride was hot and terribly uncomfortable. Libby was grateful to Mary Baker and her basket of food, a fitting and sensible parting gift. She knew that every time she used that basket in the future, she would remember the kindness of Mary Baker. Several times the three women left the wagon seats and walked on the shady side of the wagon boxes, finding that easier on their bodies than fending off the jolts from the wagon wheels.

The group stopped to rest the horses at a small creek, and Sgt. Sullivan pulled the team of horses and the wagon into a grove of quaking aspen. Captain Roberts followed suit. The tiny leaves, bursting with energy, twisted and turned on the branches as the prairie wind blew. The trees, to the delight of Katie and Libby, provided a bit of shade, and that is where they opened the basket. The contents looked like a banquet to the weary travelers.

Katie opened the wine jug first and, since they had no cups, passed the bottle to Libby who took a sip. Libby in turn passed it back to Katie. Katie then handed it to Mary Margaret.

"To our new world." The women spoke in unison and smiled at their toast. Katie handed the jug to Thomas.

"You look rather thirsty, me Lord, but would you dare to sip from me hand-crushed grapes?" At first Thomas paused. Then he recognized Katie's teasing style and he drank fully from the jug of wine.

"Roberts, take a swig. It is very good homemade chokecherry wine. The bushes grow along the riverbanks." Roberts took a long drink and passed on the jug to Sgt. Sullivan.

"Take what is left, Sully. You need it probably more than any of us. You have to keep these animals moving, and put up with the chatter of these three fair damsels in distress." All six members of the group enjoyed the sound of laughter while they settled into eating their late afternoon meal.

Thomas kept his body and mind on alert status. He worried about being alone on the trail and was hurrying the group to eat. His fear of Indians was genuine, and he wanted to discuss a guard duty plan for the night hours. He didn't want to alarm the three women, but he would not allow a fire. "We have many miles to go before dark, Libby. Why, the sun doesn't go down until ten o'clock during the summer months." He hoped to make it to the stage line rest stop where they would be safe.

Just two nights ago, while on his way to Fort Benton, he and Sully had topped a small knoll, to find Indians readying to attack a lone wagon. Robert Vaughn had become separated from the wagon train because of damaged wheels. He had several men with him, all protecting their gold pouches. Their destination was Fort Benton where they planned to catch a boat going back to the States. Thomas and Sully rode into the fracas and the Indians galloped off, thus saving the lives of some very grateful men.

She hasn't a clue, thought Thomas. *Wait until she sees the little log house in Virginia City.*

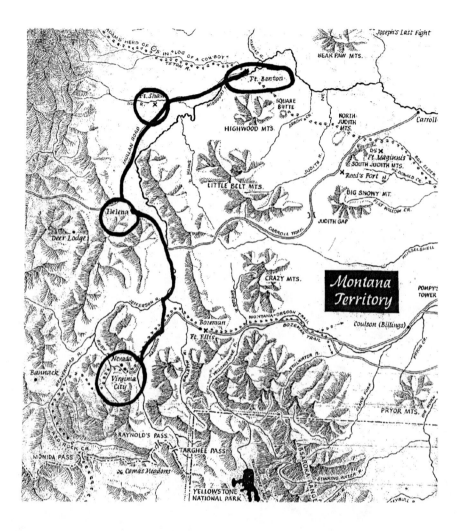

CHAPTER 29

▼

HELENA, MT. TERRITORY

The chosen route proved uneventful all the way to Helena. It was late at the end of the third day before they saw the lantern lights shining far off in the valley distance. Helena, discovered by four placer miners in 1864, was a frontier town full of wild men, a handful of women and a large canvas tent for a hotel. They would eat at the public café, also sheltered under canvas, much to Libby's delight. The streets, even at the late hour, were teaming with men starting or leaving their shifts, to work the main gold mines; some worked their own claims and used placer mining techniques.

"Say, ain't you the acting governor?" asked a bartender standing behind his makeshift bar set up in the corner of the tent. His bar consisted of a couple of rough cut boards stretched across wood saw horses.

"Welcome to my humble pub." The bearded, unkempt man made a grand sweeping gesture. Thomas reached out and shook his hand.

"You pegged me," he said. "My wife has arrived to join me in my political duties." He looked around for Libby in the tent barroom. "I am sure she is amazed and a bit perplexed at the wildness of this country." He took a swallow of the shot of whiskey.

Libby had left the tent and was enjoying her stroll with Katie. "Listen to the noises, Katie. It is like everything is a new beginning here. Men can start over and build a future." She turned around in a circle. "Look at all the room for buildings, freighting, a railroad, businesses, stores." She stopped and grabbed Katie's hand. "Katie, I think Thomas is going to be very successful here in the West. This is where he belongs. Why, he can do anything he wants to do here. The doors of opportunity are wide open." Libby clapped her hands together.

"Miss Libby, maybe my brothers will come. They could work in the mines and pick up gold nuggets. Mr. Townsend could build the railroad and there would be jobs for the Irish in the slums. We just have to convince them to move to…"

Pistol shots rang out, and a man hit in his chest fell backward out the saloon swinging doors, off the wooden plank porch, and into the dirt street. He still clutched the gaming cards in his right hand. A man ran out to aid his friend, but the rest of the men turned away, minding their own business. The piano player pounded out a louder tune and routine settled over the scene.

Libby and Katie stood frozen to their spot, mesmerized. A few minutes later, Thomas found them focused on the man in the street. Katie was pointing to a black wagon that had pulled up next to the dead man. The sign on the side of the undertaker's wagon read, *Hermann and Company Funeral Home—Coffins and Fine Furniture Made To Order.*

"Thomas should we help him?" Libby's eyes were bright with curiosity.

"No Libby. We stay put. The men have a rough life here in Helena. Nobody interferes in another man's affairs. He smiled at his wife. *Virginia City will be worse,* he thought.

Just then the undertaker pulled out the dead man's six-shooter from his holster. He checked the chambers, obviously looking for something in the barrel. He pulled out a rolled up piece of paper placed in the sixth chamber. It was a greenback dollar bill.

"Thomas, he's robbing that man."

"No, Libby. He's collecting his pay. Drifters keep a bill in the chamber to pay for their funeral."

Thomas took the elbow of the two women and led them back toward the boarding house and some supper.

"Will we have a menu choice, Thomas?"

He chuckled. The table boards were connected with an oilcloth, dirty, stained and torn. Libby and Katie hung back, but Thomas pointed them to three empty backless chairs.

"Sit, ladies." They sat.

"Here's the menu selection," he said as he pointed to a chalkboard hanging from a nail over the stove.

"All you can eat buffalo stew, $.25, coffee free, pie $.05," was scrawled haphazardly on the board.

"That's it?" asked a stunned Katie.

"It will fill you up and if you're lucky, you'll get a carrot, a potato and some onion along with a chunk of meat." Thomas ordered their meals.

A burly, hairy man wearing a canvas apron brought the large tin plates loaded high with stew, to their end of the table. He quickly returned with steaming coffee, spoons sunk in the cracked cups. A platter of hot bread came sliding down the table. Thomas reached out to stop the platter before it slid off the end and onto the dirt floor.

"Thomas, is this typical behavior and fare?" asked Libby. "Is all of Montana Territory wild and open like this place? Helena you called it?"

Thomas hesitated.

"Yes Libby, this is it." Thomas decided to give Libby a history lesson. "This is the West that once belonged to the Louisiana Territory. Jefferson's expedition, Lewis and Clark, back in 1805–06 opened up all this land for future development." He sipped the thick black coffee.

Libby was still working on her stew and bread. "Does Virginia City look like this too?"

"I'm afraid so, Libby." Thomas glanced at her. "Katie, try a piece of this apple pie," he said, shifting the conversation.

"Have you friends here, Thomas?"

"Yes, of course. And there are many in Virginia City eager to meet you. Mrs. Ronan has been very good to me, providing me with evening meals on occasion. Mary will be your next-door neighbor and she is a Catholic, active in the church groups and choir. Her husband and I have established a good friendship as well as a political one. He is interested in the Indians and their problems, especially the conflict with the white settlers and farmers." He paused for a moment.

"The church ladies are good women for you and Katie to spend time with."

Thomas looked at Libby and Katie. "Virginia City is a mining camp, Libby. It is growing and you will be happy to be a part of it, I am sure. I know I am happy you are finally here by my side." He winked at Libby hoping to make her blush.

"Tomorrow I'll introduce you to some folks and things will look brighter. Helena is only three years old and already she has more millionaires here than New York City because of the gold mines." He dug into his apple pie. "It is too late tonight, but in the morning we will be greeted properly by John Ming. You will like him and his wife and their one son. It'll be fine, come morning." He savored a bite of pie. "Umm! This pie is delicious."

The meal complete, Thomas took the two women to another tent boarding house where they would spend the night. The rooms were divided by canvas and a lumpy bed greeted Libby and Thomas. Katie was to sleep on the other side of the canvas divider on a single canvas cot. "I don't think I'll even take off my dress, tonight, Miss Libby. I'm going to flop onto this bed and sleep. I'm very tired. Goodnight."

Libby sat on the edge of the bed. "This certainly has been an interesting day, Thomas. I had no idea your conditions were so primitive. My poor darling."

Thomas rolled over to Libby and pulled her to him. "Come to bed Libby. We will spend a few days here in Helena with friends. It will be much better than your initial welcome to Helena." He stretched.

"I've made arrangements for you and Katie to travel by stagecoach to Virginia City. I'll travel on my horse and Sully will bring the wagon with your provisions." He laughed.

"What did you bring in all those trunks?"

"Well, you told me to be prepared for all seasons, and so I am. I don't want to be writing for things and bothering Bridget and Milton." Libby yawned. "Mainly, I brought first aid pharmaceuticals and Bridget sent her herbs."

A very tired Libby fell sound asleep, secure on the arm of her love. Morning dawned bright and clear. Libby reached for Thomas only to find the bed empty.

"Katie? Are you awake?" She asked through the canvas wall.

Katie stepped from behind the canvas. "Yes, Miss Libby. I'm ready for breakfast." We let you sleep in. Mr. Meagher and I have been exploring."

"This is a beautiful place, Libby. We didn't see anything in the dark last night." Katie moved quickly across the room.

"Miss Libby, Thomas's friend, John Ming found us and he is having a breakfast for us in his lovely mansion. He was scolding Thomas for not coming to his home last night."

Libby glanced into a mirror and patted her coiled hair. "Well, then, Katie, first let's find an outhouse, and then go eat." She grabbed her small satchel bag from the dresser and walked outside, still wearing her rumpled clothes from the day before.

"Thomas, good morning." Libby kissed her love soundly.

"Libby, good morning. I have a good friend for you to meet. Did Katie tell you?"

"Yes, Thomas. Can we walk to his house?"

"It's up this way," said Thomas, and he pointed to the Westside of the gulch that ran through the middle of the mining district. "John Ming is expecting us this morning."

The three of them started out at a fast pace. Libby indeed saw what Katie had seen earlier. Mountains covered in pine trees completely ringed the Prickly Pear Valley. Buildings in various stages of construction gave the semblance of a Main Street. But looming directly in front of them raised Mount Helena, a volcanic cone shaped mountain 6,000 feet above sea level.

"Ohh! How spectacular. There stands a part of the Rocky Mountains." She stopped to catch her breath. "I'm not used to this high, thin air. Thomas, no wonder you look so thin and healthy. Do you walk everywhere in Virginia City?"

How do I tell her she will be living on the side of a gulch, walking every-where, all within a couple of blocks? Thomas kept his counsel. *She'll see her new home soon enough,* he thought.

"Look, Libby. That is John Ming's house at the end of this iron fence."

Just then, a flamboyant, young-looking handsome man threw open the mansion's front door and tossed out his arms in a most theatrical gesture. He greeted Thomas warmly and kissed Libby's hand. Katie giggled but instantly warmed to this extroverted personality.

"Come in. Breakfast is ready," he gushed. "My wife is in Denver visit-ing family, but my staff is here. Meagher? Why didn't you come directly here with your beautiful wife? Afraid I'd steal her away were you?" He winked at Libby.

Libby didn't quite know how to respond. She graciously sat in her soft padded dining room chair and smiled.

Ming turned to Thomas. "You are planning to stay with me for a few days, maybe 'til after the 4th of July?" He looked at Libby. "I know we aren't a State yet, but we do celebrate our position of Territory with lots of hoopla."

Thomas looked at his wife. "What do you think, Libby? Would you like to stay in Helena for a few days? After what you have been through, staying put probably appeals to both you and Katie?"

"Ah! Governor. You've got so much work stacked up on your desk, do you?" Ming paused. "Libby, I insist you stay here in Helena. He can go on to Virginia City, but I bet he doesn't leave without you."

Libby laughed, looked at Katie and at Thomas and said, "Thomas I insist that we stay here in Helena." The four of them sipped European cof-fee from fine English bone china.

"After the initial shock wears off, Libby, you'll find cultural events are plentiful, even in Virginia City," said Ming. "I have a mercantile store and hardware store in Virginia City as well as here in Helena. You'll be seeing a lot of me this summer as I travel between the two cities." He took a bite of bacon. "If you need anything Libby, you just get a note to me." He thumped his chest. Then he checked his watch.

"A maid will show you the way to your rooms." The man never stopped talking and his energy was high. He pulled a bell pull hanging from the wall in the dining room. A young, girl, dressed in an ankle-length, black skirt, a white weskit and a little floppy hairnet type hat on her head, came into view.

"Please take our guests to their rooms," Ming requested. "Then bring them back here to me in one hour." He turned to Libby. "I want to show you my roses. I love to garden and this is just the right time for the flowers to bloom in Helena I am discovering. The vegetables, besides a few radishes and lettuce are going to need a longer growing season." He smiled. "Frost comes by the middle of September, but then we have an Indian summer into the late Fall." He shrugged. "I talk too much. Be off with you."

He gave a flourish with his hands and the maid immediately ushered the three guests out of the dining room and into the huge hall. The grand stairway appeared around the next wall and Libby caught her breath at the beauty of it all. At the top of the stairway an enormously large stained glass window glowed from the morning sun shining through it. They ascended this massive stairway and Libby felt as if she were walking into the light of heaven.

The maid directed Libby and Thomas to their bedroom suite and Katie's room was just across the hall. The plastered walls were covered in the wildest wallpaper Libby had ever seen. Long-tailed and plumed birds, their feathers hand painted in blue and green hues completely covered the walls. Plastered rounds hung in the middle of the ceiling with a large chandelier hanging from the center. It appeared to be wired for both electricity and gas, even though neither option was as yet available in Helena. Huge mahogany furniture filled the massive room. The wardrobe cabinet took up one entire wall, and the bed…why, Libby noted, they needed steps to climb up on to the mattress covered in a thick burgundy satin spread.

Katie turned in circles inside her bedroom. *Why, this is much more elegant than the Townsend mansion,* she thought. *I must be careful not to comment upon the elegance of this room. My gracious. These men must have more money from the gold mines than we ever dreamed possible back in New York City. I am going to write my brothers this very day.*

The group met again at the planned location.

"I enjoy roses; my son is a violinist with a great future, and my dear wife likes to spend my money. And you know? I like her to. We settled on Helena as the place to put our theatre. It will be so well-built dynamite won't disturb its foundation." He took a deep breath. "Of course, that theatre is in our future plans, but you and Thomas and Katie, too, will applaud some of the finest talents in the world right here in my Ming Theatre. Wait and see." He led them all outside.

"Come along. We'll walk the grounds."

Libby turned to Thomas and took his arm. For over an hour they strolled through rose bushes, apple trees, and other vegetation recently planted as a hedge around the mansion. Whenever Ming would come upon a bush in bloom, he would exclaim, "Ah! Just look at that beauty."

He picked a long stemmed red rose and handed it to Libby. Then he found a pink one and presented it to Katie. "Beautiful roses for beautiful women," he said as he bowed at the waist. Katie giggled at the antics of this delightful, friendly man. *I wonder what his son is like?"* she thought. Libby's sharp glance brought her back in line.

"Thank you for such a warm and wonderful welcome, John," said Libby. "I can see that you and Thomas have become good friends this past winter."

Thomas gave John a punch to his arm. "When did you say your wife would be returning from Denver?"

Meal Board

—Helena Tent Restaurant—
Helena, Montana Territory
June 1866

Buffalo or Beef Stew 25c

Fresh bread free
Apple Pie 5c
Coffee free with meal

Cook Wanted
Must Know How To Make Bread

Recipe for Buffalo (or Beef) Stew

Potatoes, carrots, onions, turnips, rutabagas, cabbage, peeled and quartered. Put in a large cooking pot; add water to cover the vegetables good. Pour in two pinches of salt. Put on hot woodstove. Buffalo meat, or beef meat, cut into bite-sized squares of meat. Coat the pieces with flour. Add to the boiling water and vegetables. When the meat is tender it is done. When the vegetables are tender they are done. When the water turns to thick gravy it is done and ready to serve. If company is coming, pour in some red wine before serving.

From the family recipe box of author's Grandmother, Mary Phoebe Frey.

CHAPTER 30

▼

VIRGINIA CITY, 1866

The road wound south through the Boulder Valley, parallel to the Boulder River. The hot sun and the jostling stagecoach did not make the trip pleasurable, but Libby and Katie were busy looking this way and that to take in all the new landscape. The Ruby Mountains came into view as the horses hit their rhythmic stride and the miles smoothed out.

"Ladies and gents," shouted the driver as he bent over and thumped the top of the stagecoach door. "Look over to your right and into the sky...there. See the eagle?"

Katie saw him first. "Libby, look at that magnificent bird. He has a wing span of at least six feet across." She stared for a moment longer. "Look how he rides the air currents. Oh! Oh! Here he comes close to us." Katie pulled herself back inside the coach window. "Miss Libby, come over and take a look."

Libby leaned over Katie's body to peek out the opposite side window. "Ireland used to have eagles flying everywhere when I lived there," said Katie.

Libby stretched her arms and hands a bit. "Fifteen hours in this coach...my back is telling me it is time to stop." She tried to stand, but the rocking of the coach made it impossible to find steady footing and she gave up.

Two other male passengers shared the coach. One looked like a gambler wearing his black frock coat and boiled white shirt. The other man, a merchant businessman, had the corpulent look of success about his mid-section. His gold watch chain stretched across his vest front.

Katie and Libby exchanged the complimentary "hellos" with the men, but they did not converse with them. Libby was a bit uneasy. She noticed the men occasionally staring at her, as if they wanted to speak but instead turned away.

I wonder if they have any idea who I am, thought Libby. An unexpected shiver of fear ran through her body, and it flashed through her mind that she and Katie must be on the alert for danger. Libby chastised herself for being so suspicious. She looked over at Katie and smiled. Katie bubbled with excitement and wonder at all she was seeing, so enthralled with the whole trip.

Fifty-seven days on the riverboat to Fort Benton and another month of traveling by train from New York City to St. Louis had not drained either of the women of their energy. One wonderful companion on the riverboat had been Father Pierre J. DeSmet. He and Libby discussed the plight and needs of the redskins, and he had agreed to come into the Montana Territory to teach and baptize.

The very idea of the territory being so new reminded Libby of the plans men had for this great land. Wasn't it Horace Greeley, a New Yorker, who called out *Go west, young man? Go west*. There had not been one moment of trouble among the passengers. The train filled with Confederate and Union men alike, rode the rails without incident. Libby wondered why she was now faced with inner fears.

"Look at that tumbling creek, it is so clear." Katie brought Libby back to the present moment.

"Miss Libby, did you have any idea of how the West would look?"

"I have read books, Katie, but the authors must have imagined their views of the West, This valley is as lush as the Garden of Eden. This part of Montana is spectacular. Just look at those mountains!"

Katie interrupted. "Never did I dream I would see such massive, jagged mountains."

"My dear girl, this mountain range is prettier than the Alps in Switzerland." Libby let her gaze return to the scene outside her window.

"Look at the snow way up in that crevice," said Katie.

The Rocky Mountains begin rising in New Mexico and end in Canada. They are bold and high, glacial snow remaining in the crevices year round.

"I have been thinking how smooth and sedate and worn our mountains in the east look compared to these." Libby returned her gaze to the inside of the coach where Katie sat next to her on the cushioned seat.

"What do you think is ahead for us Miss Libby? Do you think we will be staying out West for long?"

Libby closed her eyes.

Thomas is ambitious, and he has dreams of fame and fortune like all of these other independent men who are investigating living in the open west. She also wondered if Thomas would ever leave the west. *Time will answer all the questions,* she thought. "Time will tell, Katie."

The way station beckoned horses, driver and passengers. The passengers wandered to the outhouses before they entered the station house. One outhouse said "Gents" and the other "Ladies." It took a minute for their eyes to adjust to the dim interior after spending so much time in the bright sunlight, and the smell was rank and bothersome.

Inside the station house the dimness was welcome, as the building felt cool. They sat on the strange looking wire chairs spaced around rough planked tables.

"Our clothes are filthy, Katie. The dresses we brought will just not do on these dusty, unpaved roads. Imagine us walking in the streets of Virginia City after it rains." She sighed and looked at her tired feet. "Our shoes are certainly not built for this country. The narrow heel is not going to get very far when we try to walk anywhere."

Katie giggled. "Maybe we will wear men's pants and boots?"

"Men's clothes? I don't think Thomas wants to be reminded of our escapade at the pub. Goodness, that was over twelve years ago, Katie. And here we are wishing for a pair of trousers to wear and boots for our feet."

Libby brushed at her dress front. "I predict we will be doing business with Ming Mercantile very soon."

A haggard-looking woman, probably the station owner's wife, her gray straggly hair uncombed and flying loose around her shoulders, approached the new arrivals. She wore a dirty brown cotton day dress with a stained-beyond-clean white apron pinned at the breast and tied in the back. Men's boots covered her feet and cotton brown long stockings.

"Yaw wanna eat?"

"Yes, please. We would like glasses of water as well," said Libby.

The waitress raised her eyebrows at that request. "I don't have water glasses. Two coffees and two lunches. That's it?" She did not take time for chitchat. She returned to the kitchen and Libby could see her hitting at something with a large cleaver. Within minutes she brought two plates and two coffee cups. She set them on the rough-board, oilcloth covered tabletop.

"Thank you," said Libby, and she sipped at the hot cup of coffee, so stale it tasted bitter in her mouth. The plates held one boiled egg, sliced thick ham, brick cheese cut the same way, and Sour Dough bread to fill them.

"I'm going to pay for our meal and stretch my legs, Katie. Take your time. I'll be back soon."

Libby left Katie who was still munching at the bread and wandered outside. She started around the side of the station house when she heard two men talking. Before she was seen, she stepped back into the shadows.

"How's the road ahead for me today? The Vigilantes takin' stages?" asked one of the men.

"So far all stages have passed through," said the man with a bushy beard. "I'm sending a shotgunner with you today. You better watch it though seein' as how you got the Acting Guv's wife on board."

Libby froze. "*Vigilantes? A chance at being robbed or killed?* Her mind started to swirl. *I must warn Katie as well*, thought Libby as she hurried back toward the front of the building. *Where is Thomas? Is he ahead and riding into this danger?* She halted her steps. *Oh! He must know about it.*

Libby tried to remain calm as she found Katie still sitting where she had left her.

"Katie, come with me. I have to talk to you right now before we get back on the stagecoach."

"What is it Miss Libby?" Katie could see fear in Libby's eyes. "She jumped up from the chair and followed Libby outside where they could talk in private.

"All aboard! Stage is a'leavin'." A male voice shouted from the corral where fresh horses were harnessed to the stagecoach and ready to continue this last lap to Virginia City.

"Howdy do ladies. It's a long trip, but you're almost there. Climb aboard." He held out his hand to support Libby as she stepped onto the hanging stairs and entered the coach once more. "These are good, fast horses we got now." He winked at Libby and a sign of understanding passed between the two of them.

Libby bit her lip. Her news would have to wait, and maybe it would be best anyway not to frighten Katie over a rumor.

"Twenty hours in a stage coach is hard on the bottoms, Katie, but the driver says we are almost there." She hoped Thomas was ahead of them since he was traveling light on horseback.

"Can you believe how late in the day it is before the sun goes down? Why it is almost 10 o'clock at night, and we still have daylight." Katie could only stare out the stagecoach window. "I wonder…." Unable to speak for a moment, Katie pointed her finger at the sight outside her window. "Miss Libby! Look!"

There, not more than a stone's throw away stood a majestic elk, his rack well over six feet across. The animal appeared heavier and taller than a horse.

"Well, I never! Libby stared at the magnificent creature living in the pine trees, near the forest meadow. Suddenly the bull's harem of female elk and calves came out of the trees along the meadow, foraging food before darkness overtook them. A narrow creek tumbled and bubbled and sang lazily through the meadow.

Katie was beside herself in an innocent joy. She had not yet recovered from losing Seán in the war. To hear her laugh on this trip was music for Libby's ears. *Bringing Katie was a good idea,* thought Libby. *Not only has she been a helping hand to me, she has been a delightful traveling companion.* Libby shifted on the bench that was getting harder with each mile. *I can see now why Thomas wrote so glowingly of this country.*

Thomas's letters did not begin to explain the beauty that she found surrounded them. Nor was she prepared for all the different types of landscapes witnessed from Helena to Virginia City. The clear thin air not polluted by factory smoke and burning coal left a blue sky so clean it came as a complete surprise to Libby.

The late sunsets filled Libby's soul with the beauty of the colors. Sharing their space with wild animals seemed incomprehensible, but here was this new land spread before her like a wonderful banquet filled with morsels to sample.

The stagecoach rumbled on, not disturbing the scene. *Such beauty surrounds us,* thought Libby. *Thomas's health has greatly improved. He's lost weight and his life has purpose once again; and Katie, why she is blossoming ever since we left New York City.*

Libby pondered what their future would be here in this start-over place of new beginnings. Little did she suspect what life would orchestrate.

"Katie. We are all going to benefit from this mountain air and a slower pace. I am happy with the decision to move out here. Thomas is pleased, I can tell, and you just might find yourself a western cowboy." Libby noticed the surprised look on Katie's face. "Now, Katie. Don't tell me you hadn't thought about that yourself," she teased.

At last the town of Virginia City spread before them. The shock of it all hit Libby full force. *Is this where I'll be living my life?* She stared out the curtained but open windows. Libby hoped she hid her disappointment from Katie.

False-fronted business buildings stood their ground as the stagecoach rolled by. Libby read hand painted signs identifying the hastily begun businesses. She saw an advertisement for lady's shoes, hand painted on the bricks up high on the side of the wagon-freight company's building. The doors to the fire station were blocked open, and the mercantile shop stared straight ahead as they rolled on by. The buildings, built on either side of a dirt road, filled the gulch. Most of them were made from unpainted wood boards, probably rough-cut at a nearby sawmill. Some had brown paper sheets dipped in hot wax hanging in the holes meant for glass windows. None of the buildings were more than two stories high. A wooden plank sidewalk provided a place to walk above the mud when the streets were wet. Libby thought of soldiers standing at attention as the carriage rolled past them.

The Wells-Fargo building loomed ahead, and Libby saw Thomas standing in the yard. She would always remember him standing there looking anxious. *What is he worrying over?* wondered Libby as she waved and smiled and called out his name.

"Libby. At last." Thomas put his arm around Libby's waist and gave her a big hug. "I hope the trip wasn't too unbearable. Hello to you too, Katie. He smiled that charismatic smile that won Libby's heart every time she came near him. "Welcome to Virginia City, ladies."

He took Libby's hand and started to walk across the roadway. "Home is just down there!" He pointed a few hundred yards down the dusty street. Libby could not believe her eyes. *A cabin? A cabin was to be her home?*

With her head held high, Libby followed Thomas to the gate, waited while he opened it and she stepped through. No one had come to greet the wife of the first Acting Governor of Montana Territory. If Libby felt slighted, she did not let on.

Katie held back. She felt her jaw drop. *My! This is such a reverse from when I came to my new home in New York City*, she thought. *Lord in Heaven, what is to become of us?*

Meagher home 1867
Virginia City, Montana
(Used with the permission of the Montana State Historical Society)

CHAPTER 31

▼

LIFE IN VIRGINIA CITY
1866

The basket housing half-a-dozen Leghorn chickens wiggled back and forth in the corner of the room. Even with a cloth over the top to keep the birds in darkness, come the dawn they always managed to find a glimmer of light, just enough to start clucking and pecking at the bottom of the container.

"Katie, please take the chickens outside for me, will you?" Libby sighed. "They'll wake Thomas, and I want him to sleep longer this morning."

Katie, who was busy assembling the ingredients to make her daily round of Irish soda bread, wiped her hands on her pin-on apron front.

"Yes, Ma'am."

Katie grabbed the basket by its sturdy handle and carried the birds out to the yard where she released them. Each bird took a turn at flapping and stretching their wings, free of their tight nightly constraints. Pecking at seeds and grasshoppers would occupy them today, as they searched in the tall weed-like grasses that surrounded the log cabin home.

Katie reached for the metal coffee can hanging on a large hook at the side of the open porch. She noted it was still full of chicken feed and dipped her hand into the bucket.

"Here, chick, chick, chick...here chick," she sang into the July day as she broadcast the feed.

The kitchen screen door flapped behind Katie as she returned to the kitchen and her morning chore of making the Irish soda bread.

"Miss Libby, why do you want Mr. Meagher to sleep in this morning?"

She mixed the bread ingredients and flopped the mass of dough into a round lump on an iron skillet. "It is going to be really hot later on today." Without thinking of her actions, she placed the bread dough into the already warm oven.

"He has appointments with the miners to hear their work complaints, for one thing. Then in the mid-morning, the political contingency wants his time to discuss the farmers and families starting to squat on land and claiming it for their own use." Libby continued setting the table for the three of them. "He works too hard at this job." She glanced toward the bedroom. "And, the Indians were bothering homesteaders on the Bozeman Trail. Sometime today John Bozeman himself is riding in to town." Bozeman wanted guns and protection along the trail.

Katie checked her bread and noted it was about as brown and as raised as usual. She found her recipes all needed more of everything here in this higher altitude, and cooking was a challenge on many occasions. But Thomas and Libby were not fussy, and they grew more and more less formal with each passing day of living in the mining town.

"Thomas's forty-third birthday is in a couple of weeks, and I'd like to have a party for him. What do you think?" Libby walked over to the cupboard and took out plates and cups.

Katie clapped her hands at the idea of their first official party. "I think it is a wonderful idea. We could hold it at the Planter's House. That would be a lovely place for your guests...and I know the new cook. He is from San Francisco." Katie took a breath.

"I want to make the cake though, my Chocolate Sour Cream Cake. It is Mr. Meagher's favorite. At least that's what he says every time I make it.

You know the one, with the walnuts sprinkled on top?" She walked to the cupboard to check over her ingredients for cake making. She looked carefully at the supplies and frowned. "I'll need to go to the market today and order some ingredients in from Salt Lake City if Mr. Ming doesn't have them in stock."

Libby handed her a lead pencil and a note pad.

"We can hand-make the invitations, and you can deliver them for me. Most of the guests we will see at church this Sunday. The other invitations you can take to their place of business." She put her hand on her hip. "Be sure and tell Mr. Ming if you see him that he is to be in Virginia City on August third, will you please?" She sighed. "Even with the population around 35,000 people, this place is so uncivilized..."

"What's that you say? What's uncivilized about this place?"

Libby jumped at the sound of Thomas's voice.

"Good morning, Katie." He walked over to Libby and pulled her into his arms. "And good morning to you, too, my love." Libby detected a bit of a happy lilt to his voice this day.

"Did we wake you? I was hoping you'd get more rest today."

"Katie's bread always wakes me every morning just like clock work," said Thomas. "I love the smell of that bread. Katie...have you some raspberry jam and a cup of strong coffee for me this morning?" He swung his left leg over the chair seat and sat himself at the table. "How about a couple of fried eggs to go with that?"

Katie giggled. "Coming right up, sir."

Libby tapped him on the top of his head. "It's because of you and your taste for fresh eggs that we sleep with chickens," teased Libby. "What would Mother and Father think of us if they knew we did that?" She gave Katie a plate to hold the now cooked eggs, sunny side up; just the way Thomas liked them.

"At the Mercantile last week, eggs were a dollar and fifty cents each. Can you believe that?"

Thomas looked out the small window glass panes at the chickens strutting about, heads bobbing up and down in an ancient instinctive rhythm and harmony. "Something about our chickens, Libby. We have happy chickens." He smiled at Libby. "You didn't expect to be raising them now did you love?"

"No!" said Libby and Katie in unison.

"I never thought it would be my duty to collect them into a basket at night and keep them inside the house." Katie looked at Thomas. "Why, somebody would steal our chickens, and then we'd be without your eggs the next morning. That would be a real disaster. Around here, chickens are as scarce as hen's teeth."

Thomas and Libby stared at each other and burst into laughter. "Katie did you hear what you just said?" And so the bantering and teasing continued inside the log cabin now called "home." The chickens continued to scratch and roam in the weeds, totally unaware that they were the center of attention this fine summer morning.

Libby jumped up from her chair. "It's time for you to be on your way to the office," she said to Thomas. "Shoo…away with you. Katie and I have plans for the day. We will see you at noon?"

"Yes. I have meetings all day today," spoke Thomas. He kissed his wife and ruffled her still uncombed hair. *I am so happy you are here, Libby,* he thought. *I'll never allow us to be separated again, my anam cara.*

Libby watched as Thomas walked the block to his office on Wallace Street. "Now, let us get busy on that invitation list." Katie sat, poised with the pencil she had been using earlier in the morning, ready to write names as she heard them.

"Mr. and Mrs. Martin McGinnis. The Ronan's for sure. Oh! We can't forget John Ming. Mrs. Ming is still in Denver for the rest of this month." She thought a moment and Katie stopped writing. "What about Captain and Mrs. Roberts?"

"Yes. Put them down on your paper, and don't forget Father Michael." The two continued to think of people and the list grew long. Thomas was very well liked among the townspeople. Libby and Katie had only been in Virginia City for two weeks, but already they had met most of the church people and the Irish folks.

"Miss Libby. Here is what I have written for the invitation. Does this sound right?"

You are cordially invited

To Attend

A

Surprise Birthday Dinner

For Thomas Francis Meagher

August 3, 1866,

The Planter's House.

Sincerely,

Mrs. Elizabeth "Libby" Meagher

"The wording is just right, Katie. You best be off to the mercantile before the day gets any hotter."

"Yes, Ma'am. I'll finish putting things away here in the kitchen. And I'll check over my supplies list," said Katie.

"I am going to stop at Mr. Meagher's office and see if he needs me to act as his secretary during these meetings today. I forgot to ask him before he left us." Libby had often acted as his right-hand office staff during their years together, carrying out official orders when her husband was a famous Civil War General. She wanted very much to be of help to him now.

Libby looked over Katie's list. "Tell Mr. Ming to add whatever you order to our bill. We'll pay him in full when Thomas is finally paid for his services. It is a disgrace that he has not received his wages due him." Libby frowned. "I don't know how he survived alone all these months. I am so glad we came west. It will be a good place for us to live, wait and see."

Katie started to leave the kitchen when Libby stopped her. "Katie, will you also remind Mr. Ming that I want hard candies ordered in for the Christmas party I am planning for the children at church? See if he thinks he can get in any oranges, maybe walnuts?"

She checked the calendar hanging on the wall by the back door. "Oh! Ask him about the Frozen Charlotte dolls. He was going to check a sales catalog." Libby worried that Santa Clause would not find Virginia City since the mines would all shut down as soon as the freezing cold weather hit the area. "The time is getting short for ordering in time for the holidays. I want every child to receive a storybook as well. I have written Father and Mother to send boxes of marbles for the boys and some wooden block sets for the toddlers."

"I had a Frozen Charlotte doll," said Katie. "She was so tiny I carried her around in my pinafore in a tiny box that I made into a bed for her. She was maybe three inches high, but I played with her all the time. Mine came from a cake that a neighbor baked. It was a children's cake, and she hid the doll, a coin, a small pencil, and even a tiny spoon inside the cake batter and baked it. Who ever got that piece of cake got the prize." She laughed at that memory, one of the few Katie had of her childhood in Ireland. "My, but that seems like such a long, long time ago."

The day passed quickly as summer days tend to do in Montana Territory. Katie ordered her necessary ingredients at Ming's Mercantile and walked to the Palmer House to visit with the new chef from San Francisco.

"Is John-Paul in the kitchen?" she asked the hotel clerk. He waved her on and Katie found her way to the back interior of the hotel.

"Hello. What a nice surprise," said the very handsome French man, originally from Paris. "What brings you into my kitchen?"

Katie felt herself blushing. "I am here for Miss Libby. She wants to plan a surprise birthday party for Mr. Meagher on August third. He will be forty-three years old, and she thought a party would be a good way for us to meet his friends." Katie stammered. "You know, us being here only a couple of weeks and all."

John-Paul pulled out a chair and motioned for Katie to sit down. He poured her a cup of coffee and reached for a recipe book. "How many is she planning to invite?" He didn't wait for an answer, but flipped the pages until he came to a well-worn recipe. "This is perfect. It is good for hot weather meals and will feed a large crowd. Does the governor like lamb with green mint jelly?"

Anything John-Paul recommended was good enough for Katie. "We will get back to you but Miss Libby does want something very special with lots of vegetables and fruit trays and good linen and silver, and…"

"Whoa, little missie. I will prepare a wonderful feast for this occasion. Do not think otherwise. What about a French creation for a dessert?"

Katie felt herself shrinking, but she wasn't going to be intimidated by this special chef's delightful desserts. "I plan to make the dessert cake," she said. "I always make Mr. Meagher's cake for his birthday, and this year will be no different."

Katie jumped up from the chair and quickly left the room. *Why does he make me feel all funny?* she thought as she left the Palmer House by a side door. Since the death of her husband, Seán Daly, Katie had not thought of other men. *I certainly would not be interested in a Frenchman, for sure.* But, as she walked the hill to home, she realized she was day dreaming of him just a little bit.

"Hey Katie, wait up." Katie stopped and turned to see Mr. Meagher walking towards her. His day had been full and weary lines were beginning to show on his face. Katie noticed gray hairs in his otherwise black hair.

"Are you happy here, Katie? I certainly hope so. I don't know what Libby would do without you. You two have grown to be more like sisters, you know?"

Katie smiled. "I've never been happier, Mr. Meagher. It is a great adventure I am on right now in my life. There is so much to this world, isn't there?" The two of them strolled on toward the log cabin and both waved when they saw Libby standing at the door watching for them to come home.

"Isn't she beautiful standing there in that pretty blue dress, just waiting for us? I am a very happy man, young lady. *Níl aon tinteán mar do thinteán féin.*

Katie nodded her head in agreement. "Yes, sir. There's no fireplace like your own fireplace."

All through their light evening meal of vegetable soup and bread, Libby had good things to tell. She had met with several church ladies to plan a Fall Harvest supper for later in the year, in September actually. "You know how much I love planning ways for fund raising for the church, Thomas. This supper will be a grand affair, and we will make so much money for the school fund we will be able to send for the Sisters of Charity to come and teach our children." For several years there had been no school in Virginia City. "Also, we can have the sisters open a small hospital. Maybe that will put an end to Mountain Fever that I hear can be deadly." Libby frowned. "Thomas, you will put in a good word for us to get the sisters to come from St. Paul, won't you?"

"Libby, if you and the good ladies raise the money, I can guarantee you Virginia City will have the sisters here before winter sets in."

Thomas rose from the kitchen chair and walked to the small area that served as their parlor. He sat rather heavily into his favorite chair and picked up his pipe. "It is a perfect night for a quiet smoke, my dear. Would you hand me my book of Shakespeare's Sonnets? I feel like reading a while before we retire to bed."

Sour Cream Chocolate Cake

½ cup butter (or lard)—soften
½ cup cooking oil Cream these 6 together
1–3/4 cups white sugar
2 eggs, beaten
1 teaspoon Vanilla
½ cup sour cream (or buttermilk)

2–1/2 cups flour
4 Tab. cocoa
½ tsp. Baking powder Sift 7 dry ingredients
1 tsp. Baking soda
½ tsp. Cloves
½ tsp. Cinnamon
½ tsp. Salt

½ cups chocolate chips
¼ cup chopped walnuts

Cream butter, oil and sugar. Add beaten eggs, vanilla and sour milk (cream or buttermilk) and blend well. Add sifted dry ingredients and stir together. Spoon or pour into a greased and floured 9" x 13" pan. Sprinkle top with chocolate chips and nuts.

Bake at 350 degrees for about 40 minutes or until done. No frosting needed.

From the family recipe box of author's Grandmother, Mary Phoebe Frey, 1860s.

Chapter 32

▼

An Evening in the Log Cabin

"Brrrr." It's cold outside tonight," thought Libby as she re-entered the kitchen after a quick visit to the outhouse. *One thing I do miss is indoor plumbing.*

Libby was half way through her first Montana winter. The wood stoves in the kitchen and the parlor were kept burning day and night to stave off the February below zero temperatures.

The freezing wind blew up the gulch streets and snow swirled in high drifts. Getting around the slippery streets of Virginia City was tricky and dangerous, but the men did their best to keep things shoveled out around the churches and businesses on Wallace Street. *Can spring be far behind?* She thought.

Libby took off her cape and hung it on the peg attached to the wall near the kitchen door. She passed silently into the bedroom, noting that Thomas appeared to be asleep in his rocking chair in the parlor, his pipe held tightly in his hand.

The house was exceptionally quiet tonight as Katie was stepping out with John-Paul, the chef from the Planter House. *My how different it is for young people to court these days,* she thought.

Standing in front of the dresser mirror, Libby reached for her brush. Every night without fail she gave her tresses one hundred strokes before tying it into a loose braid for sleeping. *I don't see any gray hairs yet,* she thought, as she closely examined strands of hair. *My goodness, I am only…*

"Libby? Thomas softly called her name. "Are you free? Come visit with me."

"I thought you were napping." She peeked into the parlor and saw that Thomas had a ring of smoke curling around his head.

These winter days were long for her husband. The legislature had begun, demands were being made from all arenas: political, financial, social, and she noted a weariness about him. His dreams for the Territory were not progressing as planned. His letters to President Johnson remained unanswered. Statehood would be a reality, someday. Thomas wanted to be an integral part of the decisions being made now to secure the future for all Montana citizens.

Libby loved the smell of pipe tobacco. Its' pungent odor filled her with contentment, knowing Thomas was nearby. *We will grow old together,* she thought. Without planning to, Libby found herself sitting on the rag rug she'd made at the Ladies Altar Society's last meeting. She rested her arm and head on Thomas's legs.

"Libby. I've been thinking seriously about us, our future here in Montana Territory." Absent-mindedly, he stroked Libby's thick, curly hair. "What would you say if I told you I'm thinking about resigning from this appointment?" He let his hand rest on Libby's hair.

"Go on Thomas, I'm listening."

"I'd like to bring my son to live with us." The one great regret of my life is not having my son with me. He is a teen now; almost a man and I've never met him. What do you think of us taking a trip to France in the fall?"

Libby sat very still, not wanting to break into his thoughts.

"I'll write me da in Ireland and inform him of my decision. He can bring the lad to me in Paris." He stopped talking and sat puffing his pipe.

My goodness, you are pensive tonight, aren't you? I think it is a lovely idea to bring your son to America and to Montana, if that is where your future lies." She sat back on her knees and took Thomas's hand into hers. "I encourage you to write the letter and it will be a wonderful reunion for you to see your father."

Libby and Thomas had agreed a few years earlier, before the outbreak of the Civil War, that Thomas Francis, Jr. was safer in Ireland. Letters from Mr. Meagher, Sr., indicated that the boy was doing well. He was getting a well-balanced education and was growing into a fine Irishman.

"Also, Libby, I've spoken about this to John Ming. He thinks Helena is the place to live for future growth and opportunities. I've asked him to look into land. We could build you a fine mansion and I could open up my law office." He hesitated, eager to hear what Libby thought.

"Libby? Libby, talk to me."

Libby took a deep breath. "I've hoped you'd make a decision soon about our future. I know you worry about us financially but my darling man, we are fine. You know I have more money than we will ever need…"

Thomas raised his hand to protest. "I know you don't agree with me, but the money is there to achieve your dreams. Let's do it. We can have the best life in Helena." Libby stood up. "Your son will be at your side, learning the new Montana laws and you will be a powerful force in the political arena. Helena is a fine city and I would be proud to live there. As long as you are there, Thomas, that is all I want, or need, or ask of you."

"My *anam cara*. Thank you. My heart is full this night."

"When I married you twelve years ago, I knew my life would never be dull but I had no idea where the trail would take us. Never in my wildest dreams did I think about moving to the Wild West. Thomas, I am as happy as a thrush in the bush being here with you."

Libby reached down and put her arms around Thomas's neck. "Come to bed now, love. We'll talk more in the morning."

As Libby lay in the dark on the hand made mattress held by ropes tied to the braces of the log bed, she waited for Thomas to join her. *At least doors were opening for Thomas to see his son in France*, she thought. *Won't Katie be surprised when I tell her we will be going to Paris, France? Oh! Katie. Maybe she will want to stay in Virginia City with her new beau. I must talk with her about this new courtship tomorrow. I would never want to interfere with her happiness, but I don't know if I could stand being apart from her.*

Tears formed in the corners of her eyes and Libby felt them spill down her cheeks toward her ears. She reached up and quickly brushed them away, not wanting Thomas to see her crying.

She heard the kitchen door open and shut and she knew Thomas had gone outside to the outhouse. *Time and life determine our future*, she prayed as she drifted off to sleep.

Thomas left the warmth of the house to be jarred rudely back to the reality of a winter in Montana. He did not linger outside. But as was his habit, he took the time to look up at the clear blue sky and was startled to see the brilliant stars twinkling down on him.

"I'll build Libby the finest mansion in Helena, he thought. *But first, I've got to get my militia firmly in place. The settlers need to be safe.*

Thomas hurried back into the shelter of the log cabin, but it was the warmth he'd find in his bed that lured him this night.

The promise of spring arrived unexpectedly one night and brought the Robins to Virginia City. In March, Mother Nature teased them with false warm days, but when the calendar turned into April, the town stretched itself awake, like the hibernating bears waking up in the nearby mountain caves.

The miners returned to their claims and worked mines. Water trickled down the main ruts of Wallace Street and the ground was slick mud.

Libby was hanging clothes on the rope clothesline. "These towels are going to be such a delight to bring into the house," said Libby as she snapped each one before pinning it to the rope.

Katie, determined to have a vegetable garden in the back yard, chipped away at the soil. "If I get these seeds in before the middle of May we will have fresh vegetables by the Fourth of July."

"Someone someday will write a song called, *When It's Springtime in the Rockies*," said Libby. "It is so beautiful here." Way off in the distance, the mountains that formed The Yellowstone loomed, still crested with snow.

"Enjoy it while you can, Miss Libby. Summer will be here with all its glorious heat."

With a stick, Katie tried to make a straight line in the dirt.

As predicted, the sun burned with a great intensity. The thin air allowed the rays to penetrate the soil, parching the ground into uneven squares. Katie's garden prospered much earlier than predicted and she worked hard hand watering the plants from water carried from a distant yard well.

"Thomas, are you all right?" Libby had been studying his face, so much thinner than usual. "You seem self-absorbed these days."

Thomas shifted his legs, crossing the black boots he wore daily. "There have been more Indian uprisings, Libby." He paused as if trying to decide what to reveal and what to keep near the vest. "There are more pioneers moving into the territory and they need protection." He planted both feet on the wood plank floor and put his hands on his knees. "I can't be everywhere in this huge territory, and I am not getting response from Washington…and I need approval for the political moves I see necessary for this country to move forward toward Statehood."

Libby walked behind Thomas and rubbed his shoulders. He stood up, gave her a peck on the cheek and abruptly left the kitchen, slamming the kitchen door behind him. *He is so on edge,* thought Libby as she watched him walk away, kicking up dust with every step.

CHAPTER 33

▼

JUNE 1867

Libby's body barred the way through the gate. She stood with her feet solidly planted, her hands gripping it shut. Leghorn chickens scratched in the weeds and dirt, cluck-clucking around her feet.

Thomas had just stepped out of the barn, his arms loaded with his saddle and gear. Earlier he had brushed and fed Champion who now nonchalantly munched at the heads of the tall grasses within his reach.

"Thomas, don't you dare walk through this gate."

"Now, Libby. You know I have to go. I have important business to attend to. We need to collect the rifles that are coming up river from St. Louis, and I am meeting the Fenian group headquartered in Fort Benton." He smiled a wan smile. "Please don't try to stop me." He thought a moment. "You know there are at least 300 Blackfeet camped along the Missouri and that needs looking into. I have to be sure they are keeping the treaty we signed last year."

"But what about my dream last night?" Libby searched his eyes. "I am afraid for you."

"Yes, your dream." Thomas looked to the ground. "I don't take stock in your dreams. You are just tired of all of this." He made a sweeping gesture and looked about the yard. "When I return, we'll go camping in Yellowstone…"

"Then let me ride with you. I want to be with you, Thomas."

"It is so blasted hot, Libby. It will take us at least five days to get to Fort Benton with these wagons and that many days or more on the return." Thomas would not budge. "Just send me off with your kiss and a prayer for my safety. I'll be fine. My bodyguard, he'll watch out for me." Thomas knew his attempt at making a joke failed miserably.

Libby flinched at the mention of the bodyguard. "You know I don't like him or trust him, yet you keep him by your side. Why?"

"Because I *can't* trust him and you *don't* like him." Thomas laughed.

"The men will be here any minute with the wagons." Thomas shielded his hand in front of his eyes. "I see them at the end of the gulch now." He lifted his arm in salute to the men off in the distance who slowly lumbered up Wallace Street in the huge freight wagons.

"Libby, please don't say anything more about my leaving you here. You and Katie will be fine."

"Then at least take the food stuffs Katie has prepared for you." She let go of the garden gate and walked back into the house with Thomas behind her.

"Libby…Libby, I don't want to leave here on a sour word." He pulled Libby to him and kissed her. "That's my *Anam Cara*," he whispered in her ear.

A horse whinnied in the yard and the jangled sounds of the freight wagons broke the couple apart. All of a sudden it was time for Thomas to go. He would not send the men down the road without him.

Katie followed Thomas out to the gate. "Please keep yourself in God's hands, sir. Don't worry yourself about Miss Libby. I'll be with her." She handed Thomas the large gunnysack full of provisions. "God speed to you all."

"Thank you Katie. Take care of Libby for me won't you? I'll be back by the fourth of July."

Thomas tossed the sack on top of canvas tarps and ropes already in the wagon box. He spoke softly to one of the men, turned to Katie and gave her a salute. He easily swung himself into the saddle. Champion spun in a circle, lifting tufts of dust with his hooves. Thomas looked back toward the house and saw his Libby standing in the doorframe.

"There you are. At least I get one last look?" He smiled, giving Libby a very forlorn face. *God! What if she is right and I am headed into danger*, he thought. He felt for his rifle sheathed in the scabbard. *I can't change my plans now. Too much is riding on that gun shipment.*

"Thomas! Don't go!" She flew out the door and through the gate for one last kiss. "Listen to me. At church last night I heard the women gossiping about that note…"

Thomas jumped out of the saddle and grabbed Libby's arms.

"Shhh…I don't want the men to hear about that. It is just another note, Libby. I get them all the time at the office. It is a ruckus over that fellow I pardoned from jail last week in Helena. The Vigilantes are just…it will cool down." But inwardly Thomas wondered about that last note. It said, *Stay out of our business or you'll be swinging next.*

Wanting to soften Libby's fears, Thomas paused and thought a moment. "Suppose I camp in the canyon instead of stopping in Helena? Would that ease your mind a bit? I'll by-pass a clean bed and hot food." He looked at Libby and saw how sincere and worried she really was for his safety.

"*Níl aon éaló ón gcinniúint*—There's no escaping what's meant to be."

"Get on your horse and be gone with you." Libby turned and stomped up the walk and slammed the door.

"She'll be all right, sir. God speed." Katie smiled at the other men, knowing the scene had embarrassed Thomas. "Good mornin' to you all," said Katie. "*Slan.*" She also returned to the safety of the log cabin, but she gently shut the screen door behind her.

Inside the house, Libby stared out the small glass-paned window and watched the wagons lurch away from the hitching post in the front yard. This was the first time in their married life she had sent Thomas away from her without her blessings.

"Katie, I am afraid for him. My dream was so vivid." Libby's feet were like lead as she stood at the window. "Already more than one hundred men have died in this town and we've only been here a year. She pulled back the curtain just a bit and watched her beloved turn the corner onto Wallace Street and out of her sight. "He's gone."

The days passed slowly for Libby, and Katie was at a loss as to what to do for her. A pall hung over the cabin as Libby watched the road every evening. She and Katie attended church on Sundays and took food to the potluck suppers, but neither had their hearts into the events.

Tomorrow would be the Fourth of July, and the folks in Virginia City celebrated Independence Day as if the Montana Territory was part of the Union. The town's population of 35,000 men, women and children who lived in the immediate area in mining camps, would flock to take part in the activities. The town would be bulging with sweating men, noisy children, and hot, fatigued women. This was Libby's first year in Virginia City and she did not quite know what to expect, but she had overheard women at the last church supper making their plans.

Libby could not help but remember past Fourth of July picnics and family outings. Bridget and Milton would prepare a picnic and have the carriage ready to take them to Central Park where they spread out blankets on carpets of green grass, and set out food. Children ran freely under the recently planted trees. Well-rehearsed bands played in the band shell. Then, as soon as it was dark enough, the fireworks display would begin. *Oh! How I remember the night sky with the explosions of tiny colors, blotting out the stars for just a second or two.*

By comparison, the Fourth of July in Virginia City would be a celebration of contests: beer drinking, rifle shooting, horse races through the middle of town; a tossed-together band consisting of men playing accordions, fiddles and trumpets from the mining camps would be oom-pah-pa-ing down in the gully by the German brewery. A few half-grown Poplar trees were the only shelter and they provided a bit of shade into a corral for the horses and buggies.

Libby was not up to being jostled in the crowd.

"Katie, you go on and have a good time today. I'm not going to leave the house. I have a headache and it is just too hot out there for me to enjoy myself."

Katie hesitated. She did want to watch the activities.

"Are you sure, Miss Libby? I'll stay with you."

"Be gone with you, now. I'll be fine." Libby reached for the book she had started after Thomas left for Fort Benton. "I have Walt Whitman's poems to keep me company." Libby waved her away. She heard the back screen door screech as it banged shut behind Katie.

Thomas said he would try to be back by the fourth, thought Libby. *He's been gone now since the middle of June.* Feeling anxious, Libby could not concentrate on reading. She left her rocking chair and went to the kitchen to make a cup of tea.

Ka-Booom! Ka-Booom! The whole cabin shook. The hanging kerosene lamp swayed over her head, and the Waterford glasses clinked on their shelf. Startled, Libby jumped away from the stove and ran out the back door, teakettle still in her hand.

Ka-Booom! The ground shook beneath her feet. "What on earth?" She stood, confused as to what she should do.

Just then she heard loud knocking on the front door.

Libby panicked. "Who is it?" She called out. She forced herself to walk around the side of the small cabin to the front lawn. There, on her steps, stood a Wells Fargo stage driver.

"Afternoon, Missus. The men must be gettin' a little rambunctious over on the hillside shooting off the guv's cannon." He took off his broad brimmed hat and twirled it in his hand. "I have a letter for you." From his leather vest pocket where he stored his tobacco and cigarette paper, he pulled out a tattered envelope. "There's a dollar due for delivery."

Libby stared at the man as if not fully comprehending his message. "I've money in the house. Wait here." She moved through the front door into the kitchen, fumbled in her egg money jar and returned to the man still standing on her steps. She gave the man four coins. He in turn, handed Libby the envelope, and left her standing in the doorframe.

Libby stared at the white envelope in her hand. The handwriting was scribbled as if written in a hurry, and she did not recognize it. There was no return address in the corner; only her name, *Mrs. Elizabeth Meagher, Virginia City, Montana Territory.* Libby's whole body started to tremble as if she had Mountain Fever. She knew it was not a note from Thomas.

Libby put the envelope to her nose. The tobacco smell that lingered on the paper seemed repulsive to her. She sat down in a wooden straight-backed chair and looked around the room at her familiar surroundings. *I can't open this; I'll wait for Katie.* But with each passing minute, her anxiety grew.

Carefully she lifted the sealed flap, trying not to tear the envelope too much. She sensed whatever the inside message revealed, it was important to be very careful with it. A lone sheet of paper, folded in half, pulled easily out of the envelope.

> *July 1, 1867*
> *My dear Mrs. Meagher,*
> *I was in Fort Benton the night your husband drowned*
> *in the Missouri River. Please accept this loss as God's will.*
> *Sincerely,*
> *Father James O'Brian*

Only the chickens, innocently pecking at grasshoppers in the cabin yard, heard the keening that started as a low growl deep in the core of Libby. The alley cat, curled up on the outdoor rocking chair, jumped to the porch floor and disappeared over the porch railing when the soft moan exploded into a Banshee wail.

Katie walked alone up the hill to Idaho Street, humming an Irish tune, happy with the events of the day. Meeting her friends and sneaking a beer, made the day in the hot sun a fun one. As she neared the cabin, she noticed there was no light in the kitchen...*Run Katie! Run!*

Katie rushed into the kitchen not expecting what awaited her. Sitting at the kitchen table, as if in a trance, Libby sat clutching a sheet of paper.

"Miss Libby! Miss Libby? What?"

Libby stared into space. She had not heard, nor cared, that Katie was finally back from the picnic and festivities.

Katie walked to Libby and knelt down beside her. "Miss Libby? What do you have in your hand? May I take it? May I read it?" asked Katie in soft tones.

Libby opened her hand and the letter fell to the tabletop. Katie snatched it up and quickly scanned the page. "OOOHHH! NOOO! This cannot be true." "No! No! This is just another mean note, Miss Libby. Don't you believe it."

Katie didn't know what to do. *Slow down and think.* Suddenly, she remembered Libby's friend. *Get Mrs. Ronan. She'll know what to do,* thought Katie. *But I can't leave Miss Libby.*

Katie went to the wash area and dipped a cloth into the drinking water bucket. She wrung it out and laid the cloth tenderly on Libby's forehead. "There, there, Miss Libby. This cool cloth will feel good." She took both of Libby's hands. "I am going for Mrs. Ronan. I'll hurry."

Libby, finally realizing Katie's presence, nodded. "Yes, get Mary," she said.

My dearest love… Thomas? Is that you? Have you come for me?

Katie and Mrs. Ronan returned in minutes. "Do you hear me Libby?" She reapplied the discarded wet cloth to Libby's forehead. "Libby?" What has happened to Thomas?"

Katie handed her the crumbled paper. "This can't be true, can it?"

"We'll have to wait until we hear from someone coming in from Fort Benton, child."

"But we have no way to get information in this god-forsaken town." Katie walked about the kitchen, deep in thought. She stopped in front of Mrs. Ronan.

"Where will I find Mr. Ronan?"

"Peter? He's somewhere in that crowd." Mary pointed toward the brewery. "Yes. Katie. Go!"

Without wasting another second, Katie did not hesitate to run from the kitchen. *Please God, help me to find Mr. Ronan,* she prayed as she retraced her earlier steps to Wallace Street and the fun loving group of men. She would try the Bale of Hay Saloon first. *Surely Mr. Ronan will be there*, she thought.

"Libby, can you hear me?" Mary rubbed Libby's shoulders. "This letter came from someone who had business in Helena. When he realized you were not there, he scribbled this note." She stopped and looked at Libby. "Peter can send a rider down the trail. Maybe they have news at the Wells-Fargo office by now in Helena." Mary Ronan busied herself making tea.

"Oh! Where is that husband of mine? We have to talk to the stage driver who brought her the letter. Maybe he knows something more.

Libby stirred. Suddenly she realized Mary was standing in her kitchen fixing tea. "Mary, it can't be true. Oh, why didn't he listen to me? My Thomas drowned in the Missouri River? That can't be true."

"Now, now, Libby. Don't fret so. We'll find out soon enough."

In grief Libby lashed out. "Thomas, why didn't you listen to me? Why couldn't you forget the politics and Irish causes?" Libby beat the table top with her clenched fists. She dropped her head onto the tabletop and reached for her hair, pulling out all of the pins that held her bun tight to her head. She tried to run her fingers through the long strands to grab at the roots. She wanted to release the anguish and madness swirling in her brain.

Mary grabbed her hands. "No, Libby. You can't pull out your hair. I won't let you." There was no fight left in Libby. She did not resist Mary's strength.

With great effort, Libby stood up. The room swirled and she grabbed the edge of the table to keep from falling to the wood plank floor.

"Thomas needs me. I have to go to him. I must find Thomas." She staggered into their small crowded bedroom. She bumped into the edge of the bed and fell on top of the log cabin designed quilt. She began pounding her fists into the pillows.

"Thomas, oh my love. Don't go without me. Come for me. Why?" At last the dammed-up lake of tears broke through the foggy stone wall.

Katie, Peter and Mary Ronan found their mistress and friend, drowning in her own tears. Quietly, they returned to the kitchen, to sit in vigil under the lone kerosene lamp hanging from the middle of the room's ceiling. None spoke as Mary poured them each a cup of tea.

CHAPTER 34

▼

STAGECOACH TO FORT BENTON

Swirls of penetrating yellow dust swooped through the open stagecoach windows as it shuddered to a stop in front of the Cosmopolitan Hotel in Fort Benton. The horses, pawing at the hard ground, snorted and tossed their heads, as biting horse flies descended upon their sweat-lathered hides.

The trail from Sun River, the last lap of the Virginia City to Fort Benton run, seemed endless in the 100 degree July heat. Two female passengers waited inside the coach. They heard the thud of their valises and satchels as the driver tossed them from atop the stagecoach. Both women flinched with every drop.

"At last! We're finally here," said the younger of the two. She wrestled with the coach door handle and, after a mighty, unladylike shoulder heave, forced the lock to loosen its grip. The door swung open, almost pulling her with it as her hand still clung to the clasp. The hot, dry prairie wind caught at her hat and skirts as she stepped from the confined, terribly uncomfortable coach. Katie turned her attention back to the other woman still sitting inside.

"Libby, let me help you out of there." She reached inside the coach as the other woman stood. "Here, take hold of my hand." Katie's voice reflected her concern.

Libby rather clumsily exited the coach with Katie's help. She adjusted her clinging long skirts and looked blankly at the hotel. They both turned to the street when they heard a woman's voice, shouting out Libby's name.

"Libby! Libby, over here."

Waving, and at the same time trying desperately to cross the wagon wheel tracks, came Mary Baker, the woman Libby had met on her initial journey up river to Montana Territory. Libby shielded her eyes and waited for Mary. The two women embraced while Katie stood back and watched them.

"Well, you made it." Mary held Libby at arms length. "Let me look at you…" She caught her breath as dull blue eyes stared back, not connecting.

"Can you hear me…Libby?"

Libby nodded her head and forced a smile. Katie held out her hand to the woman.

"My name is Katie Daly." Mary took her hand for a second, and a look of common concern passed between the two women.

"I met you over a year ago when I came up river with Miss Libby."

Mary smiled and nodded her head, now remembering their meeting. She turned back to Libby.

"Too much commotion coming from the longshoremen unloading the cargo from the paddle boats." Mary shouted to be heard. They are forced to work around the clock for as long as the water stays high." Mary babbled on, not quite knowing how to handle this meeting. She brushed some dust from her skirt folds, giving her a minute to think.

The stagecoach driver tipped his leather hat to Mary.

"Hello, Jake." She flashed a quick smile his way. Jake knew Mary through the general store. Her husband, I.G., owned the business.

"Howdy do, Mary."

His weathered, suntanned face revealed his many years of driving stage in all types of weather. He blew into Fort Benton a few years ago, hired on at the livery, and said his name was 'Jake.' He handled horses with great skill and avoided contact with people equally well. No one thought to ask him much about his past, seeing as how he never offered up any information about himself. One true code of the West was no one cared about your past, or what you had been, only what you were doing now in this new land.

"You takin' charge of the passengers?" He winked at Katie.

Jake longed to be on his way to the stage line barn. He was anxious to cross the street to the invitingly dark interior of the Stockman's Bar. He needed a beer. The intense heat sent rivulets of sweat from the band of his hat to catch in his shirt collar. Without thinking, he reached up and worked his neckerchief over his face. He was parched and sweaty and tired from the long trail, and wanted nothing more than to end this unpleasant journey.

He stole a quick glance once more at the middle-aged woman who seemed to be frozen in a trance-like state. His had been the unhappy task of bringing Elizabeth Townsend Meagher, the days-old widow of the acting territorial governor, Thomas Francis Meagher, to Ft. Benton, Montana Territory.

Four days ago, Jake had left Virginia City, and traveled to Helena. He had made good time and finally arrived at his destination on the river's edge.

At several of the necessary overnight stage stops, Jake had tried to engage the woman in conversation but to no avail. She seemed like a really nice lady, fine character and all. The obviously distraught woman avoided his eye contact, preferring her attendant's company. She was confused, and when she did speak, it was to ask him questions to which he had no answers.

"Did you see my husband drown?" She asked over and over.

"No, Ma'am, I was in Virginia City when the accident happened."

"How do they know for sure he's dead? He isn't dead." Then she'd wring her hands, and stare at Jake, ready to ask the series of questions all over again. She tried valiantly to hold back her tears, portraying the upbringing of a refined woman.

Jake paced the pine floorboards on those nights, anxious to continue the journey. He was glad to hear the stable hands shout out early each morning, "Horses' er ready. Passengers all aboard. Driver's movin' on out!"

Now he was almost finished with this run. *Only got the six horses to take care of and then I'll be on my way,* he thought.

"Jake, I know you are hot and tired, but could I ask one more favor of you? Would you please bring the ladies' luggage to my house across the street? Libby will be staying with us for a while," shouted Mary over the constant din coming from the levee. She grabbed Libby's elbow and steered her toward the dirt street.

I could've pulled the stagecoach up on the other side of the street had I'd a known they was goin' to Mary's place, thought Jake as he struggled to keep his balance while he loaded his arms with the luggage.

"Come, dear Libby…Katie. Let us move out of the way. That's my house right over there." She pointed to the small, non-descript white house. Mercifully, Libby failed to remember that it faced the Missouri River.

"A spot of tea will freshen you two right up." Mary hoped she was right.

Mechanically, the three women weaved their way through the teams of oxen and mules, hitched to wagons loaded with freight, headed up the Benton Trail. The road was so deeply rutted on this main thoroughfare in and out of town that it was impossible to cross over the tracks in a wagon without jarring one's teeth. Trying to maneuver across those furrows presented a challenge to the ladies in their long skirts and high-topped, laced shoes.

"Be careful, now. We are almost there," said Mary. "We don't want any twisted ankles." The three women made it safely to Mary's house. Jake followed behind, large valises in his strong hands and the smaller satchels tucked under his arms. *Good thing they don't have trunks,* he thought.

A steady stream of supplies was brought upstream from St. Louis, Missouri, on steamboats and paddleboats, piloted by grizzled river captains who knew every bend and sand bar in the river. All sizes of freight wagons waited in line, to be loaded, twenty-four hours, seven days a week, during the high water season. Black workers from the Delta area had the jobs of emptying out the hulls and getting the cargo onto the levee. The wagons were then loaded with merchandise bound for the gold fields. Signs, hand painted with names like "Broadwater Freight," and "Power-Townsend Freight" were tied with ropes to the wagon sides. These freight companies carried the cargo to miners, farmers, merchants, and forts. The wagons stretched in continuous strings, like connect-the-dots across the prairie grasslands, into the foothills and beyond into the Rocky Mountains.

Even with the door closed, the noise from the dockworkers carried inside the tidy little kitchen. Libby sat, lifeless in a straight-backed wooden chair, her hands folded gracefully in her lap. She was unaware of the sweat on her brow, or that she had not yet removed her traveling hat.

Mary looked at her new houseguests. Just what was she to do with them and for how long? Finally Mary broke the silence.

"Libby, your letter arrived only yesterday with a freighter. You are, of course, welcome to stay here. Stay as long as you need to, whatever your plans." Mary sighed.

Fort Benton was not a safe harbor, nor a place for single women to spend any time. Mary Baker, the only white woman in town, longed for a more civilized home, and knew it was just a matter of time before she took a boat back east. Her sadness filled her daily at the thought of leaving I.G. Baker, but he would never give up his lucrative mercantile business. At least, not during the booming years, anyway. Blackfeet, Crows and other Indian tribes camped across the river. Hundreds of tipis faced the east in the meadow. Blacks filled the shacks built along the river's edge. The businesses consisted of blacksmith shops, whiskey traders, prostitutes houses, bars, and hardware stores, like her husband's general mercantile store.

One notorious madam, Madam Moustache, sported the finest brothel in town and was probably the richest woman in that part of the territory. Her business was all cash. She catered to the riverboat captains, as they were the men in town with money in their pockets. She allowed the pilots in next, and kept her many girls' rooms filled every night to capacity. Her bartenders served their expensive, watered-down drinks and the piano player kept the tinkling honky-tonk sounds spilling out into the night air. The river rats had to look elsewhere along Front Street for their pleasures.

Mary Baker reached up to a hook near the wet sink, and took down her floor-length, boiled clean, white cotton apron and pulled it over her head, covering her ample bosom. She tied the straps around her waist. With another sigh, she took a hard pull on the water pump handle and filled her copper teapot with the well water. She set the kettle on the wood-burning stovetop and heated up the kitchen even more.

Mary and Libby had met just a little over a year ago when Libby came up river to join her husband. Mary remembered it had been a pleasant June day when the passengers debarked. I. G. and Mr. Meagher and Mary had stood on the platform. Mr. Meagher was beside himself with happiness, ready to explode with expectation.

"There she is," he shouted. "Libby, here I am…" and he ran to her, picked her up and twirled her around and around, both laughing like little children, so excited to see each other and be together again.

But this was not the time to bring up that memory. It was time to make tea. Scooping up a corner of her apron, Mary reached for the hot teakettle. She made her tea the Irish way, pouring the hot water into a porcelain teapot, one of the few treasures she had been able to pack when she had left her beloved homeland forever.

This teapot saw only formal company use, and held tealeaves, captive in a tiny metal tea holder. She watched as the water turned a golden hue. Automatically she walked to a side cupboard and drew out three matching china teacups and saucers and three small plates. She took three starched and ironed linen napkins and placed them on the kitchen table. Next, she found three small stirring spoons, also placing them on the table. She forgot to ask if her guests needed cream or sugar and decided not to bother with it.

"Katie, if you look in the pie safe you'll find a plate of fresh biscuits." Mary poured them a cup of tea while Katie brought the plate to the table.

"Take a sip, Libby…please." Mary set the cup near Libby's right hand. "Please, Libby, just one sip."

Whether it was Mary's actions, or her tone of voice, it was enough to bring Libby back to the present. She looked about the room as if confused as to why she was sitting in this woman's kitchen. Then, focusing on Katie, she tried to talk but failed in her efforts.

"Thomas, my Thomas." In anguish she began to cry out. "Mary what happened?" Libby set down the cup and reached for her handkerchief tucked up inside her dress sleeve.

"She has not slept one hour since the letter from a priest arrived last week," offered Katie. Libby dabbed at her eyes.

"The letter didn't tell me anything other than Thomas had drowned in the Missouri River and I must accept it as God's will." Again, she dabbed at her red-rimmed swollen eyes.

Katie rose from her chair and put comforting arms around Libby's shoulder.

"This wretched country, so wild and lawless," shouted Libby. She waved her arms, making circles in the air, as if to sweep her thoughts out of her sight. Suddenly, she jumped to her feet and paced the room. Walking to the window, Libby pulled back the Irish lace curtain. It startled her to discover the mighty roiling Missouri River only a few hundred yards distant.

"That river...she pointed toward the window...swept my Thomas away. I cannot bear it. I don't believe this was an act of God."

Libby tried to control herself but couldn't. Katie walked toward her just as Libby released the curtain back over the window, willing herself not to stare at the river. She clutched the curtain hem in her fist. Then as if in resignation, she whispered ever so softly. "Thomas? Thomas. You are so close, I feel you are near."

Now it was Mary who sat unmoving, silent. She took a sip of tea and returned her cup to the saucer.

"Libby, come back and sit with me," coaxed Mary.

She did as Mary requested. The hostess reached across the table to take Libby's hand.

"He's gone, Libby…he's…gone. Your beloved husband is dead. You must accept, find it in your heart and soul and mind that he is…just gone."

Mary pulled her long white apron up over her own head, and buried in that sacred, silent space, she bowed her head and wept, oblivious to the flower-like aroma that filled the brightly painted yellow and white kitchen. Giving in to her own sorrows, Mary had unwittingly summoned herself to a place of deep private grief.

Katie, unable to watch the two women any longer, wandered into the guest bedroom and started to unpack their many pieces of luggage. She and Libby would share this one small room. For how long, Katie had no idea.

The bedroom was neat and sparse. The furniture consisted of a small chest of drawers, a stand (for a water pitcher) with an attached swivel mirror, and a large brass bed comfortable enough for the two of them. A handmade Indian star quilt lay folded on the end rung of the bed. The chamber pot was tucked discreetly underneath the bed. Two paned-glass windows gave light to the room, and thankfully, they faced away from the river. Through the glass the women would view the stubble from the browned grass on the hillside.

As the night wore on, Libby eventually found her way to the bedroom. Katie and Libby lay side-by-side, sleep eluding them. They could hear the unfamiliar sounds of a raucous town coming to life on Front Street. The low-class boatsmen (river rats) and the prostitutes called out to each other. The bartenders' jobs got busier as the men ended their shifts. Their well-developed muscles being achingly tired only made the men want all the more for a drink, and they were willing to pay handsomely for a fancy woman's company. The gamblers waited patiently at their corner table, flipping through their deck of 'marked' cards.

Libby's and Katie's final destination for this day ended in yet another sleepless night. Darkness intruded, like the lowering of a window shade, as a deep purple shadow swept across the prairie valley. The night brought a temporary relief from the sun's intensity, but it did not silence the cacophonous din of the steamboats coming and going, or the pulsating life of the ever-flowing river.

Fort Benton returned to business as usual, oblivious to the fact that the grieving widow of Montana's acting territorial governor, Thomas Francis Meagher, was a guest in the home of Mary and I. G. Baker.

CHAPTER 35

▼

LIBBY LEAVES FORT BENTON

The days passed quickly for Libby as she received visitors in Mary Baker's small setting room. They came, offering their condolences. A delegation from the Fenian Brotherhood was the first to sit with her and they offered their services in dragging the river. They told her they had joined in the search that lasted for four days. Some claimed they had ridden as far as the Marias River in the hot July days that followed Thomas Francis Meagher's mysterious disappearance. Many of these men were lifelong friends and felt helpless, unable to give their leader a Christian burial.

Men from the fort walked the river's edge to the small islands that dotted the center of the Missouri, but again the river released nothing. Next came the officials representing the territorial government. These men announced themselves investigators into the "accidental" drowning of the acting territorial governor, Thomas Francis Meagher.

Libby graciously listened to them all, as Katie poured tea, served Mary's lovely shortbread cookies, and cleaned up the remains when the company departed.

Libby anguished over the investigator's official report that he had fallen from the boat docked at the river's edge. *I don't believe them*, thought Libby. *I will never accept this explanation that Thomas drowned by his own incompetence. This mystery of how Thomas died will come out into the light.*

The reward posters offering $2,000 for the return of his body were tacked up on fences and set in storefront windows. Many men had valiantly hunted for Thomas's body. Cannons had been shot, the impact hitting the water in the hope that the body would shake loose if caught in tree stumps. In a bazaar ritual, loaves of bread had been dumped from shore to shore in the belief that if the body were in the water, it would float to the surface. Libby had done everything she could think of in her quest to find her husband's body. She wanted to give him a proper and honorable Christian funeral. He deserved to be memorialized in New York City by his troops and the Irish who had fought with him in the War Between the States. Her intention for coming to Fort Benton had been to find his remains. That was not going to happen. Libby finally accepted that reality.

Libby had decided earlier in the day that she and Katie would leave on the morning stage. Katie, abiding by her wishes, had walked to the stage line ticket office. She found Jake, sitting in a hard chair he had tipped onto its two back legs, with his feet up on the desk, crossed at the ankles, drinking a cup of coffee.

"Good day to you, sir." Katie spoke loudly.

Jake, daydreaming in the heat, had not heard her come in to the shack that served as the office. He jumped up, spilling the chair over backwards.

"Howdy, Ma'am. I didn't hear you acomin'," said an embarrassed Jake. "What can I do for ya?"

"Miss Libby and I will be leaving on your next stage out, Jake. And I want to purchase the tickets today and get the time schedule." Katie replied.

"I'll be apullin' up in front of Mary Baker's house by five-thirty in the mornin'," said Jake. "I get agoin' early for the horses."

Since there was no telegraph in Fort Benton, Libby would have to wait until she arrived in Helena to wire her father, telling him of her plans to return east. She hoped the lines were operating since she needed to ask him to wire her money to St. Louis, Missouri.

It would take her and Katie at least two weeks to pack up their belongings in Virginia City, and her first duty to Thomas was to clear out his records in the tiny office space. She would make everything ready for the next appointed territorial governor, Green Clay Smith.

She also wanted to spend a few days in Helena in August with friends. She had some ideas to honor Thomas and she wanted to discuss them with people she trusted before leaving the territory; Friends who were capable and who would carry out her wishes from a long distance correspondence.

It was late afternoon on the fifth day of their Fort Benton stay. Katie, helping to prepare potatoes for the early evening meal, glanced out the kitchen window and saw Libby walking alone down Front Street.

"Mary...Look! Libby's going out. I must hurry and catch up with her," said Katie.

"Leave her be," said Mary. "She has some private needs, Katie. Just wait a bit and she'll be back on her own." However, Mary also stared out the window.

She saw the slump-shouldered figure as she slowly made her way, walking into the dried grasses on the hillside opposite the river. The two women watched her diminish in size as she climbed to the top of the bluff that overlooked the Missouri.

Oblivious of the hot, dry winds blowing against her skirts and rippling her hair, Libby sensed the time for her to say goodbye had arrived. She needed this alone time to talk to Thomas. She wanted a bird's eye view of the river, as if her eyes would see Thomas resting along the river's edge at Cow Island downstream from the town.

Rivers are always symbolic of life, she thought, *so how is it my Thomas met his ignominious death in a river of life?* Libby stared off into the distant skyline where she could see a tiny black speck, probably an eagle, riding the wind currents, circling ever closer to the river where it soon would dip into the swirling water and find food to sustain its life. *Circles of life,* she thought.

Suddenly, as if struck from behind, Libby crumbled prostrate onto the earth, her grief overtaking her once more.

"THOMAS! Thomas…Thom…. Oh! God! WHY?" In anguish she screamed into the wind. "*Anam Cara*, my soul friend, I love you so. Come back to me…Thomas!" But the hot prairie winds continued to blow, carrying her voice toward the heavens.

The eagle, growing closer with every circle on the wind currents, screeched as if answering Libby's cry. Its white head gleamed in the back glow of the late afternoon sun. His piercing black eyes settled in on the woman lying face down in the grasses. Libby, in her pain, had not seen the bird drawing near, but the screeching sounds brought her to her knees. She looked at the bird without fear as it landed nearby, and she began talking to the resplendent creature.

"Eagle," she said boldly, "you were the first bird I saw last year and now here you are again in my sight." The bird stared at Libby, unblinking. "My Thomas stood solid in his courage and convictions, only to be misunderstood and even hated." She brushed away a tear and sighed. "His only purpose in life was to find a better way of living for his Irish brothers now in America."

A sudden gust of wind swirled around Libby. She felt a surging power within her body begin to rise up and she grew strong. She stood up, tall and proud, her back straight, her eyes clear.

"Carry on, eagle. Carry on, and I must do the same."

Libby stretched her hand toward the eagle. The movement caused the bird to rise, flapping his six-foot wingspan, making a rushing sound as he swooped across the landscape spiraling downward toward the river's edge. She kept her eyes on the bird growing smaller in its flight.

Libby faced into the wind and looked toward the river. In a clear and unfaltering voice, she returned to her soliloquy, continuing her final goodbye to the only man she would ever love.

"From this day forward, I vow I will keep your name alive, *Thomas Francis Meagher of the Sword*. I will spend my days seeing to it that the truth and depth of who you really are is known and recorded. I will keep you alive in the public's eye so that the black mark of mystery that surrounds your death will be cleared. Someday we'll know, Thomas. Someday."

"I promise you, with all of my heart, I will raise your son as you had hoped when you wrote your love letter to me…has it really been twelve years ago? I will go to Ireland and demand what is rightfully yours and mine, your son. Through me, he will grow to know you, Thomas. You are his father, and he will become a powerful man in his own right." Libby sighed and without tears she said, "Goodbye my love. Wait for me on the other side."

She forced herself to look down at that black, ominous, swirling rush of water one last time. A gleaming patch of light, from the afterglow of the late afternoon sun, marked a spot in the river. It stayed focused just below the walking bridge, about where the *A. G. Thompson* had been docked that fateful night, not even two weeks ago.

Turning around, Libby began her descent off the bluff. She stopped to pick dried grasses and weeds, and when she had an armload, she set them beside her to free her hands. She reached up and pulled a green satin ribbon from her hair; the tightly coiled tresses falling loosely around her shoulders, leaving it to the whims of the prairie winds. Libby then wrapped and tightly tied the ribbon around the natural bouquet.

The transformation had begun as Libby walked back into town, her head high, shoulders back. She crossed to the river's edge, and walked to the middle of the bridge until she came to the spot where she could still see the gleaming light in the water that spoke to her when she was on the bluff above.

"Carry these grasses to Thomas," she said as she tossed the bouquet into the ever-flowing Missouri.

Libby stood there, oblivious to the men who lined the river's edge, watching her last act of love and honor to her brave and glorious husband. Some had hats in hand, others stood, curious as to what the ceremony was all about, having arrived days later and not aware of the tragic death of Montana's territorial governor.

Libby remained on the bridge, staring down into that spot of light, until she could no longer see the bobbing green ribbon, swirling and turning, as it was swept into and swallowed up in that vortex of sunlight in the river, carrying her message to the soul of her *Anam Cara*.

The time had come. It was time for her to leave the river's edge. Libby bid her Thomas a final goodbye.

"Goodbye, love of my life, may your soul eternally rest at the right hand of the Father."

"Slán a ghrá geal, ar dheis Dé go marfaidh d'anam"

Missouri River
Fort Benton
Montana Territory
1867

©Watercolor by Merelyn K. Brubaker 2005
Shown in color on back cover of book.

CHAPTER 36

▼

LIBBY RETURNS TO VIRGINIA CITY

The sun had barely marked the horizon when Jake stopped the eager team of six horses in front of Mary Baker's white picket fence. Mary stood on her porch waiting for him to arrive.

"Good morning, Jake. The ladies are ready," said Mary. "This is all of their luggage." She pointed to four valises waiting by the gate.

Jake lifted them up to the stagecoach roof and secured the bags with ropes, pulling them tight and knotting the ends.

"God speed, Libby…Katie," said Mary. "I'll be watching for your return toward the end of August."

"Thank you, Mary. You have taken wonderful care of us. I appreciate it all, and yes, if we could stay with you until the boat leaves…" her voice trailed off. Libby turned and quickly entered the stagecoach; Katie followed and settled on the bench across from Libby. "If you don't want to ride backwards Katie, come over to this side, next to me," invited Libby.

Jake, anxious to cover early morning miles before the July heat exhausted the horses, began the torturous journey. Four days of jarring, dust, heat, thirst, accompanied the uncomplaining women. They welcomed the stage stops enroute and used the break time as an opportunity to take short walks. Libby was mentally making a list of all the work waiting for them in Virginia City.

Jake finally completed the last leg of the trip and pulled into Virginia City, near their log home. Libby and Katie emerged into the early evening and were surprised by all the activity. Wagons and people and dust and noise filled their nostrils and ears and eyes.

"Why, the town is bustling. Looks to me like hundreds of men have moved into that field over to the left." She pointed across the gulch. "See all the tents? Maybe a mine came in."

Arriving unannounced was Libby's choice. No one met the stage. No one offered her a hand, or a shoulder to cry on. No one offered her condolences.

"Come Katie, we have much work to accomplish in a short time." She pinched the top of her nose to stop any unwanted tears.

"Thank you Jake," said Libby. "We'll be freighting our belongings to Fort Benton; Katie and I will spend time in Helena the first part of August, then ride with you again toward the end of August. Our boat is to leave no later than September second if the water stays high enough. We will stay with Mary again until that last day."

"Yes, Ma'am!" Jake tipped his hat to her. "I'll be runnin' the route Ma'am." He slapped the reins, and the horses and stagecoach lurched forward, trudging toward the Wells Fargo Stage office and barn at the end of the gulch road.

"Well, Katie, here we are. Let's get inside and make a cup of tea. I'm so tired."

She entered the log cabin house that served as the official home for the Montana Territorial Acting Governor, his first lady and Katie. Looking around the room, Libby sighed.

"Katie, we have a huge job ahead of us." She took off her travel hat and cape to shake off the dust.

A noise from the kitchen startled the two women, but before they could react Mary Jane McKelvey entered the room. "Libby come here to me," said Mary Jane, a good friend to Libby since the first day she had arrived in

Virginia City. Mary Jane was the chairwoman of the Catholic women's circle and married to a mining engineer. She enveloped Libby in a comfortable bear hug, pulling her into her ample bosom. "I come every day waiting for you. Tish, tish," said Mary Jane. "Let those tears out Libby. Tish, tish."

Like a backed-up dam of river water, the force found a crack. Libby sobbed for a good while completely soaking the front of Mary Jane's weskit. Finally spent and weak, Libby went limp in her arms.

"Katie! Help me get Libby to a chair, and I'll need a wet cloth for her face and hands." Gently she placed the cloth on Libby's forehead. "She'll be all right in a minute."

Libby folded into herself, but only for a moment. "It's true, Mary Jane. He disappeared late at night in the river." Libby frowned. "We only had twelve years together. She looked her friend squarely in the eyes. "I'll never accept that Thomas slipped on deck and fell into the Missouri River and drowned. He had enemies."

"There, there, Libby. We'll discuss it all in detail. For now, you need help with a moving plan. I have news also. Just last week, James received official orders, signed by your husband by the way, to be the official mining engineer at the McKelvey Mine in Butte." She smiled. "So our lives were destined to part, dear lady. Now let's have tea."

The tears spent; the tea sipped; the daylight fading into a hot summer evening, the three women came up with a plan.

"Katie, in the morning I want you to search for some men to help with the moving of heavy items, trunks. Check with Father Sullivan at church. Then go to the freight company, as we'll need a wagon. Ask them to bring barrels. She turned to Mary Jane. "If you can keep me company as I pack up the house, Mary Jane? That will make the chore much easier." Without any hesitation, Mary Jane nodded. "Please tell the ladies I am not moving furniture, only personal items." I want them to take and use whatever they would like. I have no need for household items in New York City and there is no point in packing them and paying freight." Libby shrugged. "Whatever is left, give it to charity, to the miners.

"I will go to the office and retrieve Thomas's things, and papers. Green Clay Smith will find a clean, empty desk and files will be in order. He'll be arriving any day and he'll need this house to move into. Hopefully, he'll be kind enough to stay at the hotel until we are gone."

She noted a bitterness creeping into her voice. "Let's go to bed now, tomorrow starts a new life for us all."

At last all was packed, the barrels hammered shut, and the load weighed. She turned to Mary Jane. "John Ming is offering us his mansion in Helena for as long as Katie and I need his hospitality," said Libby. "He stopped by last night to tell me he has business in Helena, and he is riding the stage with us."

"Well, that is wonderful news. You two can visit about the memorial plans for Thomas," said Mary Jane.

John Ming's mercantile business had done well all the way from Denver to Salt Lake City to Virginia City and Helena. Over the next few years his vision was to see expansion and growth in Helena. He planned to build an opera house as a monument to his wife.

"By the 1880s Helena will be the Queen City in these Rocky Mountains." Libby smiled. "The people of Helena will have a place to assemble in a meeting hall of great caliber for entertainment for hundreds of years to come." She frowned. "We had intended to be a part of that growth." Libby quickly shut her eyes, not allowing tears to fall.

"Mary Jane, I can not even thank you enough for your help and support. If you and James have political problems, be sure you write me in New York. I still have some political clout." She tilted her head back and laughed. "Well, that might be up for debate," she added.

With a "Gee-up" from Jake, the stagecoach left Virginia City. To Jake's surprise, the women and men from the Catholic Church and the Irish community stood shoulder-to-shoulder lining both sides of Wallace Street, standing respectfully still. Most had one hand on the shoulder of child, and held a babe in their arms. A few wiped at tears as Jake deliberately slowed the stagecoach while Libby and Katie passed by. He picked up speed when he drove around the bend and out of the area. Neither woman looked out the window curtains for a last goodbye.

©Virginia City, Montana
Photo by Lenore McKelvey Puhek
2001

John Ming's carriage was waiting in Helena. The three of them transferred everything to the carriage and climbed inside. It was a short ride to the Ming's Mansion. Soft feather beds waited them, as did a welcoming staff. Hot coffee, a light supper and a wonderful apple pie energized the two women.

"Come in to my study, Libby. There is no further word as to Thomas's disappearance in the Missouri River. The reward money is now over two thousand dollars, but no one has come forward."

He waited until Libby was seated. "I have a newspaper clipping for you. The Irish Brigade held a memorial in St. Francis Xavier Church on August Fourteenth. The church was packed." He handed over the clipping and Libby scanned it. "Too bad you could not have been there."

"Well, John. It is going to take me several months to get back to New York City. There was no need to delay the service. I am content with what they put together in a memorial tribute to their Irish leader." She clasped her hands together. "At least he was honored and respected and loved for who he was in New York City. It bothered Thomas that he could not find that same respect here in the Territory."

"Thomas was loved, Libby. Not all the citizens in Montana were against his politics and ideals." He shook his head slowly.

"Libby, you need money for this trip. We can send a telegram to your father to send you money to St. Louis, but from here you will need my assistance. He took Union bills from his desk drawer and presented them to her.

"John, I..." Libby put her hand to her throat and felt the jewelry. She unclasped the beloved brooch; her first gift from Thomas "Let me leave you this brooch just in case something should happen to me. I cannot accept your money without leaving you something of value."

"Libby, you know that is not necessary. I happen to know your need for money from the government. This letter (he held up a one page letter written in Thomas's familiar script) arrived on the same stage announcing Thomas's drowning." He handed it to Libby. She read the words in disbelief. "Why would Thomas want money sent to him in Fort Benton, John?"

"He has not received any payment for the time he spent here." She picked up the money and folded it into her purse. Standing, she took John's hand.

"Thank you, good friend." She turned and left the room. But not before she set the brooch on the walnut desktop.

Ming picked it up and examined the gems and pearls. *Exquisite piece,* he thought. *Meagher had good taste.* He would make sure Katie left with the brooch to return it to Libby when they reached New York City.

While in Helena, Libby spent her time meeting with businessmen and friends. Her intent was to stir up a committee to fund a fitting memorial to honor Thomas. She wrote letters to friends, to the Bishop of the Catholic Church, and to businessmen announcing her intentions to honor Thomas's death. The time passed all too quickly and Libby had business to attend to.

"I don't want to leave any loose ends, John. The piece of property we were considering buying for our mansion when Thomas finished his term of office is up for grabs John. Why don't you buy it on speculation?"

The time for departure from the Montana territory had come, and this would be their last dinner together for many years. The conversation was stilted and Libby retired to her room.

"Katie, we leave for Fort Benton in the morning," she announced at the table.

Jake arrived as scheduled. *One more grueling trip back to Mary Baker's door in Fort Benton, and then... back to the States and civilization*, thought Libby.

"The river is very low, Libby. They are trying to get one more boat down river. You have to leave now or you won't get out until spring," said Mary Baker.

September 2, 1867 was the departure day. With a deep sadness, Libby and Katie stepped on board the riverboat. *How can I leave on the same river that carried you away from me? I'll be searching for you at every oxbow in the water. Thomas, this is the hardest day of my life.*

As the boat took her downstream away from the nightmare and mystery of the death of Thomas Francis Meagher, orator, fighter for the Irish cause, statesman, politician, military leader of the Civil War, lawyer, keeper of the faith, lover, family man, it all raced through her emotions and physically attacked her body with chills. She correctly thought of the many faceted sides of the polished diamond that summed up for her the life she had led with her love, her *anam cara*.

The two women sat quietly together as the water rushed by. Each saying their own private and sad goodbye to the west.

"Katie, you have a home with me forever if you want it," said Libby, breaking the silence.

"Yes Ma'am, and I appreciate your generosity," said Katie. "I plan to stay right by your side."

CHAPTER 37

▼

THOMAS COMES
FOR LIBBY
RYE, NEW YORK,
JULY 5, 1906

Katie and Libby had finished their light supper of tomato soup and cucumber sandwiches, enjoying the early summer evening on the patio off the kitchen. They sat, this hot July 5, 1906 day, drinking lemonade. A few days earlier, Libby had gone off alone for a few hours to remember the anniversary of her husband's death. She had done that at Fort Benton when she said her final goodbye, and every year, no matter where she was, she paused alone and remembered. Now she was back in her cottage in Rye, New York sitting across from her lifelong companion and friend, Katie Daly.

"Katie, every year when Thomas's anniversary comes around, I spend time talking to you about it." She took a sip of the cold drink. "Thank you for allowing me to do so. You never say too much about Seán Daly and sometimes I feel like I bore you with my foolishness." She twisted her napkin. "We certainly have come a long ways on this trail of life, haven't we?" She paused as she saw Katie doing a mental count of the years.

"I remember it all so well, Miss Libby. Why, we've spent a lifetime laughing, crying…living out our destiny. I think it's wonderful that we have been blessed with a long, healthy life. As for Seán Daly. Well, we were so young when we married before he joined up with the Irish Brigade and died at Bull Run. I don't like to talk about it but I miss him with that young girl's heart." She stirred her glass with the long teaspoon.

"Do you think Thomas's death was an accident, Katie?" She didn't wait for her answer. "I never believed that he fell overboard." She waved her hand in the air. "Oh, I know what they tried to make me believe…I read the investigative reports and received all the condolences from the big wigs on the political scene at the time, but you know, in my heart, I never accepted it. Thomas was killed." She grew pensive.

I had hoped to prove that in my lifetime, but nothing ever came of my inquiries. The Pinkerton men gave me no information, but I suspect they believe otherwise as to the cause of his death." She rose from her chair.

"I think I am going to my room early tonight, Katie. I want to reminisce a bit in my quiet space. Do you remember the love letter Thomas wrote me when he proposed? I want to find that."

Katie waved her away.

Libby walked to her bedroom window and raised the sash. The slight July breeze lifted the Irish lace curtains in a gentle stir, letting fresh air into the small space. *Katie certainly was right tonight in that we did it all. To think we used to take care of a Fifth Avenue Mansion in New York City and now here we are in this tiny cottage. My. My. One never knows….* Libby rummaged around in the closet until her hands rested on a beautiful hand carved wooden pencil box. *I gave this to you for our very first gift exchange, Thomas,* she thought as she ran her fingers over the carved designs. She lifted the lid, ruffled through a few letters and extracted a well-worn envelope.

"Ah! Here it is." She set the box on top of her bedcover and took the letter to the rocker near the window where the light was better. Every time

Libby read this letter she felt refreshed, alive, in love. She took a gamble marrying Thomas Francis Meagher and what a choice it was. She had once told Thomas, "Sometimes I think our marriage is like gambling on a gold mine. We hit a nugget and that keeps us going, digging for the next one. Only trouble is, we have had to move a lot of earth in between those nuggets, dear." Remembering this quote made Libby smile.

She would do it all over again with Thomas. She wished she *could* do it all over again. Life had been cruel in many ways but often, when reflecting on Thomas, she thought of him as a flaming shooting star that swept across the heavens to flare out too fast in an exploding burst. *He had so much to live for, so much to give*, she thought as she wiped away a forbidden tear.

Libby reached for her glasses. She kept them on the small round table near the rocker. This spot is where she sat each night, reading her precious Bible, saying her rosary, meditating on a daily scripture, and saying her litany of prayers for Katie, her family and friends, whatever came into her mind. Tonight would be no different. *I'll light a candle tonight and talk to Thomas*, she thought. She reached for her well-worn rosary, a gift from Thomas when she had joined the Catholic Church. She wrapped the crystal beads around her fingers and sat down.

As soon as she saw the familiar handwriting, the beautiful cursive strokes, *My Dear, Dear Miss Townsend*, Libby started reciting the words from memory. The letter lay carefully in her lap while she shut her eyes to take in the nostalgic memory of the day she received the letter from the courier.

The envelope held a fourteen-page love letter. It arrived early that morning of January 2, 1855. Thomas had proposed to her in Irish just the night before in the family parlor. "Yes," Libby had said, much to the consternation of her parents.

A blustery gust of wind blew through the curtains and Libby looked up.

"Thomas? Is that you?" she asked into the silent room. She saw him.

"Mind if I join you, Libby?"

"You are always near, my dear. Do come and visit for a spell."

"Libby, this time I have come for you, my *Anam Cara*."

Libby looked up at the young, vibrant handsome Thomas Francis Meagher standing in his Civil War uniform. The very one she had sewn with the braid trim. Oh! How handsome she thought he looked with his flowing hair just off the collar and his moustache trimmed to his otherwise clean-shaven face.

He held out his right hand, covered in white gloves. His sword clanked at his side from the movement.

In one last burst of life-energy, one last heartbeat, Libby reached up and put her still delicate, but now blue-veined hand into his. "It's about time. I'm ready, Thomas…have been for thirty-nine years you know, what took you so long to come get me?" Libby stumbled a bit getting out of the rocker and she hoped the noise wouldn't arouse Katie. She left her glasses and the letter on the seat of the rocker.

"Miss Libby? Are you all right in there? Katie knocked on the closed bedroom door." Miss Libby? May I come in? There was only silence. "Miss Libby?" Katie turned the doorknob and swung open the door.

"Miss Libby!" she screamed. She ran over to the rocker where Libby sat, her eyes closed with an expression of peace glowing on her countenance.

"Miss Libby," this time Katie spoke reverently. "Thomas finally came for you, did he?" Katie blew out the candle, folded the letter and returned it to its proper place in the tattered envelope and put it back into the box. She set the pair of glasses on top of the Bible.

"God speed, my dear friend. I'll not be too long in crossin' meself. If you see Seán Daly you tell him I love him and I am so mad at him for dying at Bull Run. Remember to come for me…all of you…when it is my time. I'll be right here waitin'."

Author's Notes

The list for the steamboat Gallatin included Mrs. Elizabeth Meagher among the 150 passengers who departed Ft. Benton for Omaha, Nebraska, September 2, 1867. This was the last passenger boat out for the season, as the water had dropped extremely low and rocks and sand bars were appearing in the river downstream.

The departure began smoothly, but only thirteen miles down river near Camp Cooke on the morning of September 5th; the boat hit rocks and was damaged beyond repair. Capt. Howe worked day and night, concerned about the safety of his passengers and for the damage to his boat.

On September 11th, the boat was pronounced unsafe and the passengers and some supplies were taken to the shore. The passengers set up a makeshift camp, only to suffer heavy downpours of rain and cold weather. Wolves were heard howling in the night. There were eleven ladies, including Libby. She suffered in this ordeal, but she tended the sick children, helped with camp duties and hoped for a rescue team.

Eventually, the steamboat Huntsville rescued the stranded passengers and on September 19th with Libby on board, the journey east began again. That portion of her return trip came to an end in Omaha, Nebraska, on October 17, 1867.

Libby Meagher and Katie Daly returned to the Townsend mansion in New York City. After a brief respite, the two women, (both widows in their thirties) left for the Tuscany Valley in Italy, "to heal there," as wrote Libby to a good friend in Helena, Montana. "We will then travel to Ireland and Waterford, where I intend to live near the family on the O'Meagher property." While in Waterford, Libby presented the city with a portrait of Thomas, a sword and sash, medals and military flags. (This gift is on permanent display, housed in the National Treasures Museum in Waterford, Ireland.)

Libby and Katie and Thomas Francis Jr., now a teenager, left Ireland and returned to Rye, New York. He was enrolled in West Point. But he did not have the military bent of his father and left school. He eventually went to California. He married and had three children. Thomas Francis Meagher, Jr. died in 1910 at the age of 55. The cause of death is believed to be from pneumonia while living in Manila, working for the Federal Government as an engineer.

For almost forty years Libby lived a full life as a widow. Katie also did not marry again, and they maintained their friendship. Libby remained active in St. Francis Xavier Catholic Church, was a fundraiser for many Catholic causes, served as President of the Board for the New York City Cancer Hospital (now Sloan-Kettering Cancer Research Hospital) and kept in touch with the soldiers from the Irish Brigade. She chaired several projects to help with fund raising for orphanages and clinics for pregnant women.

Always close to her heart were the young boys left fatherless because of the Civil War. She donated all of the battlefield flags that Thomas had collected after each skirmish, to the Perfectory for Boys as well as giving them her time and financial help.

Libby enjoyed traveling, and she did return to Helena as she had promised, in 1887, twenty years after the mysterious death of Thomas Francis Meagher. She and Katie traveled to Alaska, Washington, Oregon and California before coming to Helena. She visited with many of her territorial era friends and presented a portrait of the General to the Montana Historical Society. That portrait hangs on loan from the Historical Society in the bank in White Sulphur Springs, Montana...Meagher County is named after the Acting Governor).

Because of confusing events (and circumstances unclear today) involving the husband of one of her nieces, Libby did not receive a full inheritance from her father's estate. She was forced, in 1887, to petition the United States Congress for a military widow's pension due her because of Thomas's service during the Civil War. She was originally granted $150.00 per month, but that was reduced to $50.00 a month. The reason for the reduction in benefits is not known.

Her wishes to erect a monument to her husband were brought to fruition in July 5, 1905. On the front lawn of the Montana state capitol, Helena, Montana, is a fitting memorial to *Thomas Francis Meagher of the Sword*. The scene is typical of a Civil War statue. Meagher is mounted on a mighty steed and in his right hand is his famous sword.

The Irish population in Montana attended and an estimated crowd of 5,000 people witnessed the unveiling of the statue created by Charles "Gus" Mulligan from Chicago, Illinois. Sadly, Libby was not one of them. Her health was failing her and although she had planned to return for the ceremony, she was not able to do so. A telegram from her was read to the crowd.

Libby died July 5, 1906, at her cottage in Rye, NY from heart disease (broken heart) with her faithful housekeeper, Katie Daly, at her side. Their friendship spanned more than fifty years.

Her services were held on July 7, 1906 from St. Francis Xavier Church, New York City, NY. She is buried in the Townsend family plot. I have not been able to trace where Katie finally was laid to rest, but I assume she would have been buried with her Irish brothers.

Thank you for reading this love story. I have enjoyed every step of the adventurous trails I took, eventually leading me to Waterford, Ireland. The several years I have spent researching, developing and writing this true love story between two soul mates is as accurate as I can determine. What really happened that dark moonless night on the Missouri River in Fort Benton, Montana Territory on July 1, 1867 still remains an unexplained mystery. I will leave that to the mystery writers.

On July 5, 2005 in Helena (now the capital city of Montana), the local fraternal organization, The Ancient Order of Hibernians, Thomas Francis

Meagher Chapter, re-dedicated the statue erected in 1905 to honor the Irishman and his accomplishments for the people of Montana.

As part of that celebration, I dressed in a green 1887 traveling suit and in a living history presentation, I introduced Libby Meagher to the hundreds of Thomas Francis Meagher fans. This was my way of helping Libby to keep the vow she made when she told her *Anam Cara* goodbye from the walking bridge that crosses the Missouri River at Ft. Benton, Montana.

On the anniversary date, July 1, 2005, I stood on that bridge and tossed in a bouquet of my own in memory of that fateful day one hundred and thirty-eight years ago. While I stood there, two beautiful morning doves flew up from the corners of the bridge. The birds came together in the center of the bridge after making a complete circle around me and then settled on a handrail by my hand.

Thank you, Libby for choosing me to write your story. I have tried to be as historically correct with your past as research would give up information to me to work with. I trust I heard you...and wrote your love story the way you lived it and wanted it to be shared.

Now! Libby! Go to the light! Rest in peace.

Slán!

Lenore McKelvey Puhek
From the banks of the Missouri River
Helena, Montana
lpuhek@mt.net
November 2005

Thank You

Go raibh míle maith agat!

To Thomas Francis Meagher for penning his beautiful love letter to Libby proposing marriage. (Chapter 16) This letter was my inspiration for the novel.

To Elizabeth "Libby" Townsend for saying, "Yes" to Thomas' proposal. For without these two people there would be no book.

Although this is a work of historical fiction, this love story is as true as I can make it. I used personal letters, diaries, newspaper articles and society page articles to put together this lovely romance of soul mates who found and recognized their *Anam Cara*, if only for a little while on this earth.

To Carla Hall, Nashville, TN, for her finishing touch editing skills and her faith in me to complete the project of my dreams. Her positive energy always seems to come when I need it the most, not just on this book, but for all of life's surprises.

To Michael J. Finnegan, Pittsburgh, playwright and friend, and author of "*Meagher*," who graciously shared his research information and knowledge. His encouragement kept me writing.

To James Cullinane, New York City, writer and friend, for sharing his expert knowledge of the city where he lives.

To David Smith, author and friend, Waterford, Ireland, for providing me with important Irish genealogy. For touring me around the city of

Waterford, pointing out the houses of the O'Meagher Family, and the cemetery family plot.

To Professor Martin John Hearne, Waterford, Ireland, author and lecturer on Meagher, who also provided me with Irish information so pertinent to this book. Thank you for your friendship and guidance.

To the librarians, Waterford Library, Waterford, Ireland, for their wonderful, helpful E-mails full of research information about Libby and Thomas.

To Traolach O Riordain, Ph.D., Co.Cork, Ireland. Irish Studies Professor, Carroll College, Helena, MT who put up with me for a semester teaching me Irish phrases scattered throughout this novel.

To Donal Ward, Co. Donegal, Glenties, Ireland, for your computer skills in Irish.

To Bill Markley, Pierre, SD, author of *Dakota Epic,* for suggestions to tighten this novel, and for his eye for little details.

To my Helena writers' group, *Writers in the Big Sky*: Stevie Erving, Carol Rae Lane, Karyn Cheatham, Eva Spaulding, John Barbagello, Sandy Barker, Diana Boom.

To Mary Bell, Helena, MT writer and friend, while in the midst of her own heartache, (her son Adam injured in Iraq while serving his country) gave excellent suggestions, and encouraged me to "write on, McDuff." Thanks for all the lunches, Mary. Keep the faith.

To Anne Yellow Kidney, Helena, MT for your healing ministry and for the positive insights concerning the outcome of this novel.

To Donna Edwards, St. George, Utah, Genealogist, who discovered some interesting dates and facts to help me make sure I was as accurate as history and the past will allow me to be.

A grateful thank you goes to the knowledgeable and helpful staff at the Montana State Historical Society, Helena, Mt., for their interest and support in digging up old records, letters, newspapers, and photographs.

To my sister, Ellen K. Murphy, who contributed the artwork for the cover. Thanks to you, also, big sister for your care and concern in driving me 180 miles to Great Falls week after week, allowing me to read chapters out loud. Your suggestions about the Irish grandfather were a definite flashback to our own Grandpa James McKelvey.

To Merelyn Brubaker for your interest and ability to visualize scenes bringing alive description and detail; for accompanying me to the banks of the Missouri River, Fort Benton, Montana, and to Virginia City, Montana, for valuable information about Victorian life. It was a privilege to walk with you on the wooden sidewalks in the western towns that Libby and Thomas spent the last year of their lives. The dog loved you for feeding him ice cream, even if he wouldn't let us on the porch of the Territorial Governor's house.

To Kathryn Dietrich, age 91, for contributing her first hand information as to life in the Victorian age, and for the Matrimonial Cake recipe.

To my life-long dear friend, Nancy Ahmann, Phoenix, Az., who believes in me, in Libby and Thomas. You finally got me to "see" the Libby connection. Thanks for all the long distance late night telephone calls, E-mails, your editing skills, and your positive approach to this book's message—"Love Never Dies."

And…to Steve and Joe…Sláinte!

Buíochas le Dia!

Thank You God For Everything!

Research Bibliography

BOOKS

Athearn, Robert; Thomas Francis Meagher: *An Irish Revolutionary in America,* Boulder: University of Colorado Press, 1949.

Burrows, Edwin G., and Wallace, Mike; *Gotham: A History of New York City to 1898,* New York Oxford, Oxford University Press, 1999.
Part 4 (42) City of Immigrants
Part 4 (47) Panic of 1857
Part 4 (49) Civil War
Part 4 (51) Westward Ho! Railroading West
Part 4 (54) Haute Monde and Demimonde

Crutchfield, James A.; *It Happened in Montana*, Falcon Publishing Co., Helena, MT 1992.

Dimsdale, Thomas J., Professor; *The Vigilantes of Montana*, University of Oklahoma Press, Oklahoma City, OK, new edition, 1953.

Forney, Gary R., *Thomas Francis Meagher, Irish Rebel, American Yankee, Montana Pioneer*, Xlibris Corporation, 2003.

Homberger, Eric; New York City, *Interlink Books*; Interlink Publishing Group, Inc.,
New York, NY, 2003

Keneally, Thomas; *American Scoundrel*, Anchor Books, Division of Random House, Inc., New York, 2004.

Keneally, Thomas; *The Great Shame*, Anchor Books, Division of Random House, Inc., New York, 1998.

Lepley, John G; *Birthplace of Montana*, Pictorial Histories Publishing Co.

Malone, Michael P., and Roeder, Richard B.; *Montana: A History of Two Centuries,* University of Washington Press, Seattle, WA. 1976.

McCutcheon, Marc; *The Writer's Guide to Everyday Life in the 1800s*, Writer's Digest Books, Cincinnati, Ohio, 1993.

Moore, Ann; *Leaving Ireland*, Penguin Books, NY, 2002.

Morris, Roy, Jr; *The Better Angel, Walt Whitman in the Civil War*; Oxford University Press, New York, NY, 2000.

Moulton, Candy; *The Writer's Guide to Everyday Life in the Wild West from 1840–1900*; Writer's Digest Books, Cincinnati, Ohio, 1999.

O'Donohue, John; *Anam Cara: A Book of Celtic Wisdom*, Harpercollins (A Cliff Street) Pub. Co., Inc. NYC, NY, 1997.

Pepin Press Design Book; *Fashion Design, 1850–1895*, Design Press, New York, an imprint of Quite Specific Media Group Ltd., 1997.

Riis, Jacob A.; *How The Other Half Lives: Studies Among the Tenements of New York,* Charles Scribner's Sons, 1890:

Chapter III, The Mixed Crowd pg. 21–17
Chapter XIV, The Common Herd, pg. 159–178

Setnik, Linda; *Victorian Costume For Ladies, 1860–1900*, Schiffer Pub., Ltd., Atglen, Pa., 2000.

Spence, Clark C.; *Territorial Politics and Government in Montana 1864–89*, University of Illinois Press, Chicago, Ill, 1975.

Stuart, Granville; *The Montana Frontier, 1852–1864*; Edited by Paul C. Phillips, Bison Books, University of Nebraska Press, Lincoln and London.1925.

Swartout, Robert R., Jr. and Fritz, Harry W.; *Montana Heritage; An Anthology of Historical Essays,* Montana Historical Society Press, Helens, MT 59601, 1992.

Varhola, Michael J.; *Everyday Life during The Civil War;* Writer's Digest Books, Cincinnati, Ohio, 1999.

Vaughn, Robert; *Then and Now: Thirty-six years in the Rockies—1864–1900*, Farcountry Press, Helena, MT. 2001.

Watson, Reg. A.; *The Life and Times of Thomas Francis Meagher, Irish Exile to Van Diemen's Land,* Tasmania, 2001.

Whalen, William J., *The Irish in America*, Claretian Publications, Chicago, Ill., 1972.

Wheeler, Richard; *The Exile*, Forge Books, New York City, NY, 2003.

Winik, Jay; *April 1865: The Month That Saved America*, Harpercollins Publishers, Inc. New York, NY, 2001.

Wolle, Muriel Sibell; *Montana Pay Dirt*, Sage Books.

ART

Missouri River, Fort Benton, Montana; watercolor by Merelyn Brubaker, Helena, MT., 2005. (This painting was created exclusively for this book.) Back cover and inside.

Book cover and jacket; Computer design by Ellen McKelvey Murphy, 2005.

POEMS

Whitman, Walt: *When Lilacs Last in the Dooryard Bloomed,* 1856.
Lewis, C. S., *The Four Loves.*

MUSIC

Brahms, J., *"F.A.E." Scherzo in C minor*, October 27, 1853. F.A.E. letters are German, Frei Aber Einsam, (Free, yet lonely).

LETTERS, NEWSPAPERS, JOURNALS

Major Collection: Thomas Francis Meagher and Elizabeth (Libby) Meagher,
Library; Montana State Historical Society, Helena, Montana.
Major Collection: Fort Benton Museum, Fort Benton, Montana.
Major Collection: New York Historical Society, NYC, NY.
Major Collection: New York City Public Library, New York City, NY.

Newspapers

The Helena Independent Record
Fort Benton River Press
Virginia City

New York Times
Helena Radiator
Montana Post
Montana Post Tri-Weekly
The Helena Herald Weekly

MISCELLANEOUS
Recipes
Matrimonial Cake, *from the family recipes of Kathryn Dietrich, Lakeside, MT.*
Buffalo or Beef Stew, from the family recipes of Mary Phoebe Frey, Helena, MT.
Chocolate Sour Cream Cake, from the family recipes of Mary Phoebe Frey, Helena, Mt. (Author's grandmother)

MAP
Montana Territory, 1860 era.
ARTICLES
Robison, Ken; *Mrs. Thomas Francis Meagher's Sad Departure from Fort Benton in 1867: What a Way to Treat a Lady!* Fort Benton River Press, August 11, 2005

©Photo by Nancy Ahmann, Phoenix, AZ 2005

Biography

Author Biography:

Lenore McKelvey Puhek
1215 Hudson Street
Helena, MT 59601
1 (406) 443-2552
E-mail: lpuhek@mt.net

My interest in Thomas Francis Meagher began as a child when I played under his statue on the Montana state capitol lawn. Fascinated with the idea of a Civil War statue in Montana, I have been collecting materials for years on this man's many faceted life. I found that writing a book based on a love letter between Thomas Francis and his second wife, Libby Townsend Meagher, to be pure joy.

I write and photograph Montana history. My work appears in *Wild West Magazine, Persimmon Hill, Fence Post, Chronicles of the Old West, GRIT, Country Discoveries, Cowboy, Frommers, Moody Monthly, Catholic Digest,* and many more. I was privileged to work on and edit a book about the Blackfeet culture. A script I wrote about my grandparents won the right to become a play at Carroll College. I have articles in six anthologies.

I am a member of Western Writers of America, The Montana Historical Society, and a charter member (1982) of *Writers in the Big Sky*. I am a guest speaker performing Living History conversations as "Libby Meagher."

Past honors include: A. B. "Bud" Guthrie, Jr. Scholarship for western writing while attending Carroll College. I graduated with a BA in English/Writing. Writer's Digest Association award for western non-fiction writing, and two honorable mentions in *By-Line* Magazine contests.

Although I love to travel this earth, Helena, Montana is home.

978-0-595-37847-0
0-595-37847-1

Printed in the United States
141582LV00002B/2/A